GULA

SHADES OF SIN

GULA

SHADES OF SIN

COLETTE RHODES

COPYRIGHT © 2023 COLETTE RHODES
ALL RIGHTS RESERVED

THE CHARACTERS AND EVENTS PORTRAYED IN THIS BOOK ARE FICTITIOUS. ANY SIMILARITY TO REAL PERSONS, LIVING OR DEAD, IS COINCIDENTAL AND NOT INTENDED BY THE AUTHOR.

NO PART OF THIS BOOK MAY BE REPRODUCED, OR STORED IN A RETRIEVAL SYSTEM, OR TRANSMITTED IN ANY FORM OR BY ANY MEANS, ELECTRONIC, MECHANICAL, PHOTOCOPYING, RECORDING, OR OTHERWISE, WITHOUT EXPRESS WRITTEN PERMISSION OF THE PUBLISHER.

ILLUSTRATED PAPERBACK ISBN: 978-1-7386105-2-5 (perfect bound)
DISCREET PAPERBACK ISBN: 978-1-7386105-3-2 (perfect bound)
HARDCOVER ISBN: 978-1-7386105-4-9

ILLUSTRATED CHARACTER COVER BY:
MYA SARACHO (@A.LOVEUNLACED)

DISCREET COVER BY: COLETTE

GULA IS A MONSTER ROMANCE BETWEEN A HUMAN AND HIS NOT-QUITE-HUMAN PARTNER, SUITABLE FOR READERS OVER 18.

CW: SEXUAL CONTENT, LIGHT BREEDING KINK.

IF MUSIC BE THE FOOD OF LOVE, PLAY ON.

\- WILLIAM SHAKESPEARE

CHAPTER 1

The three Austinators sitting directly in front of the low stage were the only reason I hadn't given up on this humiliating gig. No one else in the bar was interested in listening to my music, that was for fucking certain. And with each glass of whiskey I slammed back between songs to get myself through it, the less *I* wanted to listen to myself too.

It definitely wasn't my finest performance.

Or my finest song, if I was being honest with myself. It was new-ish material, it had taken me *months* to write, and it was...

Fine.

It was *fine*. It was a very adequate song. With adequate lyrics about heartbreak and pining and a girl with sky-blue eyes and golden hair. Four-chord progression. Boilerplate stuff.

Soulless.

Which was exactly how I felt at the moment, so it was no surprise my music sounded the same way. Shit, I was getting morose. Maybe this should be my last drink. Back in the before times, I'd had a manager to keep me on the straight and narrow, but he was long since gone. Maybe I should hire my mom again, even if she was a fucking thief.

Nah. *Bad idea, Austin.* If I spoke to Mom again, then she would speak to Grandfather, and I'd be subjected to more lectures about how it was time I got my life together and became a proper Hunter.

Nooooo, thank you. I did not want to spend my nights creeping around in the dark, armed to the teeth with silver blades like a cheesy video game character. I had important shit to do.

There were gigs for three whole fans to be played.

I finished my song, wavering slightly off-key on the final note, and the three women in the front stood up, whooping and hollering in a way that was definitely meant to be supportive but just made the whole experience more mortifying since all the other patrons were now glaring at me.

"Okay, well that concludes tonight's show," I announced, calling it early. My injured pride could only take so much. To add a metric ton of salt to the open, gaping wound, *that* was what finally got the other patrons cheering.

"Austin!" one of the woman yelled, leaning over the edge of the stage and giving me come-hither eyes as I packed up my gear as quickly as I could. Shit, shouldn't have had that last whiskey. "Come party with us. That was such a good show. Even better than the one at the barbeque place in San Antonio. We were there, you know. We're huge fans."

I used to perform in front of auditoriums of *thousands.* Remembering those days felt like peering through the looking glass at a different life.

I turned on my biggest, brightest, most charming smile, my cheeks aching with the effort. "I wouldn't be able to do what I do without you. I'm so grateful for your support."

"So you'll come out with us tonight?" she asked hopefully.

"No can do, I'm so sorry, ladies." I was maybe one percent tempted—there was no doubt it would give me the distraction from the grim reality of my life that I was seeking. But even in my groggy, alcohol-muddled brain, I knew how it would go. The highs never lasted. The lows were harder and harder to come back from. The regret left a bitterer, fuzzier taste in my mouth the next morning than the liquor did.

I needed to get my shit together.

"How about a photo?" I suggested, hating the disappointment on their faces. They'd come to this mediocre bar in the middle of suburban Denver—my goddamn hometown, no less—to see me. Probably voted for me on my season of *The Headliner* four years ago, followed me on social media and tracked my flatlining career ever since, and I couldn't give them what they wanted from me.

"We'd love a photo!" one of the others squealed, and I quickly finished snapping my guitar into its case before swinging down from the stage—*whoops, why was the floor so wavy*—and standing in the middle of the three of them while a harried server agreed to take the photo.

This part of the job used to feel like an awesome perk, but I increasingly struggled with having strangers' hands on my body like this. Like I was a commodity. The whiskey told me to say those thoughts out loud, but the little scrap of common sense at the back of my brain who was doing his hardest to keep me from being a fuckup told me to be quiet.

"Thank you again, so grateful you came out," I murmured, giving each of them hugs in turn, letting their words wash over me. My vision was kind of unfocused, and that was probably as good of a sign as any that I needed water, painkillers, and a good night's sleep.

Maybe that would be enough to revive my internal muse from the dead.

There's definitely a rat in here somewhere.

Probably in the walls? It sounded like it was in the walls somehow. Fuck me, this place was a dump.

I'd stumbled back into my apartment with a box of eggplant pizza in one hand and a duffel bag of stuff from the show in the other hand, guitar case slung over my back, and almost immediately regretted my decision to come back here.

As always, my roommate was nowhere to be seen. Craig had some kind of work-from-home job that involved developing video games designed to rot children's brains, and he barely left his room. If I died on my way home from a gig, he'd only notice when my rent payment bounced or if someone brought it up in the server he practically lived on.

How did I have *thousands* of followers and barely enough money to keep this mold-covered roof over my head? My voice was good enough for me to come second place on *The Headliner*. People claimed they liked the songs I wrote. I attempted to market myself.

All I wanted was a rodent-free apartment—ideally without a roommate. A better microphone. Maybe a pair of new shoes. When was the last time I bought shoes?

If only I'd been less of an idiot four years ago. Less of an idiot, less high off the freedom of ditching my leeching stage parents, and about a million times less cocky. I'd have a record deal, new shoes, no rodents, and a mildew-free apartment to myself.

Alas, such was life.

I set my stuff down, cracking open the bottle of whiskey on the otherwise empty shelf and pouring myself a small glass while eating pizza from the box at the greige formica counter. Maybe someone had posted something nice about tonight's gig? The odds were basically non existent, but I was a sucker for punishment so I decided to go looking in the fan spaces. Unlocking my shiny expensive phone that was somehow more financially viable for me than shoes, I pulled up the browser and hit the icon for the Austin Thibaut fan forum in my Most Visited links. Whenever I was feeling down, I could always count on my Austinators to make me feel either much better or vaguely unsettled. Either way, it would be a break in the monotony.

The latest post was a picture of me on stage tonight that one of the three women at the front had definitely taken. I squinted at the screen while trying to take a bite of pizza, nearly missing my mouth. Okay. It wasn't my *best* look. There was a definite sweatiness going on that wasn't really acceptable considering I'd been sitting on a stool for most of the show and the "stage lights" had been two of the kind of LED uplights usually seen at school dances and fiftieth birthday celebrations held in hired community halls.

@ThiBoner: How was the show?!

@ForTheStans: Um...

@ThiBoner: Spill the tea!

@ForTheStans: I think it's pretty well known in this sub that he's not super happy, and you could really see that in this performance. Like, he's just lost that spark he had back when he was on The Headliner, you know? I could just see how unfulfilled with life he was.

The parasocial relationships were a real blessing and a curse. Blessing: These people had stuck with me through the highs and lows of my career, keeping my name in the public sphere. Curse: The confidence in which they asserted facts about my personal life and state of my mind on the internet as if they *knew* me.

And okay, maybe I was one percent unfulfilled, but *they* didn't get to say that.

Annoyed, I exited the thread, clicking on the next one.

Austinators! Time for a vote. Do you prefer our king rocking a beard or clean-shaven?

Surely this couldn't hurt my feelings? Taking a fortifying gulp of my drink, I opened the thread, finding the results overwhelmingly in favor of clean-shaven to best showcase my jawline.

@ThibautMyBackOut: He has the voice of a fallen angel, and he looks perfect all the time, beard or no beard.

I held my glass up to my phone in a one-sided cheers to @ThibautMyBackOut. They always posted the nicest comments.

@ThibautMyBackOut: What we should be talking about is the rumor that Austin was out with Gigi Moore. That is obviously a rumor she started herself because Austin would never be interested in a model. He likes smart, artistic girls.

I retracted my cheers. I didn't even know Gigi Moore, but would I go on a date with a literal supermodel if she asked me? I mean, sure. Sometimes, I wondered if I'd shot myself in the foot with the artsy, sad-boy songwriter persona. I *was* an artsy sad boy sometimes. But I was also just a regular dude.

@CanineOverlord: You must be joking. Gigi Moore would never even notice him. You guys need to touch grass or something.

That was probably true, but still. Ugh, @CanineOverlord was the worst. Why were they even in this forum?

@CanineOverlord: To be honest, if he was more fuckable, maybe his career wouldn't have one foot in the grave. I know you're all die-hard fan girls here, but come on. You have to admit that all the other finalists from his season have capitalized on their fame way better than he has.

Dick.

I downed the rest of my whiskey, slamming it down on the counter a little harder than necessary. Stupid @CanineOverlord. I was plenty fuckable.

Besides, I'd lost in the finals to *dogs*. If the Hopping Hounds had won that season and scored a Vegas residency because of *fuckability*, I wanted off this timeline.

@ThibautMyBackOut: Austin is a true artist. He doesn't care about superficial stuff like that.

@CanineOverlord: You keep telling yourself that, as if he didn't go on a reality show to get famous. Delusional. He's a pretty face and if he created better content and didn't get shitfaced before every gig, maybe he'd actually be successful.

Man, that one actually hurt. Probably because it was all true. Except the content part, because I hated that word. The commoditization of art into cheap *content* for internet likes from bored scrollers who'd promptly forget what they just saw was a fucking travesty.

The idea that everything about me as a performer could be distilled down to *content* and *fuckability* was so grim. Morally, I had very strong objections to that line of thinking.

But on a personal level...

I was totally fuckable. People wanted to fuck me all the time. *I* was the one who kept chickening out because I got all in my feelings about it and didn't want to feel cheap.

Maybe that was the cause of my ennui? Maybe I could fuck my way out of my boredom?

My phone buzzed, and I squinted at the blurry screen, seeing Jonah's name flashing on the stupid hyper-secure Hunter communication app I never used. Clumsily, I swiped to accept the call out of curiosity, swallowing a mouthful of pizza at the same time. Jonah was basically toxic masculinity in walking, talking form, but we'd been kind of friendly as kids and he never called me. It wasn't as though I had anything better to do than listen to him brag about his kill count.

"Austin? You there?"

Whoops, forgot to talk. My bad. "Hey. What's up?"

"Dude, you sound fucked up." Jonah laughed. The sound annoyed me for some reason, and I usually enjoyed laughter. *"Bet you're busy partying with some freaky groupies right now, huh? Your life is so fucking cool."*

"I've got a bottle of Jack and some pretty freaky company," I agreed, glancing at the patch of wall by the one lonely exterior window where it sounded like the rat was about to claw its way to freedom.

I decided to name it Gollum in honor of its tenacity.

"So badass. Shit, I hate to spoil the party, but it's all hands on deck here at Headquarters right now. Moriah has put me in charge of calling the wanderers home. We need you, man."

"Me?" I couldn't imagine why they needed *me*. I'd done the basic training like all Hunters had to do, but I'd been more focused on my music than becoming some kind of world-class Shade assassin, or whatever it was Jonah was aiming for in life.

I was pretty sure most of them resented me for not pulling my weight, and I'd only gotten away with it because Grandfather bankrolled the Hunters Council and my mom—a stage mother if there ever was one—was his favorite daughter-in-law. Jonah was one of the few who thought of my career as a plus rather than a negative.

"Everyone, dude. It's all gone to shit. You've been keeping up with the group chat, right?"

"Sure." I'd definitely muted that the moment I'd been added to it. Group chats were a scourge on humanity.

"They should have never sent that Shade-fucker Ophelia Bishop to the shadow realm. I always said that was dumb. They should have sent a real hardened killer in, stabbed all those motherfuckers right off the bat. Then again, Astrid Bishop was one of our best, and she's sided with the monsters now too. Bet she's fucking one. I mostly blame her for all this, she was the one who convinced Ophelia to go."

"Wait..." I closed the pizza box, my head spinning. "Like... *literally* fucking them? Aren't they basically ghosts?"

"Not in their *realm. I heard they look kind of like squid in their corporeal forms, but they live on land."*

Huh. I didn't know Ophelia, but I'd seen Astrid around a bit back when we were teenagers and she seemed like the most boring, moody chick ever. I definitely wouldn't have taken her for a squid-monster fucker.

"You really haven't heard about this? Dude, your own cousin has gone to the shadow realm to be a Shade sex slave."

"Which cousin?" I had twenty at last count, and I hadn't met at least half of them.

"Tallulah."

"Tallulah went to the shadow realm? By choice or by force?" Maybe I should have kept a cursory eye on the group chat. Was Tallulah okay? Why hadn't one of my bajillion Hunter-loving relatives sent me a message about this? "Does her mom know? Do my parents know?"

"By choice. She's a traitor, so don't let anyone else hear you sounding upset about it," Jonah grumbled. *"And yeah, everyone knows. Your parents are on assignment in Detroit right now, but they're definitely aware of it. Those girls are dead to us."*

"Women," I corrected absently. Tallulah was thirty years old and living in a nice condo in the city last I heard. While she was considered a failure by Hunter standards, she had a *life* here. Definitely enough of a life not to jump ship to the shadow realm without good reason.

Unless fucking shadow squid monsters *was* a good reason.

It didn't sound like a *bad* reason.

Honestly, it sounded kind of awesome. I'd watched hentai. I considered myself an open-minded dude.

"Are you listening, Austin? The portals are shut to stop any other traitors leaving, but we need to fully close ranks. Explain to dumbasses like your cousin why fucking actual monsters is a bad thing." He snorted, clearly not on the same train of thought that I was riding. *"I'm sorry, man. I know music is your life, but you've got to put it aside for now. Duty calls."*

"I hear you," I murmured, wondering if Grandfather still stored the portal stone in the locked top drawer of his office.

It was unlikely. It had been *years* since I'd gone through his study one long summer break when I'd been bored and nosy, practicing the lock-picking skills I'd learned from online tutorials. He'd definitely have put it in a safer spot since then.

Right?

But if he hadn't...

I'd been wanting a change.

I was apparently so unfulfilled inside that strangers on the internet were stating it as fact.

I was still smarting from being called unfuckable. Maybe a squid monster would want to fuck me? I was very much not opposed to fucking a squid monster.

Maybe it could just be a little holiday? A little vacation from my increasingly bleak existence?

A change of scenery, a whole new *realm*, possibly some kind of sexual awakening...

The whiskey agreed: taking a cab to Grandfather's rambling old house, and sneaking into his office to steal the portal key and go on an adventure was a very good idea. I was already fizzing with the kind of excitement that usually led to my best music.

Without saying goodbye, I hung up on Jonah and pulled up the Notes app on my phone.

I had a quest to go on.

CHAPTER 2

And there's our Lieutenant of the Guard, on duty again," Andrus said, with *just* enough respect in his tone that I couldn't discipline him for insubordination. "The schedule says you're on the evening shift, but here you are at breakfast time. We're so fortunate that you're so dedicated to your role."

"So fortunate," Galen echoed, mimicking Andrus' politely disdainful voice because he'd never once had an original thought of his own. "And how well you cleaned up the mess yesterday after Astrid saved the day. We were all in such admiration of your leadership."

"It's my pleasure," I replied, equally as coolly, not missing the thinly veiled insult in his words. *Astrid* saved the day, *you* just tidied up. "It's a privilege I'm thankful for every day, that I get to serve the realm in such a way."

"Yes, I imagine so. First member of the Guard in the history of the realm to come from Mistwood, right?"

I didn't bother answering that. To them, Mistwood wasn't a place where I'd come from so much as a strike of ineptitude against me. As far as they were concerned, no one of value had ever come out of Mistwood, and no one ever would.

Andrus and Galen inclined their heads in the barest minimum gesture of respect before heading toward the palace to eat, leaving me to monitor the gardens and portal in front of the building alone.

They were right. It wasn't my shift. But even now, having risen as high in the ranks as I ever would, I couldn't rest. Couldn't lose focus for even a second, because Andrus and Galen, and plenty of others like them were waiting for me to fail.

They'd almost gotten their wish yesterday. If Astrid hadn't seen the threat, if her aim had been any worse... It didn't bear thinking about. The captain would have probably thrown me in the Pit for my failure to protect the royals, and I would have welcomed such a punishment.

As it stood, I still walked free, and Astrid was commanding the respect she'd probably deserved long before now, despite her past.

As though I'd summoned her, Astrid appeared, rounding the building side-by-side with Captain Soren. They weren't as demonstrative in their affections, in their mate bond, as the king and queen, but I knew how deeply they cared for each other in their own reserved ways.

I'd been hard on Astrid since she arrived in the shadow realm. I didn't regret it—she'd been a famous Shade-killer in her realm—but it was time to let that mistrust go. If no one could ever change, if we were always the thing we were born to be, then what did that say for me?

I had to believe that we could all rise above our circumstances.

"Captain!" I called, pausing my pacing in front of the portal. "Astrid," I added, tipping my chin respectfully.

"Selene," Astrid replied, her voice careful and reserved.

I swallowed thickly around my pride, keeping my arms loose at my side, attempting to relay that I wasn't a threat. "You did a good job yesterday. Even if I'd been watching the rafters and seen her, I'd have never made that shot."

"Thank you," Astrid said after a moment of hesitation, while the captain nodded approvingly.

"Perhaps you could lead a training session on knife throwing?" I suggested, looking at Soren. I was his second-in-command, but ultimately, every decision fell to him. In all honesty, my role was mainly taking on the administrative tasks he didn't want. "You have knowledge we could really benefit from in that area."

"That's a great idea," Soren agreed easily, looking affectionately at his mate. "Selene, can you coordinate that? The king tells me you handled everything exceptionally well yesterday after I ran out and left you with it. You should have been given more responsibilities before now, and I intend to rectify that going forward."

"Because you're mated now and don't want to work so much?" I asked, not quite able to hide my amusement. Captain Soren was the only member of the Guard who I was confident actually wanted me here. He'd taken a chance on an orphan from Mistwood, full of vim and vigor, without any polish or training, and given me the opportunities to become who I was today. He was the closest thing I had to a friend.

"Exactly—"

The faintest flicker of movement from the supposedly dormant portal had us all moving, immediately taking up defensive positions. The portal was shut. The Hunters had closed access on their end, and the king had decreed no Shade—except for Soren, who accompanied Astrid on supply runs—was to travel to the human realm on our end. Surely, no one would be stupid enough to defy the king in general, let alone by using the portal right in front of his home?

But it was a man who came out of the portal. Or *fell* out of the portal might be more accurate. A human man. A Hunter.

I'd never had the opportunity to examine the males much before. My trips to the human realm to feed were short and efficient as a matter of safety, but now I had the chance to really *look*.

He appeared to be of a similar age to Astrid and *reeked* of alcohol. The bottle of amber liquid was still in his hand, half-empty. His pale skin was covered in black inky drawings, which was intriguing. How had he acquired them? What did they mean? He flicked chin-length wavy dark hair out of his face, blinking brown eyes with what appeared to be a large amount of effort.

There was a substantially sized leather case on the man's back that had Soren tensing in alarm, but I was fractionally less worried.

This man was no threat to us, at least not in this condition. He was barely able to hold on to the bottle dangling from his fingertips.

"Hey." He looked between us, though his eyes seemed to have trouble focusing. "I heard we're fucking Shades now."

He dropped the bottle, shattered glass spraying everywhere.

Definitely not a threat.

"Oh, shit, I can clean that up," he mumbled, kneeling clumsily in the shards. He was *less* than a threat. If anything, he was an active danger to himself.

The more time I spent with now ex-Hunters, the more I wondered why we were ever so afraid of them. Granted, physically Shades were at a huge disadvantage in the human realm, but still. Aside from Astrid, they all seemed fairly incompetent as far as warriors went.

I didn't put my blade away, though. It was better to be over prepared than under.

"Austin?" Astrid asked.

"You know him?" Soren asked sharply, the jealousy in his voice unmistakable. How fascinating. Captain Soren hadn't struck me as the jealous type before.

"Sure, he's a Hunter. Tallulah's cousin, actually."

"What is that thing he's carrying on his back?" I asked, trying to ascertain if there was any force needed here. Was it a weapon? Did he need to be disarmed? Astrid didn't look worried.

"A guitar case. Austin is a, um, musician. I guess."

"I *am* a musician. I don't appreciate your tone there, missy," Austin slurred, pointing at Astrid. "Just because I never got a record deal or became famous like everyone said I would doesn't mean I'm not a musician, mmkay?"

"Did you just call me *missy*? I could murder you in your sleep, you know."

The captain made a sound of amusement, turning his attention to me. "You did want more responsibility."

I looked from the Captain to the drunken man dropping as many pieces of glass as he picked up. "Please, no. You're going to make *me* deal with him?"

"Search him for weapons, then take him somewhere secure to sober up. That should buy you some time to figure out what to do with him. I'll mention it to the king, of course. If you need me, ask someone else. My mate needs food."

"You're such an asshole," Astrid laughed as Soren dragged her toward the palace, leaving me alone with the Hunter who looked and smelled of poor choices. *Austin*.

Great.

I'd gotten through yesterday's near miss with a promotion, and yet it felt far more like a punishment.

Austin carefully set down a small pile of glass—a fraction of the mess he'd created—beaming up at me as though he'd just accomplished an impressive feat.

What an odd creature.

"Why are you here?" I asked bluntly, letting my blade catch the light in case he got any stupid ideas.

"I'm here to fuck a lot of Shades." He smiled beatifically. "Gonna have orgies and wild parties and live my best rockstar life." His smile turned to a confused frown. "You don't look like a squid."

And then he slumped to the ground in a dead faint.

I was going to bring up my remuneration rate with the captain after this. If I was getting more responsibility—specifically *this* kind of responsibility—I deserved a pay raise.

With a labored sigh, I lifted Austin out of the glass, setting him a few feet away lying on his side in case he brought up the contents of his stomach. It wouldn't be a good look if he choked to death on his own vomit on my watch.

Satisfied his demise wasn't imminent, I patted down his body for weapons—none—and took a moment to admire the delicate long gold necklaces hidden underneath his clothing. They were incredibly valuable here. Did that mean he was wealthy in the human realm? Pondering that, I fiddled with the silver latches keeping the black leather case shut. Astrid had described him as a musician, so I guessed the wooden, stringed device I was looking at was some kind of instrument. Nothing a Shade would use, I decided, disentangling a claw from between the strings I'd been examining and closing it back up.

Where were the rest of his belongings? His clothing?

Whatever decision led to him coming here, it was clearly an ill-advised one.

"Ooh. What is this?" Vespera cooed, pausing on her way out of the palace. She was one of the highest-born females at court, who took lovers as her due. Of course, she would be intrigued by him. "Is this one a man? Let me see him."

I hefted Austin's limp form over my shoulder, hoping he didn't decide to vomit down my back. "I have orders for his care, you will need to raise any concerns with the Captain."

And good luck to you, since I had no doubt he intended on making himself scarce for at least the next few weeks. Vespera huffed in irritation, but didn't otherwise acknowledge me, which was about what I expected. Most of the members of the Guard were also from prominent court families, they just had no choice but to speak to me. If they could get away with ignoring my existence too, they would have.

I started walking just to get away from Vespera, but once she was out of sight, I paused wondering where to *put* Austin. The other ex-Hunters were staying in Elverston House, but that was a designated Shade-free area, I couldn't walk in there with him—and he certainly wasn't going anywhere under his own steam right now—nor could I monitor him there.

There were probably rooms in the palace, but unlike most of the other guards, I didn't have access to private apartments, and walking through the halls with an unconscious man over my shoulder would draw a lot of attention.

The dungeon? That seemed a little extreme, especially since he'd shown up here unarmed. The king had been very firm about making any ex-Hunters who traveled here feel welcome, and that wouldn't exactly be a welcoming reception.

I hefted him a little higher and turned toward the training grounds instead. The attached barracks for the use of the Guard were clean, comfortable, and secure. Austin could sober up there until I figured out what to do with him.

"Carys," I called, flagging down a junior member of the Guard. She had a short attention span, but I had high hopes for her career. Carys had a compassion that was important for a guard, and yet often missing. She turned to face me, doing a double take when she noticed what I was holding. "This is a Hunter who has recently arrived from the human realm. His belongings are by the portal. Could you collect them and bring them to the barracks?"

"The barracks? I mean, yes. Of course," she agreed, discreetly attempting to get a look at Austin's face before I walked away.

He was here for pleasure, and the female Shades were already intrigued by him. I supposed it was a good omen for our dwindling energy stores, but almost everything else about him and this situation screamed trouble.

The barracks were sparsely occupied as always, and I opted to carry Austin along the narrow stone corridor to the empty room opposite mine.

Like all the others, it was a square space with a plain wooden bed against one wall, some shelving, a round table and two chairs, a small attached bathroom, and nothing else. It was no wonder that where possible, most of the Guard opted to stay elsewhere.

The moment I deposited Austin on the bed—perhaps not as gently as I should have—he blinked his eyes open, groaning slightly as he rolled onto his side.

"Is this the orgy?" Austin slurred, squinting at me. The only one of the ex-Hunters I'd spent any time with was Astrid, and her odd, mobile eyes were surrounded by white. The whites of Austin's eyes were an unhealthy-looking reddish color. Perhaps he needed a healer?

Or perhaps it was just the drink?

The elderly neighbor I'd grown up next to had an unhealthy relationship with wine, and his body was sickly and aged beyond his years because of it. He'd minded my company much less than almost everyone else where I'd grown up, probably because I fetched him items he was too inebriated to source for himself.

"You're in the shadow realm," I informed Austin, just in case he'd forgotten. "You came through the closed portal on your own."

Unless the Hunters had reopened the portal? If they had, that was something we needed to know about, though it didn't look like I was going to get any useful information from *this* Hunter any time soon.

Austin groaned, closing his eyes again and throwing his forearm over his face. "Why is the world spinning?"

"Hunter, did you hear me? You're in the shadow realm. You came through the *closed* portal on your own. If the world is spinning, it is because you imbibed an unreasonable amount of alcohol."

Silence.

Did he know where he was? It was clear that he'd been *following his cock*, as my sister would phrase it, and that he hadn't fully realized the implications of crossing through the portal. The king was very adamant that the Hunters who moved here had to be here willingly of their volition, and Austin was in no state to make that sort of decision. I supposed I'd have to lug him back to the portal and shove him through if his journey here had been a drunken mistake.

This was not how I wanted to spend the first few hours of my sort-of promotion.

Austin let out a startling sound and I jumped, my hand going to my blade on instinct.

A snore.

He was *snoring*. Infuriating, useless male.

Perhaps I should throw him back through the portal anyway.

CHAPTER 3

I *was drowning.*

I was dream drowning.

No. Fuck. I was *real* drowning.

Then suddenly, I wasn't drowning. I spluttered, coughing up water and gasping for air all at once. Flailing, I tried to find something to hold on to before being suddenly plunked down on my ass on some kind of ledge, a hard ridge digging into my back.

"What the..." I began before breaking into another coughing fit.

"Your alcohol-laden scent was deeply unpleasant," a solemn, feminine voice stated. "And you needed to wake up. The king and queen wish to see you."

"The what..." After blinking some water out of my eyes, I realized I was sitting in a circular bath, and it was the stone lip of the tub that was ravaging my spine.

And standing above me was what I assumed was a Shade, staring down at me like I was a particularly grotesque insect that had just crawled out of the drainpipe.

Fucking Jonah. They didn't look anything like squids.

Not that it was a complaint necessarily. Okay, there were no tentacles, but Shades in this form—judging by the one in front of me—were still pretty fucking majestic. Her eyes glowed emerald green, and her horns were sort of U-shaped with a dramatic outward flair at the top, and they were definitely sharp enough to impale a human on. As if she wasn't lethal enough, she had vicious black claws and a mouthful of sharp teeth.

If I wasn't suffering from a perilous case of whiskey dick, my cock might have popped up to say hello. Actually, maybe not. As attracted as I was to a dangerous woman, the visible disdain in her expression didn't really do anything for me.

"Where am I?"

"You are in the shadow realm. You entered through the closed portal."

"No, no, I know that." I looked around, taking in the sparse stone bathroom, and the open door behind her that led out to an equally grim-looking room with a small bed in the corner. "What is this place?"

"You are at the barracks on palace grounds. We will go and speak with the king and queen now, and find a more permanent place for you if you would like to stay in the shadow realm."

"Oh yeah, I just got here. I definitely want to stay."

"For the orgies?"

I began coughing and spluttering again, this time choking on my own saliva. Shit, had I said that out loud?

"You were looking for orgies," she reiterated impassively. "And to copulate with many, many Shades."

Somewhere in the back of my mind, I recognized that this wasn't the ideal first impression.

"Orgies might have been a bit ambitious for me—it's day one, after all." Her face had the same general features as a human's—two eyes, a nose, a mouth—but they were so *different* from ours that it was difficult to get a good read on her expression. I was fairly sure my words hadn't helped though. "But you should know that I'm *very* respectful of women. Like super respectful. Okay, I think I'm still pretty drunk and this might be going badly. I really like women. And I'll like Shade women too. For sure. I can tell."

Those green eyes were trained on me for so long, I briefly worried that she was going to shoot lasers out of them.

She was very beautiful in a marble statue kind of way. Sort of cold and sharp and untouchable, and absolutely majestic. My long dormant muse opened one lazy eye, interested in this elegant, angular, slightly terrifying being.

"We are not women, we are female Shades. And I am less worried about you being disrespectful of them than you being eaten alive by them at this current moment, but we'll see what the king and queen have to say about that." She tipped her chin toward a gray towel lying on the edge of the bath. "Dry off. I don't intend to lose my reputation for punctuality over you, Hunter."

Shit, I didn't even ask for her name. She was gone before I had the chance, though I could hear her in the attached room and she hadn't shut the door entirely. Was I a prisoner here? I hadn't given it much thought on the journey over, but on reflection, busting into a new realm might put me on the local watchlist for a little while.

I peeled off my t-shirt and the soaked leather pants I'd worn for the show—that now felt like a million years ago—with no small amount of effort, falling into the wall twice in an attempt to find my balance, before drying off with the towel and wrapping it around my hips.

I didn't have the physical or mental fortitude to attempt putting on wet leather pants, and in hindsight, I probably should have packed some clothes.

Then again, I hadn't expected to be dunked in a tub of tepid water either.

"I don't have anything to wear," I told my guard, stepping out into the impersonal bedroom. If it was a holding cell, it was a pretty comfortable one at least.

She stared at me, expression unreadable. Had I offended her? Clothes weren't really a *thing* here by the looks of it. She had shadows floating around her body like a particularly artsy black censor bar.

She flicked her hand and I sucked in a breath as I realized my torso was now covered in black shadows too. Almost my entire body was, in fact, from the neck down. I moved an arm and the shadows moved with me, and it felt like I was wearing a wizard's robe made of air.

With a jolt, I realized I knew very little about how Shade abilities worked. I thought they just used shadows for *traveling*, not costuming. Apparently, I was woefully uninformed.

"Don't read into it," she instructed, gesturing toward the door.

"Okay?"

That was an easy promise to make since I didn't understand the symbolism in the first place. The towel was damp and kind of uncomfortable, but I'd need another bottle of Jack to ditch it and walk around clad just in mysterious shadow, butt naked underneath.

The barracks looked medieval as fuck, all dark stone and wood so black it looked like it had been burned, though I guessed that was just what things looked like here.

"I'm Austin, by the way," I said, jogging to keep up with the guard. My bare feet slapped against the cold stone floor with each step, the uncomfortable sensation chipping away at the remaining alcohol fog in my brain.

"I know."

She didn't slow down, leading me down a long corridor with doors off it that I assumed led to rooms like the one I'd just been in. Maybe I was unfuckable. The first lady Shade I'd encountered appeared to have zero interest in sleeping with me, so I wasn't off to a roaring start.

The moment we stepped outside of the building, a group of other warrior-looking Shades paused what they were doing to stare, though they seemed more interested in my outfit than me. Mysterious Guard Lady had told me not to read into it, so I guessed the shadow robe I was rocking was symbolic in some way.

"He's wearing your shadows?" someone asked sharply, stepping into her path.

I thought my jailer had been intimidating before, but she must have been holding back. She seemed to grow taller in front of my eyes, the shadows that acted as clothing swirling in response to her agitation. The mouthy dude who'd stepped into her space immediately took a step back, dropping his gaze to the ground.

Badass.

"As always, Galen, you're welcome to take up any concerns you have about the way I do things with the captain. Or perhaps you'd like to go higher up the chain of command? I'm taking the Hunter to see the king now, would you like to join us?"

"No, that's fine," he mumbled.

"Are you sure? We all know how much the king appreciates your fawning praise. I believe last time, he looked at you for a full two seconds before walking away. How honored you must have felt."

God*damn*, there was a whole lot of sass behind those emerald eyes and stone-cold exterior.

"Is he... well?" another Shade asked, leaning in close and sniffing me. "He smells sickly."

"I believe the alcohol he consumed is seeping out through his skin," my guard replied disdainfully. "If you're concerned that he'll take no interest in the Shades here, you needn't be. From what I've observed so far, he appears to be some kind of libertine."

I spluttered, trying and failing to formulate a reply as she dismissed the other Shades and ushered me away from the barracks.

A *libertine*?

I knew that word. I'd used it in a song.

For a brief moment, I was outraged. Then I remembered that I'd promptly brought up orgies the second I arrived, so maybe she wasn't being entirely unreasonable in describing me as someone who freely indulged in sensual pleasures.

"I'm really not—" I began breathlessly, scrambling to keep up.

"Save it for the king," she called over her shoulder.

We headed up a slope to an elegant garden, filled with winding paths between raised stone garden beds. Most of the flowers were gray, but occasionally I thought I saw flashes of gold and maybe even hints of maroon. So maybe it wasn't entirely black and white here...? Or maybe it was the whiskey.

The whiskey was not my friend. The whiskey had thought coming here was a totally normal and acceptable idea, and in reality, I was starting to realize just how *vulnerable* I was in this realm.

The palace loomed ahead, all dark gray stone and sort of circular in shape, with a lot of highly stylized late-Gothic features. I was very into it. I loved me some fleurons.

There were guards stationed around the garden and entrance, but they didn't attempt to stop us. From the way they responded to the guard in front of me, I guessed she was one of the higher-ranking ones.

Was that a bad sign? That kind of seemed like a bad sign.

"They're in the throne room," a Shade told us, bowing their head slightly.

That gave my guard pause, and I added that to my list of bad omens. She muttered something quietly under her breath before hurrying me along again, seemingly deeper into the palace through what seemed to be spiraling corridors, though I was completely disoriented within minutes.

Eventually, we ended up at a heavy black door that two Shades pushed open for us the moment we came to a stop in front of it.

The throne room was very grand, with more dark stone walls and patterned stained glass windows in shades of grayish silver. There was only one throne, currently being shared by the Shade king and the ex-Hunter queen.

"King Allerick and Queen Ophelia," my guard said quietly, leaning in to speak next to my ear.

Queen Ophelia was tucked into the corner of the seat, her legs draped over her husband's thigh, and while he looked smug, she looked more than a little annoyed.

"This is quite the ceremony," the Shade standing closest to the dais said. He sounded different to the other Shades I'd encountered so far. More… cheerful? His eyes were purple and glowing, but I had a feeling that if he'd had human eyes, they would have been teasing.

"This is ridiculous," Ophelia mumbled, cheeks flushing red. "We never meet in here. I don't know why we're meeting in here now."

"You are *supposed* to use the throne room to meet petitioners and for official business of the kingdom," he replied.

"Crown Prince Damen," my guard murmured helpfully. "The king's brother."

"Selene," King Allerick began, his voice loud and commanding compared to everyone else's in the room, though he didn't seem particularly engaged with the proceedings. "Would you like to make the introductions?"

Selene.

Like the Greek goddess of the moon.

It was a softer, sweeter name than I'd expected, and yet it seemed to suit her perfectly.

"King Allerick, Queen Ophelia. This is Austin," Selene said flatly. "He is the cousin of one of the ex-Hunters I believe."

"Me," Tallulah said in a small voice, raising her hand tentatively. It was a credit to how grand the throne and royal couple were that I somehow missed the three not-Shade women standing against the far wall. It was extra impressive because Tallulah was a bright beacon of color in her sky-blue vintage-looking dress and bright red heels with matching red lipstick. We both had inherited the Thibaut glossy black hair, but where mine was a bedraggled mess, hers had been styled into some elaborate-looking bouffant. I could absolutely respect her commitment to the aesthetic.

The other two looked sort of familiar, but I didn't have a great memory for the various Hunters I hadn't seen in years.

"Oh! Well, that's good, right?" Ophelia said, leaning forward to look between my cousin and me.

"You don't know him?" the king asked her.

Ophelia shook her head. "I didn't know many Hunters. I'm guessing Astrid recognized him, but I don't want to disturb her and Soren right now."

"How did you get through the closed portal?" King Allerick asked, sounding more curious than anything. He was wearing some kind of crown that seemed to almost drape around his horns, and was maybe the coolest thing I'd ever seen. Way cooler than Queen Ophelia's regular old golden crown with a star at the top, which was pretty human-looking.

Huh. Kind of wished I was wearing more than a damp towel and a shadow blanket that I hoped was going to stay in place while I met royalty. I was no monarchist, but I did feel disrespectfully underdressed.

"I, uh, borrowed the key from my grandfather."

"If you borrowed it, then presumably you *returned* it," the prince pointed out cheerfully.

I squinted at the ceiling, trying to remember exactly what I'd done with the strange obsidian disk. "I think I just left the key in there."

Tallulah sighed. It had been years since I'd seen her, but from memory, she'd always been far more practical than me. She'd have probably remembered to pocket the portal key. Or at the very least, buried it under a bush or something.

"And have you staked a claim on him, Selene?" Prince Damen asked.

Selene startled. "Absolutely not. I dunked him in the bath to wake him up, forgetting he hadn't brought additional garments with him. I make no claim on him."

Ouch. I mean, I'd come here to live my best hedonistic life, so I didn't know why I was so offended. Possibly it was the vehemence in her voice.

Apparently, I wasn't the only one who'd noticed it.

"Is the idea so abhorrent?" the prince asked, shooting her a grin filled with pointy teeth. Given his title and the fact he was addressing her directly, it wasn't exactly surprising that Selene was giving him her full focus, and yet I was feeling kind of salty about it, which was totally unreasonable. I'd always been an attention seeker, but this was next level even for me.

Whiskey was not my friend. This was whiskey's fault.

"From what I have observed and what he has said directly, Austin is in the shadow realm for the sole purpose of copulating with as many Shades as possible," Selene said, repeating her brutally honest words from earlier.

Tallulah groaned, covering her face with her hands.

For sure never drinking again after this. Drunk Austin was embarrassing as hell.

"You came here to... bang a lot of Shades?" Ophelia asked slowly, looking to me for confirmation. "I mean, no judgment. Okay, a little bit of judgment because you probably shouldn't have led with that line, but we all like what we like."

That was a way more chill reaction than I expected her to have.

"Female Shades?" the king added. "I don't care what your preference is, but there may be biological side effects if your interest is in females."

"Um... yes?" I replied hesitantly.

"Pregnancy," Tallulah whispered loudly, staring at me as though she could send me back to the human realm with the force of her glare alone. "They're worried you're going to leave a string of children in your horny wake."

That idea sent a jolt of panic through my chest. I wanted to be a dad *so* bad, but not in a sperm-donor kind of way. In a read-my-kid-a-bedtime-story-every-night kind of way.

"If I can explain it bluntly," Ophelia began, shooting Selene an apologetic look. "Conception rates between Shades are low, and there hasn't been much demand for any kind of birth control for female Shades. And from what the research says, well, Shade-Hunter couplings are very fertile. Us human-realm ladies are on birth control, so it hasn't been a pressing issue thus far…"

"Any children would be well cared for," the prince added. "But it's important you know there may be consequences to your actions. Perhaps not, perhaps a mating bite is necessary first. We don't have that knowledge yet."

Bite? I was down to try new things, but I didn't want anyone biting me. Was there an opt-out form or something for that?

"He has not demonstrated a good understanding of consequences thus far," Selene cut in. "Based on his sudden arrival here, extremely inebriated, with no supplies except a musical instrument."

Selene really did not pull her punches.

"All this is moot because he can't stay here," Tallulah said, giving the royal couple an imploring look before turning to face me. "You can't stay here."

"Because he's a male?" King Allerick asked mildly, his face giving nothing away.

"What? No. Because he's moderately famous," Tallulah replied, startled.

"How did you make that sound like an insult?" I mumbled, frowning at my cousin across the room. She rolled her eyes. This was all going kind of terribly.

"Austin came third—"

"*Second.*"

"—in a TV talent show. He was pretty popular, though I think we all knew that beating the dancing dogs was going to be a long shot."

I gaped at Tallulah, wounded by the layers of betrayal she was oh-so-casually heaping upon me.

"Anyway, he has a lot of online fans, and his disappearance from the human realm will be very much noticed," Tallulah finished, her face slightly red. Probably because both King Allerick and Prince Damen looked like they had no idea what to make of either TVs or dancing dogs.

"That doesn't really seem like *our* problem," the king pointed out, sounding bored. "The humans will just assume he died mysteriously. Maybe in a drunken accident."

As far as first impressions went, I'd really made a horrible one. "I explained my absence to everyone before I left. I couldn't let the Austinators think I was dead, that would be cruel."

I may have never met @ThibautMyBackOut in person and sometimes they were a little intense for my liking, but I cared about their well-being.

"Please, *please* tell us how you explained your absence to your legions of fans in advance," Tallulah replied, sounding offensively exasperated.

"Is he moderately famous or does he have legions of fans?" Selene interjected waspishly, drawing the entire room's attention.

There was sexy, self-assured Selene again. Were all female Shades like her?

"Moderate legions," I replied, saving a flustered Tallulah from answering. "And I wrote a statement saying that I loved and appreciated all of my fans, but I was taking a break from fame and I wanted to focus on my life as a private citizen."

Short and sweet. Super professional. Very classy.

"You... sent out a press release or something?" Ophelia asked, frowning.

"Basically. I wrote it on my Notes app and posted screenshots on all my socials."

"Of course you did," Tallulah murmured, finally looking like the always-amused cousin I remembered. "How very celebrity of you."

"Surely it would have been better to just let them think you were dead?" Prince Damen asked, bemused.

"I couldn't do that! Look, some of the Austinators can be a little much, but most of them are wonderful and I don't want to cause them any unnecessary stress."

Everyone had an opinion on this, even though—respectfully—none of them had navigated the treacherous waters of internet fame. Most of the people and Shades in the room began talking at once, only falling silent when the queen cleared her throat.

"I think what everyone is trying to say is that you may have created *more* mystery and invited *more* speculation by announcing that you intended to leave your public life behind. Even people who weren't necessarily, er, followers of your musical career may be drawn in by the intrigue and become invested in tracking you down."

"Which isn't a problem in and of itself," Prince Damen mused. "For us, anyway. Humans can't travel to this realm."

"No," Ophelia agreed. "But it might be for the Hunters. Digging around Austin's history, his family, where he grew up and so forth leads directly back to them. The Council won't like that."

"What do you think their course of action will be?" King Allerick asked his wife. From this short interaction, it was obvious that the king looked at her differently to how he looked at anyone else, and he clearly respected her opinion.

So far, I was seeing lots of positives in the interspecies relationship column, and not a lot of negatives. Well, maybe the claws. They were kind of intimidating.

And the whole biting thing. Still super not down for that. On any part of my body, but I felt more strongly about some areas than others.

Ophelia pursed her lips. "Astrid is better qualified to answer that. I suppose the Hunters could come after him, but it would be a risky proposition, since they're outnumbered and at a huge physical disadvantage in this realm. It's more likely..." she trailed off, giving me a hesitant look.

"It's more likely they'll try to get ahead of it by faking his death," Tallulah finished grimly. "Which means they'll have to kill him for real if they ever get their hands on him again. Grandfather won't like that, but the Council are ultimately responsible for the safety and secrecy of *all* Hunters."

I blanched at that. Sure, I'd always known the Hunters Council were ruthless, and I'd been careful to toe the lines they'd set out for me, but I'd never felt like my *life* was at risk with them. Maybe I'd been a little naïve where the Hunters were concerned.

The king leaned back, idly playing with strands of Ophelia's red hair. She didn't seem to mind the super sharp claws being an inch away from her throat. Maybe the claw thing wasn't a deal-breaker.

Just the teeth thing.

"Well, I offered sanctuary to all former Hunters who wanted to come to the shadow realm, and I stand by those words," King Allerick said eventually. "It goes without saying that there will be no more treaties with the Hunters Council—they have already thoroughly demonstrated that they are not good to their word."

Ophelia nodded grim-faced in agreement.

"That being said," she said in a gentle voice, giving me a soft smile. "You're not obligated to stay or to *do* anything, other than prioritize the safety of the Shades and the shadow realm. If you'd like to leave, you're free to go. Selene can escort you back through the in-between and take you to a location of your choice, you don't need to go back to the portal you came through."

"But you should probably do it now, before they decide that it's easier to just kill you and be done with it." Prince Damen delivered those chilling words factually, though I thought I heard a trace of pity in his voice. "So, what'll it be? Are you sure you can give up your... what do you call them? Austinators?"

I blew out a long breath. It's not like I'd done the full pros-and-cons process when I'd stolen the portal key, drunk off my ass, and dived headfirst into the in-between. It had seemed like a fun escape from a depressing reality at the time, a new adventure and a chance to rediscover the passion for life that I'd lost, and that was about the level of thought I'd put into it.

Selene was looking at me expectantly, waiting for an answer. Waiting for me to say I wanted to go back. I didn't know how I knew that since her face wasn't really giving me anything to go on. Maybe I was just picking up a vibe.

And maybe it wasn't the most rational reason to stay, but I felt suddenly driven to subvert her expectations of me.

"I want to stay."

Someone groaned. I was pretty sure it was Tallulah.

The king nodded once, sparing me a look before angling himself back toward his wife. Apparently, that was all the reassurance he needed. Maybe he was more of a hands-off leader.

"If I may, Your Majesty," Selene began, *definitely* sounding tense. "His safety may be an issue in the short-term while we wait for the Hunters to make their move. Plus, the fact that he's the only male Hunter here and he's already demonstrated some impulsive behavior—"

"Yes, I think it's probably best if you could keep an eye on him for now," King Allerick agreed, speaking to Selene but still very much focused on Ophelia.

"Me?" Selene confirmed. Maybe it was her shadows against my skin conveying how filled with dread she was at the idea.

"I'm sure Soren will want to add some further direction to that, but I'd like to give him some time to settle in with his mate first," Allerick continued.

There was something very *primal* about that word. *Mate.*

"We don't want you to *feel* watched, Austin," Ophelia added hurriedly, resting a hand on her husband's forearm and looking at me intently. "The shadow realm is meant to be a sanctuary for anyone who renounces the Hunters. We want you to be comfortable here. Does he really need to be watched?"

"I'd be comfortable with Selene watching me," I replied, shrugging as though I didn't really care either way. Why was I needling her? I wasn't even sure. Maybe it was because she kept implying I was some kind of degenerate. "I feel safe with Selene," I added, laying it on a little thicker for the queen's benefit.

"Admirably foolish of you since Selene could gut you in her sleep," Tallulah muttered.

"Oh, I definitely know that," I assured everyone. "I mean, that's a large part of the appeal of living here, right? The added risk, the constant adrenaline. That can't just be a me thing."

Tallulah squinted at me. "I wouldn't say knowing I could die at any moment is at the top of my list of my reasons to be here."

I shrugged. It didn't look like she had a mate. Maybe that was why?

"I'd *just* be guarding you," Selene clarified, turning the full force of those glowing green eyes on me. "Nothing else."

"Of course. You're a professional, just doing your job, I totally get that." She made a quiet noise in her throat, not sounding entirely convinced. "I swear, I'm not a libertine. You'll see."

"I'm sure I will," she muttered.

"Well, it sounds as though everything is settled," King Allerick said. "Of course, Austin will need to be brought up to speed on the, er, relationships between Shades and Hunters—both the past and the present. Selene, I don't suppose you could...?"

"Of course, Your Majesty." Selene bowed low, and I didn't think she was acting when it came to showing the king deference. Did I have to bow? The concept rubbed me the wrong way, but not my realm, not my monkeys. Or something like that. She turned her attention on me, practically vibrating with annoyance. "Come along, Austin. Welcome to the shadow realm."

SELENE

CHAPTER 4

None of this had gone how I planned it. It was a good reminder why Soren was the *Captain* of the Guard, and why I would never have that position. Even if my lineage didn't impede me, Captain Soren would have never ended up being landed as personal guard to a drunken Hunter for the foreseeable future.

I supposed he'd been charged with watching Astrid when she first arrived in this realm, but she was an actual threat.

Austin was ambling along behind me, humming a strange, though not unpleasant, tune to himself and reeking of rancid liquor. Given the challenging looks he'd kept giving me in the throne room, I'd expected him to attempt some kind of confrontation once we were alone, but apparently, he was content to say nothing for now.

The only threat he posed was to my sanity.

"You will return to the room in the barracks where you awoke. I cannot watch you adequately if you stay in Elverston House with the other ex-Hunters, it's a Shade-free zone. I would hate for you to feel unsafe without my presence," I added pointedly.

Austin shot me a lazy grin, not a trace of apology on his face. Were all Hunter males so irksome? Perhaps that was why Astrid hadn't bothered to bring any when she'd been rounding up volunteers to move here. "Very kind of you."

What was I meant to *do* with him once I had him set up in the barracks? Presumably, he would require regular sustenance and rest and stimulation, and I didn't want to give up my duties as part of the Guard. Andrus and Galen were always waiting, hovering, hoping I'd make a mistake and get demoted. I would never let anyone see how much they bothered me, but I would be foolish to ignore the threat they presented.

Austin reached for a gray flower as we passed the edge of the palace gardens, and I slapped his hand away before he could make contact with it.

"It's poisonous," I told him, already exasperated with the responsibility of full-time minding, before doing a double take when I noticed Austin was examining four thin red lines on the back of his hand. "Is that *blood*?"

I already knew the answer—I'd spent enough time with Astrid to know that Hunters bled red, but the rich, glossy color never failed to mesmerize me.

And in this case, horrify me.

"You have very sharp claws. I was wondering how I was going to feel about those," Austin said mildly, turning his hand from side to side, looking at his injury from all angles. "So far so good I think. It all adds to the edge-of-danger, raw, primal sensuality of this place, you know?"

"No. I have no idea what you're talking about. You're not… grievously wounded?" I shifted uncomfortably, holding my hands behind my back so I didn't injure him again. His scent was still too polluted for me to tell if he was afraid.

Would I lose my position if my charge was injured? Not just under my watch but *by* me specifically? I was practically gifting Andrus and Galen my job at this point. "Do you need medical attention?"

"It's just a scratch." Austin smiled, showing off a line of blunt, white teeth. They were nice teeth. Harmless teeth, but neat and pleasing to look at.

I startled, not at all pleased with that line of thought.

"You're not my type," I blurted out, immediately horrified at myself for saying it.

If anything, his smile grew wider, eyebrows rising up alarmingly high. "Aren't I?"

"I just want to be clear about that." *Why* oh why had I said that? His provoking manner in the throne room must have gotten under my skin more than I thought. "I didn't mean to injure you. You are very fragile. Your skin is like petals."

Austin's expression changed, and whatever emotion he was displaying, it was not nearly as pleasing as his smile had been. "I'm definitely more fragile than I realized, at least in this world."

"This distresses you," I surmised, making a guess based on the slight downturn of his mouth and the tone of his voice. "No need to be afraid, fragile man. I've been assigned to protect you, and I take my duties seriously. Going forward, I'll take more care with my claws around you."

"Please don't call me fragile man," Austin asked, looking slightly pained. "My ego can only take so much."

I mulled that over. I supposed I hadn't really considered he'd *have* an ego after the shameless way he'd shown up here. "I'll take care with my claws *and* not to point out your fragility in future. I would hate to shatter that feeling of *safety* you have with me," I clipped.

"You were the first face I saw when I woke up. Clearly, I've latched on to you as a figure of safety and comfort."

"No, you haven't. I think you might just be trying to get revenge for me throwing you in the bath."

Austin grinned. "It's actually for repeatedly telling everyone I'm some kind of deviant. I'm really not, you know."

"That very much remains to be seen."

When his scent wasn't poisoned by the foul stench of liquor, then we'd truly know where his intentions lay.

As Austin had nothing but his instrument, which he lovingly checked over before propping it up in its case in the corner, it took him no time at all to get settled into his room. Which meant I was immediately back at the question of what to *do* with this man.

I had far more important uses for my time than sitting here, observing him. I supposed I could have delegated someone else to watch him, but the idea didn't sit well with me. He was my responsibility, by royal decree.

"So, uh. What do you do for fun?" Austin asked, wandering around the perimeter of the room, observing the plain black wooden furniture with mild interest. His hands drifted over the empty dresser. At least there was nothing on *there* that could poison him. He was very... tactile.

"If I'm here at the palace, it's because I'm on duty or I'm training. If I'm not doing either of those things, I prefer to be elsewhere."

"Not a palace person?" Austin asked. "Or a barracks person, perhaps?"

Both.

"I'm not a person at all. I'm a Shade."

Austin grinned. "So you are. Where are the best spots in the shadow realm then when you want to get away from it all?"

I hesitated for a moment to answer. Did I want to encourage casual conversation with my charge? Having him stay here at the barracks already blurred the lines somewhat.

There was also my inherent distrust of Hunters. If Austin changed his mind and returned to the human realm, he would take all of the information he'd gained here with him.

"You don't have to tell me," Austin laughed, sitting down on the bed I'd dumped him on when I'd brought him back here. "I can see you giving it some serious consideration."

How irritating that he'd managed to read me when I was struggling to get a read on him.

"You could be lying about how and why you came here. After all, you had access to the portal key, which I assume indicates some level of authority."

"Not even a little, I'm just a great thief." Austin paused, looking thoughtful. Or that was my best guess of his expression, at least. "Actually, I'm probably not a great thief because I left quite a lot of evidence that it was me going through that office. Like, there will be *zero* doubt about who took the key."

"It sounds like you're a terrible thief."

"It does, doesn't it? Okay, never mind. I don't have any level of authority and I'm not a good thief. Maybe luck was on my side. I'm usually a pretty lucky guy, unless dancing dogs are involved."

"The human realm sounds like a very strange place."

"It probably is. Have you spent much time there?"

I tilted my head to the side, examining him. The question seemed genuine, and I wondered if this ex-Hunter was made in the same mold as our queen. Namely, born into the Hunters, but separate somehow. Seemingly oblivious to how the mercenaries they were blood connected to worked.

"Until the treaty fell through and the Shades retreated to the shadow realm, I traveled to the human realm regularly under the cover of darkness to feed, as all Shades do once they come of age. It was an extremely risky task. I spent as little time there as possible."

"Right. I guess the whole being hunted thing probably didn't make it the most enjoyable experience." Austin frowned, and it did seem as though he was giving my statement some genuine reflection.

Perhaps he was a very good actor, but it seemed more likely that he was uninformed. Or perhaps a little dim.

"Will you feel adequately protected if I lock you in this room? No one will be able to unlock it except me."

Austin blinked at me, and I noticed most of the redness around his eyes had faded. "No."

I huffed, not quite able to disguise my frustration. "Can you not entertain yourself for a couple of hours? There is a feast in the palace every night, it is where the ex-Hunters take their meals. Keep yourself occupied until evening time and I will escort you to the dining hall."

Austin leaned back on his hands, giving me a somewhat sheepish smile. "I suppose that's only fair since I did sort of force my company on you."

"Sort of," I agreed flatly. It was far more than *sort of* and we both knew it. "Do you require anything before I go? Sustenance, perhaps? The water from the tap is drinkable, and there is a cup there for you. Food is brought down to the barracks three times a day from the palace kitchens, I can see if there is anything left."

Austin sighed, flopping backward onto the bed with a thump and staring up at the ceiling. He was still covered in my shadows, and they shifted with him, his movement exposing the entirety of his vulnerable throat to me. It was definitive confirmation that this man was no threat to anyone's safety but his own.

"I definitely, er, overindulged on the whiskey. I don't think I could stomach any food right now. I'll just wait until dinner. I don't suppose I could get an extra blanket?"

I could hardly begrudge him such a reasonable request. Especially as he *was* so fragile, even if he didn't want to admit it.

"I will bring you a blanket and demonstrate how the lock works for your peace of mind."

My shadows secured the lock in place, and only my power signature would release them, which Austin appeared satisfied with even if it was clear he didn't understand it at all.

After fetching a blanket from my room, Levana appeared in the hall with a bundle of clothes that the other ex-Hunters had assembled, pulled from their own collections.

"It is unlikely they will fit, but at least you won't need to cover him with your own shadows," Levana commented, not bothering to hide her curiosity. Of all the guards aside from Soren, I found her the most tolerable. Levana was sensible and minded her own business, which was personally guarding the queen.

"That will be preferable to my shadows," I agreed.

Levana waited for a moment, likely hoping I'd elaborate before conceding that I wasn't going to say anymore, and headed back to the palace.

"Austin, I have clothes for you," I announced, unlocking the door with my shadows and waiting for him to open it. I didn't want him to feel as though he had no privacy.

"Awesome." He pulled the door open with a beaming smile, still wearing a towel around his hips and nothing else, since I'd moved far enough away for my shadows to dissipate.

I all but shoved the clothes and blanket into his arms, not wanting to look too closely at the inky drawings on his chest.

Though I couldn't stop myself from looking just a *little*. They appeared to be serpents—one either side—slithering up over his torso toward his neck.

"I will leave them with you, do my rounds and return shortly. Are you comfortable here? I can assure you that you won't be disturbed."

"I'll be fine." Another one of those absurdly cheerful smiles. Not a drop of caution to be found.

I shut the door in his face, locking it behind me before doing two rounds of the grounds, informing the guards as I passed that there was an ex-Hunter staying in the barracks and he was not to be disturbed. They were clearly curious, but mentioning the king and queen was enough to get them to cooperate. For now, at least.

None of them ever gave Captain Soren as much grief as they gave me. They respected him because he was one of them, even if he did his best to interact with them as little as possible.

After an hour, I headed back to the barracks, unlocking Austin's door and announcing my presence again.

"Come in!"

His voice was odd and muffled, and I shoved the door open in a rush to make sure he hadn't injured himself somehow. Perhaps leaving him unsupervised was a mistake.

For a long moment, I just stared, trying to make sense of what I was seeing. Austin had laid out the spare blanket I'd given him on the ground, and was sitting on it in a position I couldn't even begin to comprehend. His legs were all twisted and his entire upper body was contorted to face the wall behind him, arms bent in all kinds of unnatural ways.

"By the night, what are you *doing*?" I asked, faintly horrified. Was this what happened if you left a human man alone? Had he tangled himself into a knot? Was he able to untangle himself?

"Yoga." He maneuvered his limbs back into a more sensible-looking position, pushing up to stand without using his hands.

"You can't go to dinner in that," I said flatly, taking in the clothing he'd put on since I left. Or lack thereof. The gray pants were *obscenely* tight, and didn't quite reach his ankles, and he'd foregone a shirt altogether.

I looked away, focusing on a spot on the wall behind him. It felt rather indecent to look at him wearing so little, and the tight fit of his pants left nothing to the imagination.

"It's not ideal," Austin agreed. "The ladies are all a lot shorter than me, so even the baggiest sweatpants aren't the best fit."

There *were* some clothes here in the shadow realm. It wouldn't take me long to go and fetch some from my sister's house. But he could hardly show up

0

to a feast in the dining hall wearing them—they were considered barely better than rags. No, that wouldn't work.

I was pacing, my shadows flickering in agitation around me.

How was I meant to mind a human man without any resources? Especially one who contorted himself into strange positions the moment my back was turned?

"I'll make it work," Austin said, smiling as if he didn't have a care in the world as he tipped out the bag of clothes onto the bed. "I'll layer and call it boho. Have you see these cheekbones? This jawline? I look good in anything."

"I can't tell if you are teasing or not."

"I'm teasing. Well, mostly. I consider myself fairly blessed in the bone structure department."

By the night, what was I going to do with this infuriating creature?

Eventually, he was ready to go, having ripped some of a shirt so he could pull it down to cover his torso and squeezing himself into a tight sweater over the top. He'd also wisely tied another sweater around his waist, hiding the most distracting of body parts from view.

"My boots are still wet." Austin gave me a pointed look, and I supposed I did bear some responsibility for that. "But I'll just go sans shoes. Shades don't wear shoes, right?"

"Our skin is not as fragile as yours, but it will have to do for now." We needed to get to the dining hall before the royals made their nightly entrance. Austin was going to draw enough attention as it was without being late.

Fortunately, he seemed content to keep pace with me in silence as we made our way up the winding path to the palace. Had he bathed again while I'd been gone? The stench of the liquor seemed to have lessened, though I still couldn't make out his natural scent underneath.

He grew more fidgety as we entered the palace, and I twice had to give him warning looks for reaching out to touch decorative sculptures in the hallway.

"In here," I instructed needlessly, gesturing to the open double doors where the low hum of voices was coming from. Austin looked rather green. Humans were so interesting.

"Alright." He straightened, rolling back his shoulders and shaking out his arms. I imagined he was still tense from having tangled himself in a knot earlier. "Let's do this."

He'd been following a step behind, but now came to stand at my side. Perhaps I should have encouraged some distance, but his pallid complexion had me taking pity on him, and we walked into the hall together.

Usually, I wandered around the palace happily invisible. I was here to do my job, after all. It didn't matter to me that the fancy high-born Shades who lived at court looked right through me.

They weren't now, though. Granted, mostly they looked at him and dismissed me as Austin's personal guard, but it was still a jarring amount of attention compared to what I usually experienced.

"Is this normal?" Austin whispered, speaking out of the corner of his mouth while leaning in close enough that his arm brushed mine. I glanced at Kael—a male I'd once coveted as a potential father for a future child—seeing him watching us intently as we passed.

"No. You are an oddity, and they will stare at you accordingly."

"Oh. Maybe they're staring at you."

He was teasing, I was almost certain. I'd never experienced it firsthand—Astrid didn't tease—but Austin had that same glint in his eye that I often noticed the queen had.

"I am not the sort of Shade that others stare at," I told him bluntly, focusing hard on keeping my shadows in place when they were eager to give away how restless and uncomfortable I felt with all this attention. "I will deposit you with your cousin."

"Ooh, come sit here, Hunter man!" Vespera cooed as we walked past her table, shuffling over and bumping into the female next to her to make room for Austin.

"Unless you'd prefer *not* to sit with your cousin," I added. With Vespera's penchant for passionate, short-lived romantic affairs, and Austin being a libertine who was solely here to fornicate, they seemed to be a match written in the stars.

"I don't know that I want to sit with Tallulah. She wasn't the most supportive about me moving here."

For very practical reasons, I thought to myself.

"Oh, do hurry and sit down, I've been so excited to meet you all day!" Vespera said, gesturing for him to come closer, no question in her mind that he would do as she wished. "A *man.* How exciting. My name is Vespera. Come— sit, sit. Right here next to me."

Austin hesitated. "Where will Selene sit?"

Vespera tilted her head to the side. "Who?"

Austin looked at me, startled. "Selene. This is Selene. She's right here."

"Oh!" Vespera laughed. "Well, she's not here to *dine.* She's here to guard."

"Precisely," I agreed hastily, taking a step back.

"Though he hardly needs a guard at this moment," Vespera added, tugging Austin down next to her and turning her back on me. It was clearly a dismissal, but I didn't take orders from the courtiers, so I stayed where I was. I was Austin's guard, I was hardly going to abandon my charge to be fondled to death by admirers in the middle of dinner.

"I need Selene around," Austin said, discreetly tugging his forearms out of her reach as Vespera went to stroke them again. Probably wary of getting another set of claw stripes on his delicate flesh. "I'm completely dependent on her, I told the king that myself. I'd be lost without her."

"Well, male Hunter, you've only just arrived. You haven't experienced a variety of company yet," Vespera managed, a waspish edge to her voice.

"Here," Lucienne said from Austin's other side, pushing a plate piled high with the best meat on it in front of him. "Some dinner. My name is Lucienne."

"Oh, er, thank you. You really didn't need to do that—"

"Here! I poured you some wine!" Cosima interjected from across the table, the liquid sloshing over the sides in her rush to shove it toward him.

"Cosima!" Vespera chided, angling her body further toward Austin's. "You're embarrassing us. Sorry about that, they're so... eager. It must be so overwhelming for you. Tell me about yourself, male Hunter."

"Um, well, most people just call me Austin. Also, I'm pretty sure we're going by ex-Hunter here...?" He twisted to look at me, as though I was the authority on these things. I gave him a tentative nod since he seemed to expect a response, and he repeated the gesture with more confidence as he returned to his conversation. "Right, ex-Hunter. In the human realm, I was a musician."

"Like in a choir?" Cosima asked hopefully, leaning forward.

I almost laughed. Where I was from, music was a major form of entertainment. It was boisterous and informal, and every song had a dance to match. These Shades had all grown up among the stuffy upper class that resided at court, I doubted they'd ever heard anything other than the subdued choir music that was occasionally employed on special occasions.

"Not quite like a choir," Austin replied slowly. "I was a solo artist."

"Wow, that's so interesting," Vespera said absently, piling her plate high with meat from the platters in the center of the table. "I do hope you'll perform for the court sometime. Perhaps I could suggest it to King Allerick? The traveling troupes of entertainers are so boring these days."

"I totally agree—" Lucienne began, but Vespera wasn't done yet, cutting her an impatient look before launching into some long-winded complaint about the tiredness of traveling troupes.

I shifted my attention to my surroundings, scanning the hall for anything unusual, making sure to check the ceiling rafters this time after the close call Astrid had saved us from. Tuning out the conversation of the courtiers over dinner was a skill I had perfected during my time in the Guard. At first, I had found it fascinating to see how they lived, the things they did and ate and enjoyed and took entirely for granted, not realizing how privileged they were.

It was the *complaining* that had taught me I was better off not listening. They complained at least twice more than the Shades of Mistwood who had half as much, and I'd found it increasingly difficult to hold my tongue.

Austin idly played with the small silver knife on the table, occasionally setting it down to twist the dinnerplate in slow circles or swirl the wine in the goblet, though he never actually consumed anything, nor ate any food. In fact, he almost appeared a little squeamish when he looked at the pile of meat, but then again, his features were difficult to understand.

By the time the meal had ended, I was more than ready to get back to the barracks and fix myself a plate of whatever had been sent down from the kitchens no matter how cold and unappetizing it was. It didn't matter. So long as I got to eat it alone in my room in perfect silence, I would be content.

"Shall we go?" Austin asked, standing and turning that guileless smile on me that he'd been using all night. If I hadn't been watching him so closely, I might have thought it was genuine.

"Yes. We'll return to the barracks."

Austin's dining companions seemed loathe to let him go, and I was prepared to intervene if necessary, but he was surprisingly adept at extricating himself all while charming them with assurances that he'd see them again soon and how much he'd enjoyed their company.

Moderately famous, his cousin had called him. Perhaps he was used to graciously escaping a fawning retinue?

I was begrudgingly impressed with the deviant. Not that I'd ever *need* that skill, but I always admired anyone who could adeptly navigate delicate social situations.

The moment we were outside the palace doors, Kael approached, as though he'd been waiting for us. I'd admired him since I came to the palace as a guard ten years ago—he was handsome, strong, and intelligent. A sure bet for the Council of Shades someday, when he was older. That admiration was somewhat dulled now, but he still had a *presence* about him that commanded attention.

"Friend of yours?" Austin asked casually.

"I don't have friends."

"What? None?" He sounded shocked, and I was glad that Kael interjected, giving me a reason not to answer.

"Selene. Are you well?"

He'd never asked me before. Austin really did draw attention.

"I am well, thank you. Did you need something?"

"Just the pleasure of your company."

Austin made a strange coughing sound, and I glanced at him to make sure he wasn't at imminent risk of death. It was so hard to tell with humans. Perhaps he was ill because he hadn't eaten anything?

"Well, I need to return Austin to the barracks, so that will have to wait," I informed Kael, gesturing for Austin to follow me. Whatever Kael wanted, it was certainly *not* the pleasure of my company. He'd made that very clear two years ago.

"That guy not your type either?" Austin asked, jogging to keep up with me as we made our way through the garden.

"I'm not his type."

"It didn't sound that way."

No, it didn't. But I knew better than to believe him.

CHAPTER 5

I didn't sleep well. Possibly because I'd had a wicked nap right after I arrived here, but also because the empty gray room in the barracks that I'd been magically locked into was not the most relaxing of spots.

Then again, I couldn't hear any rodents dancing the tango in the walls, so I guess I shouldn't really complain.

Was it Stockholm syndrome to be silently praying for Selene to come back soon? Of all the Shades I'd encountered so far, she was the one who I felt the safest with. I hadn't been totally facetious when I'd said that.

Well, maybe I had at the time, but after being surrounded by pushy Shades at dinner, my words had turned out to be a more accurate prediction than I'd anticipated.

"Are you awake, Hunter?" Selene asked suddenly from the other side of the door, startling me upright in bed. I grabbed the now-dry t-shirt I'd arrived in, yanking it on in case my chest made Selene uncomfortable. From what I'd observed yesterday, Shade fashion was pretty gender-neutral with some kind of shadow covering around the chest and groin, though the shapes which the shadows took differed, and some left more skin exposed than others.

Tying a sweater around my waist to make the tight sweatpants I was wearing less X-rated, I pulled open the door, giving Selene a smile that was entirely genuine this time because I was so happy to see a familiar face. She looked the same as she had yesterday in a tunic-style shadow arrangement and an unimpressed expression. She was carrying a tray of food that made my stomach churn unhappily almost instantly.

They were serious carnivores here in the shadow realm, which wasn't ideal for someone who hadn't eaten meat in a decade.

Selene set the tray down on the small two-person table, taking a seat and giving me an imperious look that all but demanded I do the same. Resigned to remaining hungry until I figured something else out, I took the seat opposite her.

"Here," she said, turning the tray so a couple of thick, gray, square mystery items were in front of me. "You don't like meat, correct?"

"That's right." I felt my eyebrows shoot up in surprise. I honestly hadn't realized Selene was paying that much attention at dinner.

"This is a hard bread that we usually stack meat on top of, but there's none inside it. I enquired about more food from the human realm—Astrid and Soren are doing a supply run today, they tend to bring back an assortment of non-meat items. She is also going to source you some pants that are... more suitable."

That was probably best for everyone. I had clothes in my apartment, of course, and I'd need to collect them at some stage. Then again, maybe not? If the Hunters Council put out that I was dead, I'd really scare the shit out of Craig by showing up to grab some underwear.

Drunk Austin had really made a lot of work for me.

"Thank you for enquiring about the food. That means a lot."

Selene shifted uncomfortably. "I just don't want you dying on my watch. Humans are very fragile. Who knows how long you can go without sustenance before your life is forfeit."

"A couple of months?" I guessed, putting some serious muscle into snapping the "bread" in half. A mouthful of vicious fangs would come in pretty handy right about now.

Selene made a dissatisfied noise, chewing on a piece of what may have been bacon. "What else can kill you?"

"Looking for ideas?"

She scoffed. "As if I'd need them. I'm trying to keep you *alive*, which is far more challenging."

"I'm really quite resilient."

She looked pointedly at the faint scratch marks on the top of my hand.

"These are really not a big deal. I've gotten scratch marks from the zippers on my clothes before. Scratches are very commonplace."

"You are only further proving my point."

"We also *heal* from scratches very quickly."

"You cannot convince me that Hunters are satisfactory healers. I've seen Astrid's hand."

I wanted to reply, to ask what about Astrid's hand indicated we were bad healers, but I'd just taken a bite of the bread and my entire focus was directed to chewing without cracking most of my teeth.

Selene was watching me closely again, and I made a valiant attempt at a closed-mouth smile that I hoped didn't look too much like a grimace.

"Yes, we most certainly need to source you more adequate food," she sighed, pushing her own plate away. "The food sent to the barracks is barely edible even by Shade standards. You will need to take your meals in the dining hall—"

"Please no," I interrupted, hastening to explain at her questioning look. "I mean, does it have to be every meal? It's just that the hall is quite intense. I'm a social guy, but that was a *lot*."

"I expected you to enjoy it, given the reason you journeyed here in the first place." I cringed slightly at the reminder, distracting myself from the thought by crumbling the bread in my hands onto the plate. "Perhaps if you see a little more of the grounds and get more of a sense of your surroundings, you will be more comfortable. The barracks is no place for you."

"Does that mean you're going to give me a tour?" I asked hopefully.

Selene's shadows rippled and flickered in what I was pretty sure was irritation, and I did my best to tone down my natural Austinness. It wasn't for everyone.

"Yes, I suppose so. I can hardly carry out my regular duties with you in tow, I've already delegated them elsewhere. Come, leave that. We'll find you something more palatable in the palace kitchens."

I had been *so* excited about the idea of visiting the kitchens. Between the hangover appetite and the failed attempt at bread, I was ready to eat basically whatever I could get my hands on so long as it didn't have meat in it.

But that was before I'd *seen* the kitchen, which was basically a shrine to carnivorism, and Calix, The Demon Butcher of Meat Street, otherwise known as the palace chef.

"Why are you in my kitchen?" he asked, pointing a cleaver the size of my whole torso at me.

"You know better than to point knives at the ex-Hunters who have been given sanctuary in this realm, Calix," Selene clipped, icy cool. So badass.

Calix twisted so the cleaver was pointed somewhere slightly to my right. "You know better than to bring one into my kitchen. Only the queen is allowed in here."

"This ex-Hunter doesn't eat meat."

"Another one?" Calix threw down the knife on the counter in disgust. "The sad one doesn't eat meat either."

Which one was the sad one?

"What do you feed her?" Selene asked as though they were discussing the best brands of pet food for their puppies.

"Soft breads, mostly. They have very dainty teeth." I ran my tongue over the blunt tips of my teeth protectively. *Don't listen to them, you're perfectly adequate teeth. You do great chewing.* "But she prepares much of her own food, and is trying to establish a garden of edible human realm plants outside Elverston House." Calix gave me a long, unimpressed look. "Can you cook?"

"Sure." Not really. I'd been on the road a lot over the past few years, traveling for gigs. I'd never really had the time or resources for home cooking.

"No, you can't." Calix snorted, seeing right through my lie. This guy was fucking terrifying. Like a TV-show head chef but with fangs and claws and a knife as heavy as an axe. "Lucky you've got the only guard in the palace who knows their way around a kitchen."

"I don't expect Selene to feed me. I've inconvenienced her enough as it is."

Calix's annoyed expression morphed into something vaguely wicked. "Yes, it's not usually the ex-Hunters who are feeding—"

"Calix! The bread," Selene demanded impatiently. "Don't touch that," she added, shooting me a withering look as my hand inched toward a weird looking tool on the countertop. Chastised, I clasped them behind my back.

"Fine, fine," Calix grumbled, chortling to himself as he disappeared into some kind of store room.

I didn't quite understand the vehemence of Selene's response. Of course, the *Shades* were the ones who fed. The whole reason they came to the human realm was to feed on human fear, and I assumed we were fulfilling that role here. If the other ex-Hunters hadn't seemed so comfortable, I might be worried about it.

"Here you go." Calix set down a small bundle of what I guessed was bread, wrapped in gray fabric, sliding it along the counter toward me. "You've created a lot of work for me, you know."

"Me?" I asked, picking up the light bundle. It already felt more promising than the titanium I'd been gnawing on this morning.

"Yes, for your party tomorrow. Very last minute."

"What party?" Selene asked, voice filled with dread.

"Vespera has been busy all morning arranging a special gathering to welcome the *man* to the realm. If she had her way, it would be a one-on-one event, but alas, the king said that it had to be an open invitation. Every single female in the palace will probably be there. It's a lot of last-minute food preparation for me," he added, clearly irritated about it.

"Sorry?"

"Don't apologize," Selene said instantly. "You didn't know."

Not for the first time, I realized that she was more than happy to rail at me herself, but didn't seem to like it when anyone else did. She'd even gotten a little snappy with Tallulah yesterday.

"I'm surprised *you* didn't know," Calix said to her.

"Are you?"

The silence didn't feel comfortable. Then again, there had definitely been some weirdness in how the Shades at dinner had spoken to Selene.

And the Shades we encountered on our way to the throne room.

Maybe Selene wasn't very popular among Shades?

The royal ones seemed fine with her, though. And Calix, for all his general air of menace, was speaking to her far more respectfully than the other guards had.

We made our awkward escape from the kitchen, and Selene led me through the palace while I tried to eat my bread and not spill any crumbs on the smooth stone floors.

"Are there a lot of parties at the palace?" I asked Selene, valiantly attempting to make small talk. She gave me a look that made me wish I hadn't asked, and I winced at the memory of the pronouncements I'd made when I'd arrived here. She probably thought I was asking for orgy organization purposes.

"That's the library," she said, pointing at a set of double doors without pausing, continuing at the same breakneck pace she'd been leading me around by. She was kind of a terrible tour guide, honestly. I'd love to go in and have a look around—presumably the shadow realm had its own body of literature, and I'd love to read the Shade version of Dostoevsky or Dickens or Jackie Collins.

"Next, we will go through the gardens so you know the way to Elverston House where the other ex-Hunters are staying. And so you know where the portal is."

"Why would I need to know that?"

Selene glanced at me over her shoulder. "In case."

In case I wanted to leave? That was probably wise, though I felt a sort of immediate gut reaction *nope* to that suggestion that was almost definitely motivated by pride. I wasn't going to just *leave*. I especially didn't want Selene, who I'd already embarrassed myself in front of repeatedly, to think I was going to just leave.

"You shouldn't be stubborn about it, you know."

"I'm not being stubborn," I replied automatically, seriously questioning whether Shades could read minds. That hadn't come up in Hunter training. Had it? It had been a while.

"If you insist. There's no harm in admitting you made a hasty, ill-advised decision in coming here, that's all."

"Sure. And if I'd made a hasty, ill-advised decision, I'd be totally fine with admitting that," I lied.

"So, arriving here drunk with no clothing or supplies of any kind was well-thought out and intentional?"

Damn it. "I brought my guitar."

"Ah, of course. That will surely keep you warm and provide you with the meat-free sustenance you require to live."

"Touché," I laughed as we exited the palace through a discreet side door, able to admit when I was outwitted. "Do they have potatoes in the shadow realm? I'll be fine if there's potatoes. They were the first food grown in space. And they're a great source of vitamins, minerals, fiber—"

Selene paused suddenly, midway down a path that led through the gardens.

"Look at this," she breathed in awe. She'd probably been talking to herself, but I sidled up next to her to look anyway.

Nestled in among the black foliage was one single dark red flower shaped a bit like a rose, though its petals were more pointed. It was beautiful and distinctive among the sea of gray.

My hand twitched, itching to touch it just to see if it *felt* like a rose, but Selene shot me a warning look before I could even try. She really didn't miss anything.

"It's for this reason that I can't encourage you return to your world, even though it's clear your decision to come here was made hastily," Selene murmured, mesmerized by the bloom. "The color is returning to this realm because of the former Hunters who have chosen to live here. You bring color with you. It's an alluring prospect."

Yeah, I could absolutely see how it would be.

There was far more to us being here than just Shade fucking, like Jonah had made out. If I was going to stay here, then I had a moral obligation to take that seriously, even if I didn't entirely know what it entailed yet.

For the first time in months—maybe even years—I felt something akin to a sense of responsibility. And maybe that hadn't been what I'd come here for, but I may have stumbled upon something better.

CHAPTER 6

Is this really necessary?" I mumbled to Selene, dragging my feet as she led me to an antechamber off the dining hall where the event was taking place. My newfound sense of responsibility was rapidly fading in the face of this ordeal.

"Apparently so. Vespera is quite the force of organization—not even the royal couple were able to fend off her petitions for longer than a day. I asked around and her argument is that, as you weren't present for the recent ball, this event should be held to give you and the Shades interested in you a chance to talk."

The fact that Selene sounded as unimpressed by prescribed socialization as I felt helped slightly. I'd only been here two nights. This whole thing felt super intimidating.

"You're not going to leave me there, right?" I asked, only a smidge desperately.

Selene turned to give me a withering look, and I metaphorically patted myself on the back for getting better at interpreting her expressions. "What kind of guard would I be if I *left* you there? It's a ridiculous question. I will be watching you the entire event for your safety." She hesitated for a moment. "Though if you *desire* privacy with someone—

"That's not going to be an issue," I interjected firmly, not entirely sure where my vehemence had come from. Selene looked doubtful, and I didn't blame her, and yet, the idea of her thinking of me as some easy fuckboy was abhorrent. Which was stupid since I'd basically stamped *fuckboy* on my forehead the moment I stepped foot in this realm.

I respected Selene. I wanted her to respect me too, if only a little.

She looked at me for a long moment, hand resting on the door handle as voices filtered through the wood. "Let me know if you change your mind."

I wouldn't, but she didn't give me a chance to reiterate that, throwing the door to the chamber open.

The chatter died down to complete silence for a long and uncomfortable moment, before picking up again, the tone even higher and more excitable than it had been.

"After you," Selene muttered, gesturing for me to enter. "I believe the throne-like seat at the front of the room is yours."

Please no.

"This is mortifying," I whispered back. The seat—which looked to be carved from stone and laden in silky cushions—was ludicrously opulent, and in front of it was a plain black wooden bench, I guessed for the ladies to sit on while we conducted our awkward conversations.

I'd performed live on stage in front of *millions* watching at home and felt at least three times more comfortable than I felt now. Then again, this situation was more akin to the awkward meet and greets the network had organized. While it had been gratifying to hear people tell me they loved me— they didn't, they didn't even know me—I'd always found the situations forced and weird.

The seating that lined the walls of the room didn't look so uncomfortable. It was almost like the bench was there to contrast with the not-quite-throne, to create a stark visual reminder of distinction. Except no part of me was throne material, nor did I want to be.

Was I even allowed to sit on a throne? I mean, it wasn't as grand as the one in the throne *room*, but it was still giving me vague airs of treason.

"It is mortifying," Selene agreed. "I feel very embarrassed for you. Good luck."

"Gee, thanks." I shot her a dark look as I made my way up the mini dais to the throne seat that Vespera was eagerly gesturing me to sit on.

"Do you like it?" she asked as Cosima came to stand behind her. "It was my idea."

"It's very... grand," I settled on, words failing me for maybe the first time in my life.

"As befits your station." Vespera gestured again for me to sit, her and Cosima taking seats on the stupid interview bench. I glanced at Selene, who was watching with what I was pretty sure was wry amusement as I finally gave in and sat down on the throne, sinking into the silky cushions.

It was pretty cushy. If I got guillotined for treason, at least it was in service of a comfortable seat.

"I don't really have a station," I pointed out, softening my words with what I hoped was a relaxed smile. It felt like a grimace.

I kind of *wanted* a station. Not in a weird, archaic rank kind of way, though. More like an actual *job*. Did they have troubadours in the shadow realm? I could be a troubadour.

"Of course you do! The only ex-Hunter male in the realm. You should have an apartment of your own in the palace. I know the other ex-Hunters are in Elverston House, but that building is *dreadful*. Captain Soren mentioned there were some safety concerns with the Hunters which is why you have temporary protection." She paused, shooting an unreadable look at Selene.

"I'm sure Captain Soren knows what he's doing," Cosima volunteered. "Though it does seem exceptionally cruel that you should be housed in the barracks."

"The barracks are totally fine—"

"Very cruel," Vespera agreed. "Do the barracks even have running water? I'll petition the king to have you transferred to the palace. In the meantime, Austin, I'd like to tell you more about myself."

"Um. Okay."

Vespera launched into a long list of her accomplishments in life, and it was a weird mixture between speed dating and a job interview, with Cosima occasionally attempting to say something about herself, though mostly bolstering her friend. It was rude as shit, but I just could not convince my brain to pay attention to what they were saying.

I'd experienced my share of groupies when the show had been at its peak, but whatever this was, it was far more intense than any groupie situation I'd ever found myself in. Then again, I'd never been the only rockstar in the human realm. Safety in numbers and all that.

Selene cocked her head to the side, and I swore I could hear her silent question. *Isn't this what you wanted? Isn't this why you came here?*

And she wasn't wrong, that *was* why I'd come here. Except all it did was remind me of being a piece of meat the way I'd been in the human realm. No, it was worse than that. When fans of my music had offered to let me do absolutely depraved things to their bodies that I had no interest in, I'd sort of been able to write it off as an over-the-top response to my music. Being a shit-hot rockstar was all I'd ever wanted, right?

But this was different. This wasn't about talent, or art, or fame. This was purely about my dick.

I liked my dick just fine, it was a great source of pleasure for me, but I did hope to be defined by slightly more than *just* that in my life.

"So," Vespera said, leaning in uncomfortably close and inhaling me like I was a freshly baked batch of cookies, startling me back to attention. "I'd love to smell your mating scent."

I choked on my saliva, coughing until I was probably bright red in the face. "My *what*?"

"Vespera," Cosima whispered, glancing around the small but crowded room. "I don't think you're allowed to ask him that. The king explicitly said we weren't to pressure him."

"I'm not *pressuring* him. I'm expressing an interest."

"In his *mating scent*." Cosima shook her head, leaning forward and resting a clawed hand on my arm in what I assumed was meant to be a comforting gesture. It was not. I didn't feel threatened per se, but I didn't want anyone touching me either. Cosima reeled back, her nose twitching. "I hope that's not your mating scent."

Vespera whipped her with a shadow. "Of course it isn't. Remember, the queen used to emit foul scents when she was distressed? You distressed him!"

"*I* didn't," Cosima objected, flicking out a shadow whip of her own. "*You* were the one that raised inappropriate subjects. *You* distressed him!"

I shot Selene a pleading look, though she seemed determined to pretend her excellent observational skills were suddenly malfunctioning. Apparently, she wasn't going to intervene unless I was in actual danger, and the bickering Shades in front of me didn't qualify.

"Move it," a bossy new voice interjected. A slight Shade in a flowing cascade of shadows forced herself into the middle of Vespera and Cosima from behind the bench, half shoving them off either end. "Your time is up. I wish to talk to talk to the male."

They both looked like they wanted to argue, but tilted their heads in deference to this newcomer before quietly excusing themselves. That was... unexpected, especially since the new Shade was significantly smaller than them and Vespera in particular didn't seem afraid of authority figures.

The new Shade stared at me with unsettling pink eyes, silver chains, and black jewels dripping from her curly, delicate horns. She was *so* small. Almost like she hadn't finished growing yet.

"Are you... are you a *kid*?" I asked disbelievingly.

"I'm nearly of age," she replied haughtily. "Which is why I was invited, but I'm not interested in you, sorry."

"Please don't be, the feeling is entirely mutual, actual child," I muttered.

"I'm not a *child*. I'm *almost* of age."

"Right, right. How come Vespera and Cosima ran off? Are you like... really important at court or something?"

She huffed, a sound that was eerily similar to how a human teenager sounded. Apparently, some things were universal. "I'm *quite* powerful. No one appreciates it because I haven't reached my majority yet, but they'll see. In the meantime, I suppose they're just afraid of my brother. My half brother, if you want to be technical. He and I have the same mother, but he and the *king* have the same father."

I sketched out a family tree in my head. "You're... Prince Damen's half sister?"

She startled. "By the night, no. The king has many half siblings—the last king had many, many lovers, even when he was *ancient*." Well, this conversation was getting uncomfortable. "None of his other children are as powerful as King Allerick or Prince Damen though, so there's no point in them making a play for the throne. My brother has his own grand estate, far from court."

"Right." I nodded slowly. "So you're, like, royal adjacent and that's what scared the others away."

She didn't respond, but Selene nodded once in the background. I knew she'd been paying attention.

"What's your name anyway, kid?"

"I'm *almost* of age," she emphasized, tapping her foot impatiently on the floor. "And my name is Melody-Rainywillow."

I stared at her.

She stared back.

"Your name is… Melody-Rainywillow?" I confirmed, running through a list of all the Shade names I'd heard so far for comparison.

"Yes. My brother chose it based on words he'd heard in the human realm that he liked." Melody-Rainywillow seemed very smug about this, so I decided it was probably good self-preservation not to comment on it. Even a teenage Shade could gut me if the mood took her.

"Do you ever go by Melody?"

"*Never.*" She paused for a moment, thoughtful. "You can call me Rainy, if you want. From what I've heard, Hunters are extremely delicate in this realm. I don't want to tax you too much by forcing you to say so many words. Apparently, you die without *air.*" Rainy giggled to herself like this was the funniest, most absurd thing she ever heard.

"I'm glad you find my delicate constitution so amusing," I replied dryly, staring longingly at Selene's profile, willing her to come over and rescue me from this conversation. Or this whole event. I'd be fine with either.

"Did that make you feel bad? Sorry." Rainy didn't sound sorry at all. "I guess I'm trying to figure out what the big deal is. How come everyone wants one of you ex-Hunters so badly?"

"Maybe it's the novelty." I shrugged, pouring myself a cup of water from the jug next to the mini-throne.

"My brother thinks it's to do with your breeding potential."

My sip of water bypassed 'Go' and headed straight down my airways, nearly giving Rainy a firsthand example of death-via-no-oxygen. She stared impassively as I coughed up at least most of a lung, and I contemplated going into a full faint when I noticed the attention I was garnering from Selene.

Help me, oh brave guard! I'm in grave danger! Rescue me and I shall be forever in your debt!

Damn it, nothing. I wondered if it was because of Rainy's presence—it was certainly doing a great job at deterring everyone else. Vespera was still hanging around the bottom of the dais, making no secret of the fact that she was intending to resume our conversation.

"Anyway," Rainy continued when I fell silent, as though she'd been waiting for me to stop with the hysterics so she could keep talking. "My brother is very territorial over his castle, so he doesn't like to leave unless he absolutely has to which is why he sent me to scope you out. I will be returning home to tell him that I am unimpressed."

"Good to know. Hey, can you hang out a little longer? Everyone is too scared to approach with you around."

"Of course they are, they can sense I am going to be *very* powerful one day. Maybe even more powerful than my brother, and then I'll challenge him for the castle. He's already told me he would expect nothing less."

"He sounds very supportive."

"Very," Rainy agreed solemnly, surveying the room imperiously. "Why do you *want* them to be too scared to approach? Isn't the whole point of this for you to find your preferred breeding partner?"

"I really wish you'd stop saying breeding."

"I think I might. I've noticed you emit an awful smell whenever I do. That's quite interesting."

"I live to entertain," I deadpanned, the words feeling truer than they ever had when entertaining had been my actual, full-time job.

"So why do you want them to be too scared to approach?" Melody-Rainywillow was persistent, I'd give her that. "Do none of the females here appeal to you?"

I hesitated. "They're all great."

Rainy nodded solemnly. "I see. Your weak, human heart belongs to another."

"That's not what I said. Are all Shades your age like you?"

Rainy tipped her chin up, staring imperiously down her nose at me despite being at least a head shorter. "I am far superior to Shades my age. I am going to be *very* powerful."

That was a no then.

"Which Shade female has captured your heart?" Rainy stood, making a show of looking around the room. Fortunately, everyone seemed too afraid to make eye contact with her to stare back. "My guess is Lucienne."

"Why?" I asked, startled. Lucienne was one of the Shades I'd sat near at dinner, and it had been a real exercise in patience not to just stand up and leave mid meal when I was talking to her. The conversation had reminded me so much of the painful diatribes I'd heard from Grandfather over the years about the glorious history of our family, that I could have sworn I'd gone back in time to childhood dinners around the oversized formal dinner table.

"Well, she's very rich. And powerful, though I will be *more* powerful, obviously."

"Obviously," I agreed dryly.

"And she has already borne a child. That's something some males value when looking for a breeding partner."

"Again with the B-word."

I'd come to the shadow realm for orgies, but I'd basically encountered the exact same issue with sex that I'd been experiencing in the human realm, just with a different driving reason behind it. Was it too much to ask that someone would want to fuck me for my personality?

"All in all, there are many reasons why she would be a suitable candidate to be your companion. Or "mate" as they're now calling it. If I were in your position, that is who I would choose to br—, *reproduce* with."

"Right. Well, I don't really care about any of those things."

Rainy scoffed. "That is ridiculous. Nothing is more important than finding a powerful mate. A weak Shade is nothing. A drain on our resources who contributes little of value to our world."

Big yikes. Maybe hanging out with Megalomaniac-Rainywillow wasn't such a great plan after all.

"I'm more of a personality guy," I said, though the words kind of surprised me. Was I more of a personality guy? Historically, I hadn't been a *relationship* guy, so I didn't have a lot of experience to draw from.

Then again, sex was always readily available. Finding someone I actually gave a fuck about, and who gave a fuck about me in return, was more challenging.

So yes. *Yes,* I decided, feeling something settle into place at the acknowledgment. *I was a personality guy.*

"Personality." Rainy scoffed. "That attitude will land you with weak children."

"Whom I will love with all my heart."

"I'm definitely warning my brother against ex-Hunters as breeding partners. You are very strange creatures."

Out of the corner of my eye, I almost thought I caught Selene smiling.

SELENE

CHAPTER 7

Poor Hunter man.

Not words I ever thought would cross my mind, but looking at Austin on his ostentatious fake throne surrounded by a room of admirers, I couldn't help but pity him a little.

Eventually, a few of them ventured back onto the dais to try speak to him again, but did they not notice how forced his smile was? How he cringed away from their touch? Surely, they at least noticed how he kept the crazed Duke's child sister nearby, using her as a buffer between himself and anyone who tried to speak to him. It was an effective method—Melody-Rainywillow had already developed a reputation for parroting the unhinged views of her recluse brother, and most Shades at court gave her a wide berth.

She appeared to grow bored acting as his shield, abruptly wandering off the dais and descending the stairs, leaving Austin alone with an excited Cosima. He could do worse as far as company went. Cosima was involved in all sorts of charitable endeavors, and was easily one of the kinder Shades at court, if not a little self-absorbed.

"I hope you're being well compensated for this," Melody-Rainywillow declared, pausing next to me and staring me down as though she wasn't a child. I hadn't possessed even one quarter of her confidence at that age. It was admirably unnerving. "If you're not, then you should consider taking a position at my brother's estate. He is very generous with his staff."

That was the complete opposite of everything I'd ever heard about Duke Theon of Lindow, but I wasn't about to argue with this small, imperious terror.

"You should consider taking him for your own mate," she added, tipping her chin at Austin and thankfully lowering her voice so only I could hear her mortifying words. "His seed is likely valuable, but he seems rather sweet and dim. You have already demonstrated that you are capable of managing him. I will be telling my brother as much."

With a dramatic flounce, she was off, leaving me standing stunned in her wake.

Ignoring most of what she said, Austin was neither sweet nor dim. He shot me a pleading look from the dais, and I realized from the outside that it might *not* look pleading. That he might be misleading everyone, intentionally or otherwise. He was a curious creature. The more time I spent with him, the more I understood that he experienced a wide variety of emotions, but his expression was almost always one of cheerful contentment. Or it was at first glance. On closer inspection, it was obvious when the muscles in his cheeks looked strained from forcing that lazy grin, and when his eyes didn't shine like they did when he was genuinely amused.

His scent would eventually show more nuances of feeling, but for now, it still seemed a little muddled by the vestiges of alcohol. If I had to guess, the night he came here wasn't the first night he'd been roaring drunk.

"Time to go," I announced, shaking off the strange encounter with Melody-Rainywillow. The idea of taking Austin as my own mate was ludicrous. Aside from the fact that he had not shown any sexual interest in me, the females in this room would probably revolt.

Shades like me did not get to have mates like him.

"He just got here!" Vespera argued, keeping her voice low as she stormed up to me.

"It's been an hour and thirteen minutes."

"That's hardly any time at all!"

It had felt like several hours longer than that.

"You take all your meals in the dining hall. Austin knows where to find you if he'd like to get to know you further," I replied, shifting so Austin had room to stand next to me at the bottom of the dais. I hoped I hadn't interpreted his pleading look incorrectly.

"Austin, you can tell her you don't want to leave—"

"Oh no, I really do have to go." Austin's voice seemed to magically smooth over the feathers I'd ruffled. What a gift. "Thanks for organizing all of this, it must have been quite a feat to pull it all together at such short notice."

Vespera preened, all agitation forgotten. I wished I possessed whatever talent it was that Austin had that made others easy in his company.

"Well, I'll be sure to organize another one at your earliest convenience. I really would like to get to know you better." Vespera's sincerity was clearly genuine, and who could blame her? Austin was bright and interesting, and far more complicated than he presented himself. Who wouldn't want to get to know him better?

While I didn't feel upset about it exactly, I was certainly feeling *something*. It was probably just annoyance at all the supervision I'd be doing.

He turned his most bright and brilliant smile on her as we left the room through a side door that the guards used, avoiding walking through the crowd.

"Thank you," Austin sighed heavily, shoulders slumping and that painful looking smile disappearing the moment we were alone in the narrow, empty corridor.

"Of course." I hesitated. "Perhaps I should have suggested leaving earlier?"

Austin hummed. "Probably not. It wasn't exactly an enjoyable experience, but it would have felt rude to leave early. I don't want to make a bad second impression."

"It would take an impressive spectacle to erase your *first* impression," I pointed out. Austin laughed, and I surprised myself with how much I liked the sound. "If there's anyone you wish to spend more time with, it can be arranged separately. You don't need to put yourself through another such event."

Austin's laughter faded. "Right. I mean, that's why I came here. Right?"

"Yes," I replied after a pause. "That is more or less what you said."

"More or less," he murmured in agreement, trailing after me as we exited the palace and headed toward the barracks.

Perhaps, having spent some time with the Shades, he'd changed his mind? He had come here thinking we had tentacles, it wasn't a stretch to believe that he may be experiencing some disappointment at what he'd found instead.

"Where to now, boss?" Austin asked, shaking off his melancholy as though it had never been. It took me a moment to catch up to his suddenly optimistic energy.

"I have an errand to run. I was hoping you'd be content for me to lock you in your room for an hour before I return to take you up to the dining hall for dinner. You can amuse yourself with your strange stretches."

"What kind of errand?"

"I'm expecting a food delivery. It is very unexciting I assure you."

He seemed to perk up further. "That sounds like a very safe errand."

I sighed.

"Come on, Selene. Let me come along. I'll be the best company. Want me to sing for you? I'll totally sing for you."

"I do not want that." That wasn't strictly true, I did want to hear him sing. But I didn't want to encourage his nonsense either.

"You totally do, I can see it in your eyes."

"My eyes don't broadcast my every passing sentiment the way yours do."

"I know, it's very inconvenient. So, where are we going? Are we leaving now? You're about to use safety as an excuse, I can tell. But I'll be with you. You'll keep me safe."

"You seem very certain of that." He'd said that in the throne room too when he'd first arrived, and while I knew he was just trying to antagonize me, there was a small part of me that was flattered by his confidence.

"I am."

I paused at the fork in the path where we could veer left to the barracks or continue straight on to the entry room. "Are you so opposed to spending some time alone in your room?"

"No. I don't really want to go to dinner, though," Austin admitted. "I need a little time to recharge, you know? That whole event was... a lot."

Curse him. If there was one thing that could weaken my resolve, it was that. I knew what it was to feel trapped at court, constantly surrounded and needing a break.

"You'll have to stay at my side the entire time."

"Absolutely."

"And don't do anything stupid."

"I'll be *so* good." There was a strange fluttering in my abdomen, and I quickly strode in the direction of the entry room, willing it to go away.

"Fine. Come on then. Don't make me regret this."

I pulled Austin into the entry room, keeping one hand firmly wrapped around his wrist as I tugged the door shut, plunging us into darkness.

Austin's pulse picked up slightly beneath my fingers, but his scent didn't indicate any sense of fear. He really was far too trusting.

"Oh, we're moving," Austin said in surprise as I walked us forward into the in-between. His head swiveled from side to side, though it would be far too dark for his human eyes to see anything. Did he know that I could see him perfectly? "Where'd the wall go?"

"The wall is where it was. *We* have moved."

He didn't seem overly satisfied with that answer, but I didn't know how else to explain it. It just *was*. The in-between was just another pathway for us to walk, like the path that had led us from the palace to the entry room.

"You don't smell afraid," I observed, directing Austin along the familiar route. How did he stumble so much over nothing? Was he really so impacted by the lack of sight here?

"Should I be?"

"I don't know. I can traverse shadows. I have nothing to fear in darkness."

"That's a very good point," Austin agreed. "Maybe this is my long-lost training coming back to me. Hunters don't really have the luxury of being afraid of the dark. It's trained out of us as kids in varyingly traumatic ways."

Austin pulled an odd face that I didn't think he would have done if he hadn't thought the darkness hid it. He was usually far more careful to conceal his emotions.

"I can see why that was a component of your training. You'd be useless to the Hunters otherwise."

"I was useless to the Hunters anyway." I didn't want to say that I'd assumed as much, but it certainly didn't seem as though Austin had any killer instincts. "I was always more focused on my music. In hindsight, I was given a lot more freedom to follow my passion than other Hunters—"

Unfortunately, our arrival at the entry room cut off Austin's words. As always, there was muffled voices and laughter from outside, and a noticeable rise in temperature before I even got the door open.

Austin blinked at the silver orb light suddenly flooding the room. He looked so very human that I practically threw shadows at him, covering him in a head-to-toe veil, and attempting some makeshift horns. They were wispy and insubstantial, but it was a short walk and we weren't venturing near the busy restaurants and bars. So long as we didn't get too close to anyone, it would probably be fine.

"Holy shit. Do I look like a Shade?" Austin whispered, holding up his hands, covered in shadows that moved with him like drapey sleeves to hide his blunt human fingers.

"No." I leaned in, sniffing him. He smelled the same as he usually did, and it was a pleasant scent underneath the slight sourness of alcohol, so I presumed it indicated contentment. Which was a perfectly good and acceptable way for him to be feeling, so I wasn't sure where the swooping sensation of disappointment came from. "Try not to get too emotional."

"Got it. You have nothing to worry about, I'm feeling super relaxed. This is going to be great."

"And remember to stay next to me at all times," I added warily, maintaining my hold on his arm and pulling him toward the door. "Maybe don't speak. And don't let anyone touch you."

"You're the only one I want touching me," he assured me solemnly. "That came out sleazier than I intended. I'm usually a very articulate guy, you know—"

"No talking."

"Got it. Wait, just tell me where we are first. And then I swear I'm done."

"Cartava." We stepped out into the thick, humid air and I led Austin along the dusty packed-earth streets, angling myself in front of him as much as possible. I loved the sticky heat of Cartava. The region the palace was located in had a permanent chill in the air which I found difficult to relax in. Here, with the air heavy and the smell of cooked meat that never let up, time itself felt like it was moving slower. Cartava never slept, the establishments never closed, the laughter from the table-lined streets never ceased, and yet the pace of life here felt idle compared to court.

"Is this a *city*?" Austin whispered, physically incapable of not speaking.

He leaned behind me as we walked, catching glimpses of the crowded laneways lined with bars and restaurants. There were tables down the center of each street, filled with Shades making merriment, illuminated by small orbs of silvery light that were suspended from posts above.

"It is."

"I didn't know there were cities here. Where are we going?"

"You really should stop talking. You sound unusual."

"Do I really, though? Because I'm pretty sure I heard some different languages back there."

"Yes, that's true. Some from the human realm, some from the shadow realm. Your voice is particularly distinctive though."

I ushered him onto a much narrower street, where buildings at least four stories high loomed on both sides, sometimes tilting forward over the road so the balcony on one almost touched the balcony opposite. It was so different from where I'd grown up that I'd fallen in love with this street at first glance.

"Woah," Austin breathed, looking up. "This feels like an amusement park ride designed to mess with your equilibrium. Then again, I guess you don't need space for vehicles here, so you can just go ahead and build houses like a particularly ambitious game of Jenga."

"I don't know what half of those words mean. We're here." I maintained my grip on Austin's arm, pulling him between two of the leaning buildings and up a winding flight of stone steps, holding onto him the entire way just in case. There was no railing, and he would probably die if he fell between the edge of the stairs and the neighboring building.

It really was quite a lot of work to keep a human alive.

"No OSHA in the shadow realm, huh?" Austin muttered, keeping his other hand on the stone wall to steady himself. For once, I didn't mind his willingness to touch everything. "I've never really felt breakable before, but I've got the durability of a butterfly in this realm."

"Haven't I been telling you as much since you arrived?" I asked, sending out a vine of shadows to unlock the heavy black doors. "You are very fragile. You really should take more care with your delicate body."

"What is this place?" Austin asked, ignoring my warnings as he followed me inside. I let the shadows around him dissipate the moment I'd shut the doors, watching him examine the high black brick wall that led up to a soaring domed ceiling. There were silvery orbs of light suspended every few feet across the wide-open space which were always glowing to stop anyone shadow-walking directly into my apartment. The kitchen took up most of one wall—though I doubted it looked the same as a kitchen in his realm—and a large wooden table divided it from the comfortable seated area on the other side.

Heavy shutters with slats lined the front and back walls, allowing the small amount of breeze that was blowing outside to filter through the room.

"This is my home, of course." I headed for the front wall, sliding open a few shutters, allowing more airflow into the room. Couldn't humans die from overheating? I was sure I'd heard that somewhere. Too hot was dangerous, but too cold was also dangerous. Their bodies had to be kept within an optimum range to avoid mortal peril. It was really a wonder their race had survived. "Make yourself comfortable, I suppose. But don't sit too close to the open windows or the neighbors will have questions."

The food delivery wasn't due for another few minutes, and I made for the kitchen, busying myself with taking stock of what I had. Damius sourced only the very best ingredients from all around the realm, and I would never purchase from anyone else.

"If you aren't in a rush to get back for the feast, we could eat here. You can say no, of course—"

"I would love that," Austin interjected, shooting me his prettiest smile yet.

Oh, this had not been a good idea. Not at all.

I knew Austin wasn't interested in me—his scent, or lack thereof made it very clear—but there was still some kind of territorial instinct that arose in me where he was concerned. Having him in my space, seeing him in my home...

Austin was the perfect recipe for disaster.

CHAPTER 8

There was something almost illicit feeling about being in Selene's apartment. Like I'd snuck behind a curtain and seen something I wasn't supposed to see. This place wasn't what I'd expected from the prickly Lieutenant of the Guard. There were pretty patterned rugs on the floor and squashy cushions everywhere. Along one wall were shelves that seemed to hold all kinds of knickknacks, like shiny black shells and dried flowers and charcoal sketches of every kind of landscape imaginable.

This wasn't just an apartment she used when she was off duty. This was a *home*.

"Do you want wine?" Selene asked, pulling an earthenware goblet off a shelf as I took a seat at the long table that divided the kitchen area from the living room.

I shook my head, still recovering from how much I'd overindulged before I came here. "I haven't been in the mood to drink these past couple of days."

"I noticed." She pumped some water from a faucet, filling up the goblet for me before pouring herself a wine. "No wine and no meat. Which is fine, I can prepare you a meatless dish."

"That would be amazing, thank you. I'm guessing not a lot of Shade food comes in meatless form."

"It doesn't at court. In other parts of the realm, meat is not abundant," she replied in a tone that strongly cautioned against further questioning. Duly noted.

Rather than risk pissing her off while we were being sort of friendly, I sat in silence and observed. At some point, there was a knock on the door, and Selene opened it just enough to collect a crate of what appeared to be ingredients, speaking in murmured voices before returning to the kitchen to unload things. While the appliances may not have looked like anything *I* recognized, they were definitely there. The stove was a black cast-iron contraption that Selene lit a silvery flame in the base of. There was a small stone room in the corner that I guessed was some kind of larder to keep food cool. She also had a collection of butcher knives that looked easily hefty enough to carve me up, which was slightly intimidating.

"You can speak now, you know," Selene said eventually, glancing up at me from the bowl she'd been mixing. I startled, realizing I'd been staring. There was something quite entrancing about watching Selene in the kitchen. Maybe it was just that she usually moved with such unyielding determination, always striding from place to place with her head held high, daring anyone to challenge her. But here, pottering around, grabbing bowls, cutting things I didn't recognize, and mixing mystery substances, Selene was a totally different Shade.

Relaxed. Content, maybe. Above all else, she was confident. I could cook, but I needed a recipe book and my phone on hand to search things like 'how to test if egg is fresh' or 'how long to roast vegetables'. Selene seemed to just have all the knowledge she needed up in her head.

"Or perhaps you don't want to speak?" she asked, tilting her head to the side. She pulled out some weird-looking contraption I'd definitely never seen before, using it to stir and fold the mystery gray goop in the bowl.

"I was just admiring your technique. You're very comfortable in the kitchen."

"Food brings me joy." She fell silent after those surprising words for a long moment before speaking again. "It's an... indulgence of mine, I suppose. I like to source rare and interesting ingredients. Fine ingredients. The very best, if I can. Cartava has many dining establishments—the most highly sought-after in the realm. Visiting them brings me great..." Selene trailed off, seemingly at a loss for words.

"Happiness?" I suggested.

"Happiness seems a rather extreme reaction for something as simple as food."

"Food is a big part of life. It's not just sustenance—it can represent a whole host of different experiences and emotions. And even if it didn't, who cares? Happiness can be whatever you want it to be."

Selene covered the bowl with a thin black cloth, setting it aside and looking at me across the table. "What brings you happiness?"

"Music," I replied instantly. "For as long as I can remember, music has been the language of my soul. I *understand* it, I can express myself through it. It nourishes me and brings me joy, like food does for you."

"I doubt my connection to food is as strong as all that," she mumbled, busying herself with a haunch of meat I didn't want to examine too closely. Without the nuances of expression, body language and intonation were everything when it came to reading a Shade's mood, and Selene was definitely feeling embarrassed.

"How'd you get into cooking?" I asked, imagining her coming home from Shade Soldier School and flambéing some mystery gray meat. On reflection, I didn't really know anything about Selene at all. And I guessed it wasn't a big deal—she was just doing her job by guarding me—but I *wanted* to know more.

"I come from a region where food production is the main industry." There was that don't-ask look again. "Considering what I was eating and where the ingredients came from has always been part of my life. When I reached my majority and left to join the Guard, I suppose I was... *surprised* to find that not everyone cared about such details. Calix and his staff prepare the meals for the court each day. No one really cares about the how's or why's so long as it tastes good."

I was so here for this impassioned, talkative Selene. Who knew that food was the secret conversation starter I'd been missing?

"How did you discover your passion for music?" she asked, challenging me with my own question though asked in far more eloquent terms.

I shrugged. "Honestly, I don't remember ever not having it. I was apparently a toddler prodigy from the moment I started muscling my way into my older sister's piano lessons. My mom kind of liked the idea of me being famous, I guess, and she encouraged me a lot but it became less of a positive thing as the years went on. More manager, less mother. More performances, more videos of me singing online, less family trips to the beach. We're not close these days."

It still left a slimy feeling on my skin when I thought about falling out with my parents over the money I'd earned from performing as a teenager. They hadn't *needed* it. Grandfather bankrolled all of his children to a certain degree throughout adulthood, they were more than comfortable.

My parents were just the first in a long line of people to see me as nothing more than a commodity.

"What about your older sister?" Selene asked, crossing to the sink to wash her hands—and claws, fascinating—before pulling out some gray plant-looking things. As she ripped them into smaller pieces, a fragrant smell filled the air, so I guessed they were herbs.

"She's close to our parents, so we sort of drifted apart. She's married, has a kid or two last I heard."

"Do you think they'll be petitioning the Hunters Council to get you back?"

I snorted. "No. Grandfather probably will—it'll be a blow to his reputation, especially with Tallulah already here. Two grandkids voluntary in the shadow realm? He'll hate that. Though so far, so good, right? It doesn't seem as though they're making any attempts to get me back."

Maybe because I'd written such an excellent statement in my Notes app.

"It's early days yet. You haven't changed your mind about returning?"

"Nope." I grinned at her. "You're still stuck with me, sorry."

"You're not even a little bit sorry." Selene scoffed, though she sounded more amused than annoyed. "However, your presence isn't quite as aggravating as I expected it to be. Aside from your chronic need to touch everything with no regard to your safety."

"That was one time!"

Maybe two.

"It was at least two. Aside from that, you are not so terrible, even if the amount of attention you draw is rather alarming."

I grimaced, unable to refute that. "Were there meet and greets with thrones for the other ex-Hunters who moved here?"

"There was no need. They had a ball," Selene replied thoughtfully. "Which served the same purpose, but everyone was invited so it felt less artificial than this afternoon felt. Of the single ex-Hunters, Astrid and your cousin disappeared almost immediately, Meera seemed uncomfortable making small talk, and Verity had the room entranced."

That sounded a lot less bug-under-a-microscope than my experience had been. Then again, even if I'd been around for the ball, I still would have been the only Hunter dude, and likely drawn some extra looks.

"I don't suppose you have some writing materials?" I asked.

Selene blinked at me. "Sure. Second drawer down under the shelves."

I rummaged around, finding a piece of paper that was thicker than anything I'd ever used in the human realm, almost parchment-like, and a thick pencil that was definitely better suited to Shade hands rather than human.

But that was fine. I was just scribbling. Experimenting with the bare bones concept of a song. Feeling alone in a crowded room wasn't exactly a revolutionary concept, but it was one that held universal appeal. And if my muse was finally willing to come to the table, then I wasn't about to say no on the basis of lack of originality.

I was so lost in what I was doing that I nearly fell off the chair when Selene set down a plate in front of me, while keeping a bowl of gray meat-looking stuff in front of her.

"Wow, this smells amazing." I set the pencil and paper aside, leaning forward over the plate and inhaling the aromatic, herby scent.

"It's only bread," she replied, looking uncomfortable with the praise. "A soft bread that's a delicacy where I grew up. It's filled with herbs. We used to have it at festivals."

She began constructing some elaborate open sandwich type thing with the meat on her plate, so I picked up my piece and pulled the bread apart. It was a pale silvery color and so light and fluffy that it was like a cloud between my fingers, and practically dissolved on my tongue when I put it in my mouth.

The only thing I could think to compare it to was a bao bun, but the herbs throughout gave it a slightly different texture. It was easily the most delicious thing I'd eaten in the shadow realm.

"The herbs are given to children to help them grow healthy and strong," Selene said offhandedly. "Not that you're a child, but I thought your human body might require the extra supplements."

"If I wasn't so grateful, that might have hurt my ego."

"I'm not sure your ego is capable of sustaining damage."

"Seriously, though, this is delicious. Thank you. I really appreciate you making something specifically for me."

"It wasn't much effort, you don't need to mention it," Selene mumbled, taking a bite of her admittedly impressive-looking meal, even if I didn't eat meat. "What is that you're writing?" she asked, nodding at the paper.

"I had an idea for a song. Or a collection of random ideas that may or may not end up in song form."

"Oh." Selene looked at me for a long moment. "I didn't realize you wrote the words to them yourself."

She looked begrudgingly impressed, and I was kind of proud. That was weird in and of itself. I'd gotten pretty accustomed to everyone assuming I was a pretty face, a nice voice, and no depth, but apparently there was still some part of me that longed to be recognized as something more.

"It is not so common here," Selene continued. "The choir music at court is in a very old language that no one speaks any longer, and the words haven't changed for centuries. Similarly, there are songs in other parts of the realm that are used to tell stories, especially in regions where a formal education is less common." There was that discomfited look again. "They are sung in a range of languages and most have dances that accompany them, but the words don't really change. They aren't written by any one Shade, but added to over time."

"Like folklore? That's cool. I don't know why it never occurred to me that Shades would have their own long-standing traditions. I guess, before I came here, that I didn't give Shades much thought at all outside of their visits to the human realm to feed on fear. In my head, you all just vanished into the ether when you weren't actively ghosting around for a meal."

"Ghosting around." Selene snorted. Was she amused? I liked the idea of amusing her. "I didn't give much thought to your world either even though I regularly visited to feed. It was a necessary experience, not an enjoyable one. I take it that you didn't spend much of your time actively hunting?"

"No, definitely not. I think, when I was young at least, my parents convinced the Hunters Council that I was going to become this, like, global superstar or something, and that I'd give all my money to the Council to support the cause. It takes a lot of private investment to maintain a secret army."

"I can imagine," Selene replied dryly. Maybe it wasn't the best idea to remind her repeatedly of my Hunter background? Then again, there wasn't much use playing coy about it. She knew by looking at me what I was and where I'd come from, and if she could tolerate Astrid's presence, then presumably mine wouldn't be too offensive. Astrid had been a *real* Hunter.

"So what do you do now to feed?" I asked, taking another bite of bread. "Since everything kicked off between the Hunters and the Shades, and the portal closed."

Selene froze. Had I stumbled onto a sensitive topic? I couldn't really imagine how. Feeding was the sole reason they visited the human realm in the first place.

"We have energy stores," she replied eventually, speaking slowly as though she was choosing her words carefully. "Where excess energy from feeding is siphoned for the use of those who need it. Originally, it was just the elderly, the very young, and the infirm. Now, it is the whole realm."

Okay. That definitely made more sense than everyone in the realm taking turns terrorizing the few Hunters that lived here to get a hit. No one had made any attempt to scare me yet, though it seemed to be because they were more interested in getting in my pants instead.

"We shouldn't stay here long," Selene sighed, finishing her meal and collecting both of the plates. "They will wonder where you are."

"Will they? Everyone seemed pretty content to just leave me for you to deal with."

"Yes." Selene's body language was very much broadcasting irritation, and I internally face-palmed for reminding her how annoying my presence was again, just as we were starting to get along. "I understand that the king and the captain are distracted with their new mates, but I expected a little more interest in you and how you're adjusting to things."

Oh. *Oh*. Her irritation *wasn't* directed at me. It was... on my behalf? That was kind of nice. Selene had said she didn't have friends—and honestly, friendship wasn't one of my strong suits either. Friendship required time and effort, and I wasn't good at prioritizing time and effort for things that *weren't* music.

But maybe I could start.

"Want to be friends?" I asked Selene. She dropped the plates into the sink a little harder than necessary, looking back at me over her shoulder.

"What did you just say?"

"Friends. Do you want to be friends? I think we should be."

"Why?"

I shrugged, standing up to help her wash the dishes. "I kind of think we both need one. Don't you?"

She was quiet for a long moment, focused on filling the sink with water. "Perhaps we do. For now, until you find your permanent place here in the shadow realm, I'll be your friend."

I couldn't help but think she was already saying goodbye.

AUSTIN

CHAPTER 9

I need to attend a training session but I don't want to lock you in your room," Selene announced, hovering in the doorway while I finished my morning yoga practice. I used to *love* yoga, and I didn't know at which point I'd stopped. Not stopped loving it, but stopped *caring* about myself. How had I let that happen?

"Okay. Shall I come with you?" I asked hopefully, lying in Savasana and staring up at her.

"Absolutely not." She peered down at me. "Why are you always on the ground? I have never intentionally laid on the ground in my adult life."

"You're missing out."

She looked at me for a long moment. "No, I don't think I am. I will escort you to Elverston House where you can bond with your kin. I've already assigned extra guards to watch the exterior today, and rerouted my circuit so I can check in personally."

"You didn't need to go to that much effort. I'm sure I'll be fine," I told her, standing and rolling up the blanket to use tomorrow. Maybe I could ask Astrid nicely to pick up a yoga mat next time she did a supply run? She'd already sourced me a bag full of clothes—sweatpants, t-shirts and hoodies, all in black.

They were a little drab compared to my usual style, but they were comfy, they fit, and my dick was sufficiently hidden from public view.

"Are you telling me you don't need me to personally watch over you to feel safe?" she asked dryly, handing me a small cloth. I unwrapped it, finding more of that delicious herby bread from dinner last night.

"Wow, thanks. You didn't have to bring me this."

"You need to eat," she replied dismissively. "Can you eat and walk? Is that a safe activity for humans?"

"Sure," I replied, quickly pulling on my socks and shoving my feet into my boots. So long as I didn't trip and choke or something. I was going to make a joke about it, but Selene seemed anxious enough about my fragile humanness as it was, so I resisted the urge.

After all the assurances about how Hunter defectors were welcome here and they weren't going to be pressured et cetera, et cetera, I'd expected Elverston House to be some kind of ex-Hunter paradise, full of as many creature comforts from home as could be safely stored without electricity or decent insulation.

Alas, I had been very, very wrong.

If anything, Elverston House was kind of shit hole? It looked as though it may have been nice at one point. Like it had once belonged to a grand family who'd had it for generations, but then a wayward son with a gambling addiction had lost everything, and all the servants had been let go, and there was no one left to patch the holes in the roof or cut back the vines that were taking over the stone exterior.

Actually, it sort of looked like a physical manifestation for how I felt inside. Something that had once been shiny and promising, that was now a tragic story of lost glory and wasted potential.

Or maybe it was just a house and I was getting in my feels over nothing.

"That is not your most pleasant scent," Selene remarked, coming to a stop a few feet away from the path that led through a decrepit garden to the front doors. "Are you displeased at the idea of visiting here?"

"Visiting," I laughed, making air quotes. "You're depositing me here for safekeeping and we both know it."

"Yes, well, Astrid is running a training session on knife throwing today, and given your penchant for touching things, it seems inadvisable to bring you along."

"I'm hardly going to play catch with a flying knife," I pointed out, grinning at Selene's obstinate expression. I had no idea why it brought me so much joy to needle her. While I was a baseline level of annoying to most people always, I usually attempted to pull it back rather than embracing it.

"It's the stationary knives I'm worried about," she replied primly. "They are shiny, and will be tempting for your grabby fragile hands."

"You have so little faith in me."

"You arrived here and almost immediately touched a poisonous plant."

I laughed again. "I didn't *know* it was poisonous. I am aware that knives have pointy bits, make ouchies on fingers if touchy."

Selene looked torn between doing some deep breathing exercises and throttling me. "You are a most aggravating creature, did you know that? Not because you're ridiculous, but because you *act* as though you're ridiculous, which is far worse."

"I'm extremely ridiculous," I assured her. "Everyone says so."

She gave me an unnervingly long look. "No. You're not. Go inside. I will return for you later."

I felt as though I should argue, but I didn't really have a good comeback for that. Maybe it was just the close proximity, but Selene seemed to be paying more attention to me—the *real* me—than anyone else ever had, and I wasn't sure how to respond to that.

For all my years of lamenting that no one ever wanted to look beyond the surface level idea they had of me, a not-insignificant part of my brain worried there was nothing beneath that surface worth looking at.

I put on my most carefree expression and whistled loudly as I set off down the path toward Elverston House, feeling Selene's stare burn into my back until I'd entered the foyer and shut the heavy oak doors behind me.

Was I meant to knock?

Oh well, too late now.

"Hello! Anyone here?" I called out, my boots echoing on the stone floors with each step. The foyer was enormous, with a circular staircase disappearing up into the high arched ceiling and doors leading off either side on this level. It was also devoid of furniture, decorations, and personality in general. The only thing in here were the orb lights on the walls that illuminated the space.

That settled it. If I had to lie my ass off to stay in the barracks with Selene, I'd do it. If I had to weep in front of King Allerick to convince him that the only place I felt safe was at her side, then I'd sacrifice my dignity for that cause.

"Austin?" Tallulah appeared halfway down the stairs with her black hair in rollers, a blue-and-yellow polka-dot silk scarf holding them in place. She'd always had a very retro aesthetic—even her pajamas were a sort of monstrous, flouncy-looking mini dress and shorts combination that looked straight out of the ear-piercing scene in *Grease*. "What are you doing here?"

"I've been dropped off at Hunter Daycare for a playdate with my favorite cousin to give my long-suffering guard a break."

Tallulah blinked. "Well, that I can believe. Want some tea? The kitchen here is pretty basic because we all eat up at the palace, but we've got some staples."

"Sure."

Twenty minutes later, Tallulah had shrugged on an enormous fluffy robe and slippers to ward off the incessant chill, and was getting a fire going in the open grate in the kitchen.

"Do you know what you're doing?" I asked dubiously, doing a cursory scan of the roof in the hopes that there were sprinklers dotted throughout the coffered ceiling.

Tallulah gave me an impatient look. "Yes, I know what I'm doing. I was living in an off-grid cabin in Idaho Springs before I came here."

"You were?" I pulled a small wooden stool over to sit near the fledgling fire. "I didn't know that. Last I heard, Mom mentioned you'd moved into some upscale condo. She was trying to convince me to do the same."

"That was a while ago," Tallulah laughed, picking through the pieces of wood in a giant basket at her feet and selecting one to add to the flames. "Once I got the boot from the Hunters, I really felt like I needed to get away, but I had no money and nowhere to go. An old friend from college had the cabin and said I could house-sit since they were too busy with work to maintain it."

I wanted to ask why she'd been booted from the Hunters in the first place, but it seemed like the kind of information I should wait for her to volunteer.

There was an uneasy churning in my stomach whenever I thought about the Hunters these days. In the human realm, I'd been pretty adept at not thinking about them at all—I was too caught up in my own problems to pay them any mind. These days, I realized that not everyone born into that organization had been given the same privilege.

"Anyway, it prepared me well for life here. I worked as a cashier at a grocery store—because Mom was right, a fine arts degree is not practical in the real world—and learned to do things the old-fashioned way. I even got myself a treadle-powered sewing machine, which turned out to be a great investment, since I lugged it here to the shadow realm with me."

"That's awesome, Tallulah."

"Oh." She blinked in surprise, apparently not expecting the compliment. "Well, thank you. I'm a very everything-happens-for-a-reason person, so I like to think that I was always moving toward this outcome. This life. This experience."

I was more of a nothing-is-predestined, everything-is-pointless kind of a person, but no judgment. Live and let live, and all that.

"How did you come to be here? I got the cliffs notes version, but I didn't realize you weren't an active part of the Hunters when you left."

Tallulah gave me a wry smile. "Astrid basically has a list of everyone who failed at being a Hunter and might have a good incentive to leave."

"So, what, she tracked you down to a cabin in the woods and squirreled you away to the shadow realm under the cover of darkness?"

"She just slid into my DMs actually, but your version sounds cooler. My house-sitting gig was coming to an end and the idea of moving in with roommates to be able to afford rent made me break out in hives, so I thought why not?"

"You have roommates now," I pointed out with a grin, leaning back as the fire started spitting. Was that normal? I'd really feel a lot better with a smoke detector or two for peace of mind.

"I'd never thought about it like that, but yes I do." Tallulah laughed, shaking her head. "Though this house is obviously more than big enough to accommodate us all, and Astrid has already moved out. Meera is trying to start a vegetable garden, so she spends most of her time outside. It's just Verity and I for the most part. Unless you're going to move in...?"

"The barracks are pretty comfortable. And I'm moderately famous and therefore in very grave danger..." I teased.

"I'm sorry, Austin," Tallulah said with a grimace, her cheeks flushing pink. "I was very harsh when you first arrived. I didn't think you'd be happy here, and I was trying to get you to leave without, you know, insulting the shadow realm in front of all the head honchos."

"Oh. *Oh.* That is not what I thought you were doing. At all."

"I know, I know." Tallulah sighed. "On reflection, it wasn't right—I was making a lot of assumptions about what I *thought* your life was like, what I *thought* you were giving up. But maybe you weren't as happy there as I assumed you were."

She was leaving room for me to decide how much I wanted to say, which I appreciated. I hadn't seen her since tenth grade, but Tallulah had always been the least annoying of my relatives.

"What did you think my life was like?"

"I don't know. Different. I watched your season of *The Headliner*, I saw people losing their shit over you on social media. And you were being voted through every week, so you were obviously popular. And right after, you were traveling around the country, drinking champagne on jets, partying in Vegas. Didn't you get a record deal and everything?"

I grimaced. "Yes and no. Mostly no. I *did* get a legit offer, but I turned it down in favor of this super cool, new label. Very boutique, very fresh and modern approach. Total creative control over my work. Total scam, obviously."

"Oh no, I'm sorry, Austin."

"Don't be—it was my own ego that landed me in that situation. By the time I realized, I'd made such a mess of things that the legit label wanted nothing to do with me."

It had been a much-needed lesson in hubris, that was for fucking sure. Just because people had been screaming my name for weeks on a TV show didn't mean I wasn't one-hundred-percent expendable to corporate executives because there was always someone else. Someone younger and hotter and more willing to take orders.

"So you weren't living some luxurious jet-setting lifestyle before you came here?"

I thought of Gollum the rat, wondering if he'd clawed his way through the plasterboard to freedom yet. "Not quite. So that's why you didn't want me to stay? You thought I'd miss all my human world creature comforts?"

"You have to admit, it isn't the easiest life here. It wasn't as much of an adjustment for me as it has been for the others—and I have a hobby which helps a lot—but I still miss the internet and tacos. Verity has been brainstorming frankly terrifying experiments to figure out how to harness electricity in the shadow realm, even though she failed high school physics. I might need to hide all the metal, just in case."

"Do you want to go back?" I asked, sitting up a little straighter. "If you want to leave, I'll help you. I don't want you to ever feel stuck here."

"No, I don't want to leave." Tallulah smiled a little sadly, adding a bigger log to the fire. "Maybe I'm just a little jealous, seeing Ophelia and Astrid all loved up and happy. I kind of thought… well I thought I'd met someone at the ball. He was so different from me but he also seemed to understand me so well, and we had great chemistry." Her cheeks flushed an impressive shade of crimson. "Though I'm definitely not discussing that with my cousin. Anyway, I guess it was just a one-night kind of thing for him."

"Have you seen him around court since then?"

"I haven't. Maybe he's avoiding me." She laughed, but the sound was high and false.

"Well, you're great. If he doesn't see that, he's an idiot, and it's his loss."

Tallulah nodded firmly. "You're totally right. I need to get back on the horse. I doubt he's pining over me, I'm done pining over him. I'm going to put myself out there again."

"If you want a speed dating party all to yourself, I know an event planner."

Tallulah's laugh was genuine this time. "I heard about that. My immediate reaction is god no, but there's a little petty part of me that I'm not proud of that wants to show Mr. One-Night Stand that I'm doing just fine, bathing in the attention of many, many Shades. That's probably really bad, right?"

"You're definitely asking the wrong person. I live for attention." I paused for a moment, considering my words. "Maybe not all attention. That party was pretty terrible."

"Oh no, all the prettiest, wealthiest lady Shades in the realm fawning over you. It sounds *awful*."

She was joking, and I totally got that—maybe it *was* whiny and self-indulgent of me to complain about it—but it hadn't mattered who those Shades were, what they looked like or how wealthy they were, I'd still felt like the last flat screen at a Black Friday sale.

"Austin? Shit, sorry, that was really insensitive. I didn't mean to make light of your discomfort—"

"It's fine," I interjected, shooting her my most charming, carefree smile. The one that put people at ease, assured them that I was fine and everything was fine and there was nothing to see here. "Tell me more about your sewing. Can you jazz up these sweatpants?"

SELENE

CHAPTER 10

I awoke early, heading to the kitchen to make a tray of food for Austin and me. It couldn't be good for him, subsisting off all of this bread. If I returned to the valley today I could get him other things to eat...

If.

My ten-day rotation was done, which meant my day off coincided with the Fest of Labor back in Mistwood, and I had no good reason not to attend.

Well, that wasn't strictly true. Austin was a reason. But I'd left him alone in Elverston House yesterday, assigned extra guards to the area, and no harm had come to him. He'd obediently stayed where I'd put him, and his kin was there to keep him company.

It was perfectly acceptable to leave him there again.

Though I'd stayed on palace grounds yesterday, nearby in case he needed me. If something went wrong, no one would come to Mistwood to alert me. I doubted any of the Guard even knew the way.

I was still mulling over my conundrum by the time I arrived outside his door, knocking and unlocking it with my shadows, waiting for him to pull it open.

"I didn't expect you to be so awake," I said the moment I saw him. He was standing in those obscene pants Tallulah had given him again, not a shirt in sight. "What happened to the clothes Astrid brought you?"

"What? Oh. These pants are actually super comfortable for yoga."

I looked away from the distracting sight he made in the tight fabric, my eyes falling on the blanket laid out on the floor. "Your strange stretching thing?"

"It's not *strange*, it's yoga," he laughed, stepping back so I could set the tray down on the small table. "If anything, you're the strange ones. You're telling me that you work out all day long and don't stretch before or after? That can't be good for your muscles."

"Feeding heals our injuries." I swallowed thickly, doing my best *not* to think about feeding around Austin.

"Right, right. Shit, you must really be missing going to the human realm then. Aren't you... hungry?"

I froze in the middle of piling the now-cold and overcooked bacon on my plate. "I take enough from the stores to keep the hunger at bay."

"Which I'm guessing is less than what you would have taken when you were feeding in the human realm? Aren't the stores getting low?"

Please can we talk about anything else?

"Yes."

The king had asked me to explain all of this to Austin the first day he'd arrived. I wasn't in the habit of disobeying my monarch, or at least I hadn't been before now.

I just don't want him feeling pressured to use his lust to fuel the stores, I told myself. After all, Austin was plenty willing to copulate with Shades— he'd been very clear about that when he arrived. There was no *need* to further incentivize him when it would happen naturally when he found someone he connected with.

Austin did a double take, looking at me across the table as he ripped his bread into pieces. He was fidgety and tactile even when he was eating. "You look different today."

His gaze dropped from my face, down to the lower-than-usual dip in my shadows at my collarbone.

"I don't have duty today. I prefer a more relaxed style on my days off." And less shadows when I visited home, so as not to seem like I was flaunting my abilities.

"It suits you." He swallowed thickly, eyes lingering for a moment before he shook his head as though he was trying to flick water out of his hair. I couldn't imagine what he was thinking—certainly nothing in his scent gave it away. "Wait, you have the day off?"

"Yes."

"Do you have plans?" he asked, sitting up a little straighter.

"Maybe."

Austin's shoulders slumped, his expressive human face falling. "Oh. So, I'm going to Elverston House again?"

His souring scent clearly demonstrated that he didn't like that idea. Perhaps he hadn't enjoyed spending time with his kin after all?

"There's a festival. Near my family home." I had no idea why I was elaborating, it was very unlike me. His sad scent was making me feel odd. "I usually visit my family on my days off."

Some of the sadness vanished from Austin's expression. "A festival? That sounds awesome. I'm guessing they don't have festivals at the palace."

"Not like this one," I admitted, shifting uncomfortably. "Of course, things here at court are much more formal than where I'm from. This fair is rural." I cleared my throat. "Poor."

I had no idea why I'd told him that. It wasn't something I talked about at all if I could help it.

"A rural festival sounds much more fun than a formal palace party. Especially if it was anything like the one Vespera organized," he muttered, clearly still embarrassed about the makeshift throne she'd constructed for him.

It was strange that he hadn't reacted to my admission of poverty at all. Then again, from what I'd gleaned from Astrid, the social hierarchy in the human world was less clear-cut than it was here. He probably didn't realize how *abnormal* I was. That my very existence here was strange and unwelcome.

I didn't fit in here.

I didn't fit in there either.

"You can come, if you want," I mumbled, the words escaping me before I could hold them back.

"Really?" Austin was on his feet, practically bouncing in place before I could make up an excuse to change my mind. I stared down at the table to avoid seeing something I wasn't meant to see in those tight pants. "I'd *love* that."

"You would have to stick by my side at all times, of course—"

"There's nowhere I'd rather be," he interjected with slightly unsettling certainty. "I'm not worried, Selene. I know you're more than capable of keeping me safe."

His confidence in me was baffling. Nice, but baffling.

"You'll need to put more clothes on," I pointed out. There was no need to cover him in shadows for this trip. He'd look far more out of place wearing shadows than not.

"I can manage that." He dashed around the room, opting for the clothes he'd arrived in rather than the ones Astrid had brought him. I concentrated on finishing my tasteless meal as he dressed, not bothering to excuse himself to the privacy of the bathroom. I had assumed there were extensive modesty habits in the human realm, based on all the many layers of uncomfortable-looking garments they wore, but perhaps not.

"Why do you have serpents on your chest?" I asked, still staring determinedly down at my plate.

Austin paused, his arms in his shirt sleeves, though he hadn't yet pulled the garment over his head. Not that I was looking.

"Snakes shed their skin," he said after a long moment. "There's something transformative in that. Sloughing off the old, moving forward renewed, that kind of thing. I don't know. Maybe I just thought they looked cool."

I hummed, deciding not to push him. It was clear that the transformative symbolism *had* meant something to him, but Austin didn't like to show that part of himself. And could I really hold that against him? I knew what it was to hide my vulnerabilities from the world.

"Are you ready?" I asked, piling everything back on the tray to leave in the kitchens on the way past. "We're going to the entry room, the same as we did to go to Cartava."

Austin shoved his socked feet into boots, scrambling to tie the laces, and I watched him discreetly now that he was mostly covered, fascinated by all his human trappings. He ran his blunt fingers through his messy black hair, pushing it back off his face before shooting me a beaming grin. "Ready."

There was a strange aching feeling in my chest in response to that trusting, open smile. That smile that I hadn't seen him give anyone else. But I wouldn't be so foolish as to read into it.

Austin wasn't like Astrid, who was so reserved in her feelings that her scent rarely broadcast them. Austin's scent—now free of the sickly tinge of old liquor—changed plenty, and it never once approached the mouthwatering equivalent of human fear. It had never once screamed *feed*.

If he desired me, I'd know. And he didn't.

Friends, I reminded myself. He'd suggested that we be friends. It was certainly more than Kael had ever wanted, not that I was putting Austin in the same category as Kael. Austin had never rejected me.

"Come," I ordered, striding out the door, knowing he'd follow.

I'd already been apprehensive about today. Visiting my sister's home—my childhood home—was one thing, but seeing all the inhabitants of the valley was a far less pleasant experience. They didn't understand me, I didn't understand them, and that was how it would always be.

We paused at the kitchen to deposit the tray before continuing out past the walls of the training ground. Austin hummed quietly the entire time, jogging to keep up with me, and always spared me a smile whenever he caught me looking at him.

"Why do you smile so much?" I asked, trying to figure out what he could possibly be so happy about.

Austin laughed, confusing me further. "What isn't there to smile about? It's a nice day, and I'm off to a festival with a beautiful Shade."

Presumably he was teasing me, so I didn't bother acknowledging it. I barely understood Shade humor, let alone that of the Hunters. Perhaps that was why Astrid was the only one I had some form of connection with. She didn't have a sense of humor either.

"Stay near me at all times," I reminded Austin as I pushed open the door to the entry room, holding it so he could slip into the confined space behind me. I rested a hand on his forearm as I let the door fall shut, encasing us in darkness. As with last time, Austin's expression was entirely serene as he patiently waited for me to guide him through the shadows to our destination, the same way he'd done when I'd brought him to Cartava.

How could he be so trusting? He didn't even know me.

Perhaps it had been careless of me to leave him at Elverston House yesterday. Austin clearly had no sense of self-preservation whatsoever, and I needed to watch him more closely. If I had been a less scrupulous sort, he'd be in grave danger in my presence right now, with no witnesses to look out for him.

"It's very irresponsible of you to be here alone with me," I told him seriously. "What if I had ill intentions?"

Austin's eyebrows rose. "Do you have ill intentions?"

"No, but that's what I'd say if I *did*, so it proves nothing."

"I don't think so, you're the very honest sort. I think you'd tell me."

I huffed in frustration, walking us into the darkness. "You're very trusting, and I feel certain this must have caused you many problems in the human realm."

Austin laughed, not taking my advice seriously at all. "A very astute observation. I like to see the good in people. And Shades."

"That's the most ridiculous thing I've ever heard. You should be looking for the *bad* in people—and Shades—because that's what will cause you harm. This is very basic knowledge, do they not teach you this as children in your realm?"

"I mean, I guess so." Austin shrugged, and I tightened my grip on him in response to the jostling movement. "My mom hates confrontation and negativity of any kind. She could be standing in the middle of a war and she'd be smiling at everyone, probably offering them lemonade and cookies. What's your mother like?"

"She died giving birth to me."

Austin stumbled slightly, and I held on a little tighter to his arm. His scent was changing in response to that information, and not for the better. Perhaps it distressed him?

Of course it distressed him. We were friends now.

"You don't need to feel sad for me," I assured him. "It was a very long time ago."

"That doesn't mean it stops being sad."

No, it didn't. But it had always felt like it *should* make it stop being sad. After all, my childhood had been comfortable enough. My sister was a fierce and devoted protector. It could have been much worse.

"We're here," I murmured, grateful that I didn't have to formulate a better response. If nothing else, Mistwood would serve as an excellent distraction.

AUSTIN

CHAPTER 11

Woah," I breathed, stepping out of the entry room behind Selene. We were definitely not at a fancy royal court anymore. As I looked around, I decided we must be in a valley, since there were enormous trees rising up as far as I could see on either side of the long flat plain we were making our way across. The festival was a little way in front of us—a sea of gray tents that were clearly tall based on the Shades next to them but looked tiny compared to the towering trees.

"What is this place?" I asked, almost jogging to keep up with Selene. She briefly shot me a startled glance, and I guessed she hadn't expected me to ask. I was treading lightly because I didn't want to upset her, but it was clear that Selene felt some kind of way about her hometown.

"This is Mistwood. The bottom of the valley was once forest, but it has since been cleared for farmland. Farming is the occupation of most of the Shades who live here."

She wasn't saying it explicitly, but even I could read between those lines. Selene had grown up here, surrounded by farmers, and she no longer lived here and wasn't a farmer, and that journey had definitely come with some baggage.

Maybe in the way I'd grown up as a Hunter and was no longer a Hunter? Both of us had been destined for a certain kind of life before persuing something that we liked better.

As we drew closer to the crowd, I noticed that these Shades weren't wearing shadows as clothes like the Shades at court did. They instead wore toga-type garments, draped in various different ways, made of an almost-sheer fabric but layered over the important bits to preserve their modesty.

I wanted to ask about it, but my presence had started drawing attention, and Selene was clearly uncomfortable enough already.

"Should I have worn a shadow disguise?" I asked.

Her lips twitched in amusement, some of the tension easing from her posture. "That is only even somewhat effective from a distance if no one bothers too closely."

"Aunty!" A child barreled out of the front entrance, sprinting toward Selene with a beaming smile on their face, showcasing an impressive mouthful of baby fangs, with teeny curved horns poking out of their head. "You're here! And you brought a Hunter!"

"Former Hunter," I said hastily, holding up my hands placatingly as the Shades who'd been drawing closer out of curiosity made a rapid retreat. "Ex-Hunter. I never actually hunted anyone, so I don't even know if you can call me that—"

"He's with me," Selene said coolly, surveying the surrounding crowd and all but daring them to disagree with her as she scooped the kid off the ground. "Austin is no danger to you, and I'm confident none of you are going to endanger him."

"Not bloody likely," a female Shade laughed, shooing the spectators out of her way as she navigated the crowd. "Where's my daughter gone? Ah, there you are. Oriana, what have I told you about running off? The Dalromar will snatch you up."

The *what*?

"The Dalromar isn't real," Oriana told me confidently, half hanging off Selene's neck so she could lean around her to speak to me. "It's just a scary story they tell little kids, but *I'm* not a little kid."

"You'll always be little to me," Selene stated, adjusting her hold to get Oriana comfortable on her hip. While the words had been delivered without any particular affection, Selene's expression was slightly softer than usual, and Oriana stared up at her aunt like she'd hung the moon. Selene twisted to look at me. "Today is the Fest of Labor. It is believed that the spirits of creatures from the time before the Shades emerge from their hidden tombs to terrorize the populace."

It was very clear from Selene's tone that she did *not* believe this.

"The Dalromar being one such creature. Austin, was it?" Oriana's mother said, giving me an appraising look. "I'm Selene's older sister, Callista."

They didn't look anything alike, except for the bright green eyes that Oriana also had. Callista was shorter and paler than Selene, and her horns curved up and back like a goat's where Selene's formed a sweeping U-shape.

"It's a pleasure to meet you, Callista. And Oriana," I added, bowing with a small flourish to Oriana's delight. Selene stared at me.

"Is he like... your pet?" Oriana whispered loudly in Selene's ear. Selene's eyes grew wide and I waggled my eyebrows at her. Life was too short not to try out being leashed and crawling around the floor at the whim of a female who could murder me in her sleep.

"No," Selene sputtered eventually, while Callista fairly wheezed with laughter. "Austin is, um..."

"Her friend," I supplied with a victorious grin. "I'm Selene's friend. We're friends."

"Well, any friend of Selene is a friend of mine," Callista announced, still giggling to herself. "Even though Selene doesn't have friends, but we'll let that slide for now. Come, come, cousin Thane is dancing with one of the troupes on the middle stage soon and I promised him we'd be in the crowd."

She ushered us forward, down one of the many rows of tents. While I'd been a vegetarian for the past decade, the smell of roasted meat definitely brought back childhood memories of barbecues and running around with my cousins—one of the few family memories that wasn't encased in a thick layer of generational trauma. Fortunately, it looked as though there were also a few dessert stands sprinkled throughout that I might be able to find some food at. There were also plenty of makeshift bars—not that I intended to indulge. Some had comfortable seating and bottles of wine on display while others were more like beer gardens with Shades milling around large barrels to converse.

My head was on a swivel as I attempted to see everything at once. I guessed Selene's warning had spread since the Shades were being a lot more discreet in their avid staring now.

"What did you say this celebration was called?" I asked Selene, though it was Callista who answered.

"It's the Fest of Labor. The hard work of harvesting the feed for the beasts to eat in the cold season is done, and today we celebrate with food and dancing in merriment. The spirits—the *Rolvaren*—are said to be jealous of all this merriment and come back from the plane of the dead to haunt us."

"Superstitious nonsense," Selene mumbled. Callista snorted.

"It is a very old tradition," Callista conceded. "By night, there will be fires burning throughout the grounds to ward off the spirits."

"We'll be gone by then," Selene said firmly. "They burn the bones of animals that have been collected up for months. The smell is repulsive."

"It is," Oriana agreed. "It's very, very bad."

It was subtle, but I noticed that Selene's accent had changed ever so slightly, and I got the feeling that more informal tone she'd slipped into here was her natural one.

"Is this place far from court?" I asked, looking up at the seemingly endless sea of black trees rising on either side of us.

"Court?" Callista laughed. "Oh, aye. About as far as you can get—both in distance and in feeling. You won't find any hoity-toity fancy Shades here." She glanced at Selene, shifting uneasily. "Well, not very often."

Did she mean Selene was a hoity-toity fancy Shade? That wasn't the impression I got from Selene at all, but maybe it was a matter of perspective.

"What do you eat, Austin Not-A-Hunter? Shall I get us some skewers?" Callista suggested. "I don't want to accidentally kill you with Shade food you can't eat."

"He doesn't eat meat," Selene answered for me. "I'll get the food."

"You don't eat meat?" Callista asked. "I didn't think they had anything other than meat at court."

"The options are pretty limited, but the other ex-Hunters have already brought vegetables back from the human realm. There's talk of starting a garden."

Callista scoffed. "Well, you'll be on your own with that. I doubt any of the Shades at court know how to grow anything."

That was a pretty safe bet, based on everyone I'd met so far. I was blown away by how different things were here compared to the palace. It wasn't the kind of lifestyle that would suit me—I was a city boy right down to my soul—and I could see why Selene hadn't made her home away from the barracks here, but that didn't mean I couldn't appreciate it. Mistwood was a lot more *human* than the world of the court, or even of Cartava. There were clothes. There was agriculture. They appeared to have to earn a living here, rather than however the finances of courtiers worked. Feudalism, probably.

"Wait here," Selene ordered, giving us both a stern look before heading to a stall a few feet away, keeping us—me, more specifically—in her line of sight.

"She's very good with Oriana," Callista murmured, watching her daughter clamber up on Selene's shoulders, gripping her aunt's horns for balance. "Always has been. Selene even tried to convince us to move into her apartment when Oriana was born, but no good would come of it and I told her as much. We're not like her, Oriana and me. There's barely a whisper of power between us. We're better off in Mistwood. Safer."

We're not like her. I could admit that I didn't know much about Shades, but I'd gathered that they were all born with different levels of ability, and the top dog with the most power was the one who wore the crown. I doubted Selene would have the position in the Guard she had if she didn't have substantial reserves to draw on, so she must have gotten more than her sister somehow.

"You said you're Selene's older sister?"

"Oh, much older. I raised her."

I blinked at Callista in surprise, not expecting that answer. Selene had told me her mother died in childbirth, but I assumed that her father had raised her.

"It was a difficult birth. Our mother knew she wasn't going to make it, and begged me to look after the baby. I was just shy of reaching my age of majority at the time—eighteen—still young. Selene's father had been a Shade passing through, I never saw him, still don't know who he was."

"That must have been really hard on you." I thought of plucky Rainy, also just shy of eighteen, and how very young she'd seemed. Yes, she was a tyrant in the making, but I'd also been a dark edgelord at seventeen so I kind of gave her a pass on that—true empathy took time to develop. It was a hell of an age to lose a parent and inherit a baby sibling to raise.

Callista hummed. "I doubt I would have withstood the pain of losing Mama without Selene. She needed me, and I survived for her until I was able to survive for myself again."

She fell silent as Selene returned, handing me what appeared to be a flatbread and giving Callista a skewer of meat like the one Oriana was already chewing on.

"It also has herbs in it," Selene said, nodding at the bread. "But it's denser than the one I made you. More filling."

"It's a proper peasant meal that," Callista laughed. "Then again, Selene has such a talent for finding the most delicious food at these things."

"You know I'm particular about what I eat," Selene replied dismissively.

"She always downplays her talents," Callista whispered theatrically.

"Have you noticed that?"

"I have."

"I imagine she's much worse about it at court. I'm glad she has a *friend* there now to keep her in check."

I flashed Callista a charming smile, one that she didn't question, but Selene clearly saw right through it based on the unimpressed look she shot me. She wasn't fond of my people-pleasing—or Shade-pleasing—smiles, I realized on reflection. Somehow, to her, they were always obvious.

No one in my entire *life* had been able to differentiate my stage smile from my real one. How come Selene always could?

Was she the only one who'd ever paid attention?

Selene had made it clear I wasn't her type from the second I got here, and I'd been totally fine with that. I *was* fine with that. Wasn't I?

Were my feelings as strictly platonic as they were meant to be?

There was something very intimate about feeling *seen*.

"Will you get us dessert, Aunty?" Oriana said before Selene could tell us off, looking at her with what I was pretty sure was the equivalent of puppy dog eyes.

"Of course. Finish your meat first," Selene instructed, already scanning the food stalls. Oriana happily went back to her skewer, though she'd already demolished most of it. Those sharp teeth really came in handy.

Callista snorted. "There's no point in me arguing. When Aunty is here, I am basically invisible. Selene is her hero."

Unsurprisingly, the bread was fucking delicious. Dense but somehow fluffy, and filled with herbs throughout, slightly sweeter than the ones in the bread Selene had made. We ate as we walked, and my neck started to hurt from trying to take everything in. There were things that were "familiar"—in a sort of ren-faire way—but there was also so much that was unique to this realm. The clear glass orbs filled with pale gray smoke that could hold small amounts of energy were the most fascinating. They seemed to function as top-ups to carry around when it was inconvenient to feed and came in all different sizes with different kinds of attachments to wear them around the neck or across the body.

"Are these popular?" I asked Selene in a quiet voice, not recalling seeing anyone wearing something like this. Shades at court wore jewelry, but it was all silver chains and onyx stones.

"They're not very practical—"

"Very popular," the stall owner interjected, openly staring at me. "Though I've had to put my prices up what with the portal being closed and energy scarce on the ground. We'd be in real trouble if it weren't for you ex-Hunters coming here to keep the stores running," she added, giving me an appraising look. "I bet you're popular at court."

"Me? I—"

"Thank you," Selene interjected, giving the merchant a warning look. She snorted dismissively, not put off by Selene's glare at all. "Or perhaps not. You look hungry, Lieutenant. No good comes from someone in your position going without, you need to keep your strength up."

"That will be all," Selene said curtly, dragging me away.

"Wait, what did she mean by that?" I asked, looking back over my shoulder. "Are you hungry? I'm not keeping the stores running. Am I meant to be?"

"Of course not. You aren't obligated to do anything you don't want to do."

"Maybe I do want to. I mean, I want to be helpful—"

I didn't think it was a coincidence that Selene dragged me to the heart of the fair, where the music and sounds of revelers were so loud that we couldn't speak.

Why wasn't I being scared for Shade food? I should have asked Tallulah about it, but we'd gotten distracted by other topics. Honestly, it hadn't been something I'd given much thought to at all. Maybe I'd been too reliant on Selene to tell me where I needed to be and what I needed to do.

I really didn't like the idea of her going hungry. Selene had gone out of her way to make sure I had the sustenance I needed. I should be returning the favor. She could scare me if it kept her healthy, I wouldn't mind.

"What a good idea!" Callista yelled over the noise, twirling Oriana around. "A dance! Go on you two."

Selene's jaw dropped as she shot her sister a faintly appalled look. "I don't dance."

"Last time I saw you, you didn't have friends either. But alright, I'll see if Isadora will dance with Austin then—seems an awful shame for him to come all the way out here and *not* get to experience The Vigger, it's the best part. Now, where is she? You'll like her Austin, she's the local beauty. Half the males around her would give up their farms for a chance to feel her—"

"I'll dance with him," Selene announced loudly, grabbing my forearm and yanking me into the fray.

"Let's get this over with," Selene gritted out, spinning me around and planting herself in front of me, looking as though she was about to march into battle rather than engage in a supposedly fun country jig.

"Is my company that awful?" I asked, feeling both amused and slightly offended. "We really don't have to do this, you know. I'm thoroughly enjoying the festival, with or without the dancing."

"It's fine. I just don't usually bother with this." She was directly opposite me, lined up alongside a row of Shades, while I was the only human in my row, attracting some pretty blatant sniffs and stares from the Shades either side of me. It felt very Regency era, though the two lines didn't seem to be strictly divided by male and female the way they probably would have been in the human realm.

The music started, and I devoted as little attention as possible to copying the dancers either side of me because I was far more interested in the song itself. The words weren't in English, but it had a flowing, lyrical style that made me think it had to be telling a story. The melody was folksy, though entirely reliant on woodwinds and percussion, I guessed because string instruments could pose difficulty for the claws. It was just... really fucking cool. Totally unlike anything I'd ever heard before, and yet weirdly familiar. Maybe because the concept of oral traditions set to music was such a timeless, universal thing, that even in a different realm, in an area I'd never heard of before today, I could find something in it that was relatable.

I clumsily looped around the dancer next to me before coming to my original spot in front of Selene, who was watching the Shades either side of me closely.

"What is this song about?" I asked, startling her.

"Hunger," the Shade next to me replied. *Hunger.* That seemed to be the theme today. "The agonizing need to feed. The yawning, aching emptiness when our energy runs low. The desperation that makes it impossible to think, to heal, to act sensibly."

I was going to point out how grim that was, then I remembered that *London Bridge is Falling Down* may have been a reference to a human sacrifice buried in the base of the structure, and we taught that song to children so maybe I shouldn't be so judgmental.

"I did want to ask you about that, *Selene,*" I added pointedly, because my nosy neighbor was leaning in awfully close. "I'd love to know what that energy orb vendor was talking about."

Selene usually had no problem looking at me—except when I was wearing *The Pants*—so the fact that she was so fidgety, looking at everything *but* me was a dead giveaway that she was feeling sheepish about something. With an impressively dark warning look from her, the Shades either side of me gave me some space, and I hadn't realized how uneven our line had been until they'd gotten back into formation.

"Shades can feed off the sexual energy of Hunters," Selene muttered eventually, the words all tumbling together. "It doesn't appear to be detrimental to the Hunters. We absorb energy from you during the act, and we can then siphon that into the stores that are currently fueling the entire realm."

I was vaguely aware of copying the movements of the Shades around me—albeit half a beat later—but my mind was whirling.

"So, this whole time... I was meant to be—"

"*No.* You weren't *meant* to be doing anything. The king was very clear that any contributions should be entirely voluntary."

"Contributions, huh?" I laughed, drawing the curious eyes of the Shades around us. "Quite the euphemism. Why didn't anyone tell me about this?"

I was carried away with the dancers at that moment, turning through my row in a figure eight that briefly took me away from Selene before returning me to my spot in front of her.

"Of course, Austin will need to be brought up to speed on the, er, relationships between Shades and Hunters—both the past and the present. Selene, I don't suppose you could…?"

That's what King Allerick had said when we left the throne room. I'd completely forgotten about it.

"You were supposed to tell me," I surmised, watching her small flicker of a wince. She looked as though she was bracing herself for an angry reaction, but I wasn't mad.

I was, against all odds and probably unwisely, kind of hopeful. There was a sort of fizzing, fluttering feeling in my stomach that I'd never experienced before.

Selene had never looked at me as anything more than a friend— and even that was a stretch. But she was very good at hiding her emotions. Did this… mean something?

"Selene, why didn't you tell me?"

She grabbed my wrist, tugging me out of the formation and away from the crowd. Not for the first time, I noted how much she dragged me around places, and how much I kind of *loved* it. Selene never bothered with coyness, never tried to make herself smaller or less intimidating in any way. She was who she was, and she *owned* that.

I'd sung on stages in front of thousands of people and put every piece of my soul into those performances, and I didn't have one-tenth of the confidence she did.

"I didn't tell you because I didn't want to," Selene said, stopping abruptly and releasing my wrist as she turned to face me.

"Okay. Why?"

We were standing behind a canvas stall, and she paced back and forth in front of the piles of empty wooden crates in neat stacks lining the tent.

"I don't know why," she said lamely, staring at the ground.

"Because you're protective of me?" I hedged, giving her an easy out. "As my guard?"

"That would be the most logical explanation," Selene agreed, though it didn't sound like it was the *right* one.

"You're hungry, that's what that merchant said. Did *you* ever consider feeding from me?"

The question was out before I could hold it back, but I needed to know.

Selene shifted her weight, still refusing to look at me. "Of course not."

"Am I that unappealing?" I teased, trying to lighten the mood and the blow to my ego.

"Don't be ridiculous." She threw up her hands in frustration, resuming treading a path into the grass in front of the crates. "Look at where I'm from. I doubt most of the Shades at court have even *heard* of this part of the realm. I am very clearly not suitable for anything but guarding you, Austin."

That's what she was worried about?

"So, you *have* thought about it?"

"You don't understand Shade society," Selene continued, ignoring my question. "The disapproval you'd face—"

"I understand it just fine. Shades don't have the monopoly on elitism, Selene. But I don't care about anyone's opinions except yours. What do *you* want?"

Because it was suddenly very clear to me what *I* wanted. Or was it? Because I wanted to kiss her—more than kiss her—but I also wanted...

What did I want?

For her not to be starving, that much was certain. But there was more to it. A complex minefield of feelings I wasn't sure I was qualified to explore.

"It's not that simple."

That quiet whisper, the slightly broken quality of it, had me getting my shit together. From everything I'd seen, I could get away with a lot more here than Selene could. It wasn't fair of me to dismiss the very real consequences she could face just because I had realized my feelings had changed. Because there was something *here*, something that had been growing right beneath our noses, except neither one of us had been open to seeing it.

"Okay." I blew out a breath, nodding once to affirm my own sense of calm. "Okay, it's not that simple."

Were we talking about the physical act of feeding or something more? I didn't think Selene knew either, but I doubted one could be entirely separated from the other. Selene had snuck behind my defenses and made herself important to me. If something were to happen between us... Well, it wouldn't be meaningless, that was for fucking sure.

"Don't rule me out," I said quietly, forcing myself to drop the mask of careless confidence I'd grown accustomed to wearing.

"It's not a good idea."

"If it makes you feel any better, my track record of not-good ideas turning out pretty well is quite promising."

"There you are!" We both startled as Oriana appeared through the gap between tents. "We've been looking everywhere for you. What are you doing?"

"Talking," I replied easily, giving Selene a moment to get her bearings. "Hey, what was that thing you wanted to show me?"

"Oh, the bonebranch! Can we go now?" Oriana asked, grabbing Selene's hand and tugging her back toward the festival. "Please? I want to show Austin the bonebranch."

"Yes. Yes, of course," Selene rasped. "Come on, Austin."

SELENE

CHAPTER 12

Fortunately, Oriana was both the perfect distraction and entirely enchanted by Austin's unusual humanness because I needed a moment.

What had just happened?

That conversation had taken me entirely by surprise, and I'd already thought of six different things I probably *should* have said but didn't.

Starting with: I'm not interested.

It wasn't true, of course. Austin was handsome, interesting, and far more perceptive than anyone gave him credit for. And even those misconceptions about him were his own doing—a mixture of poor decision-making and his deliberate attempts to play everything off as a joke.

That was intriguing too.

But it *couldn't* happen—no one in the realm would accept it—though telling him that was a mistake. If anything, I'd laid a challenge down at his feet. I should have said that I didn't want to. That I didn't like him. That I wasn't attracted to him. *Anything* would have been better.

I'd handled it sloppily. If he'd ever given me any indication that he was interested in me, I would have prepared an answer in my mind, but he hadn't.

"He seems nice. For a Hunter," Callista added, coming to stand next to me as Oriana and Austin built a tree out of a pile of animal bones, competing against other Shades to see who could build the most elaborate one before it collapsed.

One of the males I'd attended the schoolhouse with growing up was inching closer to Austin's back, trying to get a better look and smell as though Austin was an interesting object to be examined rather than a sentient being. I flicked a long whip of shadows out, silently warning him to back off.

"Too nice," I clipped. "And not aware enough of his surroundings."

"Well, that's what he's got you for."

"Exactly. I'm his *guard*." I wasn't sure if I was saying it for her benefit or mine.

"Anyone with eyes can see you're more than that."

"Callista—"

"You clearly like one another. The realm needs energy. You don't look as though you've been feeding enough. What's the harm?"

"It would be inappropriate."

"You told me yourself that the captain has taken his Hunter charge as a mate."

"That's different."

"Why?"

"Because..." I trailed off in frustration. It *was* different. Soren was the captain and from an illustrious family, he was one of the king's closest confidantes. If *my* sister had done what *his* sister had done, I'd be exiled forever by association.

"This is because you're from Mistwood," Callista guessed flatly. I adored my sister, but on the subject of Mistwood, we would always disagree. She'd had a wonderful childhood here, was a popular member of the community, sold preserves that she bottled herself, and got along well with Oriana's father even though they were no longer together. Callista *was* Mistwood, she exemplified everything good about life in an agricultural, close-knit community.

And because she loved me, she struggled to see that I wasn't treated the same way. She couldn't comprehend *why* I was always looked at like an outsider because she never saw me that way, and the Shades who did were her friends.

This particular struggle had always been mine to bear alone.

"I don't know how it all works at court, I'm just simple country folk and I like it that way. But I do think you'll regret it if you throw Austin at one of those spoiled court beauties because you think they're more worthy than you."

"That's the kind of Shade he *should* be with. Someone wealthy. Powerful. Prestigious. Close to the throne."

"He's having an awful lot of fun entering a bonebranch contest with a poor, nearly powerless child for someone who *should* be swimming in wealth at court."

"Oriana is a delight. It's impossible to be unhappy in her company," I countered, hating the idea of anyone calling her poor and nearly powerless, even her own mother.

Even if it was accurate.

"I certainly think so, though I'm a little biased," Callista agreed with a laugh, relaxing slightly. "But Austin seems the unpretentious sort. I think you might be projecting your own fears onto him, Selene. I don't blame you for it—I know you've suffered at court because of your lineage, and it hurts my soul that you don't feel like you belong here either."

Feeling had nothing to do with it. I didn't belong here, and that had been made very clear to me since birth. No one had ever been outright cruel to me—even in childhood, I was far more powerful than the adults of Mistwood—but they were intimidated by me and they wanted me gone. Off to who they saw as my own kind—Shades who were blessed with power in abundance and didn't even know places like Mistwood existed.

"Selene!" Austin called. "Come join in. Oriana doesn't believe that I can beat you at this."

"You can't beat me."

"Big words. Can you back them up?"

I didn't play games. I watched Oriana play games, but I didn't join in. And yet...

"Fine."

I dragged Austin away as some of the local Shades began piling up wood for the bone fires.

"Oriana will never stop pestering me now," I muttered, gripping Austin's arm as I led him through the in-between. "Why did you tell her you'd play your instrument for her?"

"Because she wants to hear me play, of course. She had a lot of questions about it."

"You... you're willing to see her again?" I asked hesitantly, hating the idea of letting Oriana down.

"Of course." Austin's tone was suddenly solemn. "I wouldn't have said it otherwise. Are we going to Cartava?"

"What?" I paused, close to the entry room at the barracks. "I'd intended to return to the barracks. I thought you'd want to go back to the palace."

"Not really, but if you have to get back—"

"No. I don't. We can go to Cartava instead." I turned, guiding Austin in a different direction. Already, the weight on my shoulders was lifting at the idea of going to the one place that felt like *my* home. Not the valley I'd grown up in or the palace I worked in, but the humid city of indulgences that I'd *chosen* for myself.

"Oh good," Austin said on an exhale. "I'm not ready for today to be over just yet."

I was glad his eyesight wasn't strong enough to see my features in the in-between, because I had no idea what he'd find in my expression. When we'd set out this morning, I hadn't envisioned having the conversation about feeding. And I certainly hadn't envisioned him offering himself up to me.

Don't rule me out, he'd said. But how could I do anything but? It would be highly inappropriate, given where I was from and the fact that I'd been assigned to guard him.

And all of that was irrelevant anyway because he *wasn't interested in me.* If he was, I would smell it.

We didn't speak on the journey back to Cartava, nor when I cloaked Austin in shadows for the short walk to my apartment. The silence wasn't uncomfortable necessarily, but it did feel charged. And the moment we were in the apartment and I'd removed his shadows, I couldn't help but think that Austin looked different. Taller, even. More self-assured.

"Well? Have you ruled me out?"

I spluttered slightly, scrambling for a response. "I hadn't given your words any thought."

"Liar." How inconvenient that he'd immediately seen right through me. "Are you not at least a little curious? About my unusual human body, if nothing else?"

"Of course I'm curious about that. Everyone in the *realm* is curious about that."

Austin spread his arms wide, magnanimous and inviting. "So explore me."

"It's a bad idea," I reminded him, though I was struggling to remember my exact reasons why when we were alone, the privacy of my apartment shielding us from the outside world. If anything happened...

No one had to know.

"Not even a kiss?" He was teasing, but he wasn't, that much was obvious. "Shades don't kiss."

Austin's eyebrows shot up, his face so charmingly mobile and expressive. "They don't? Right, right, the teeth."

I hesitated for a moment. "The Shades with Hunter mates do. Or Captain Soren and Astrid do, at least. I may have seen them once. At the training grounds before anyone else arrived."

"Did you watch?"

I looked at him, trying to figure out if he was still teasing. There was no secretive smile on his face though, just plain curiosity.

"A little." My shadows shifted restlessly around me, a reflection of my embarrassment.

"And? What was your verdict?"

It was foolish to have this conversation. I knew that. Austin had declared some kind of intention, and I'd denied him. It was a dangerous game indeed to be talking about kissing with him.

The problem was that I hadn't *wanted* to deny him.

I *wanted* to keep him all for myself. To strip him bare and explore every inch of his body, to find out if and how we'd fit together.

The fact that he'd never shown any interest in me had meant it was a harmless passing fantasy, until it wasn't.

"Selene..." Austin rumbled, pressing me for an answer. There was an edge of impatience in his voice I'd never heard before that sent a pulse of pleasure straight between my thighs.

Happy Austin was desirable, but Frustrated Austin was *sexy*.

"It looked... enjoyable."

"Just enjoyable, hm? Was that really the word you meant to say?" There was a flutter in my abdomen at the warning tone in his voice. What was wrong with me? I hated males telling me what to do. I had a very strict set of rules that I abided by when it came to sex to ensure that I was never vulnerable, and Austin was already breaking them.

And I wasn't going to have sex with him.

I repeated the words silently in my head for the benefit of my pussy, who didn't seem to be getting the message.

Often, I'd wondered if Austin's scent didn't work the same way as it did for Hunter women. Why else would his scent not have broadcasted his desire at the gathering of female Shades held in his honor?

Except right in front of me, it was changing. Sweetening. Growing thicker and more heady by the second.

"Selene..." Austin's voice was a deep rasp, nothing like his usual mischief-filled tone.

"Stop that," I ordered weakly, feeling my limbs shake.

"I'm not doing anything."

My cunt clenched, a warning of slick incoming. "You're definitely doing something."

"You're just feeling what I'm feeling."

There was that clench again and it made absolutely no sense because I didn't *like* being told how I was feeling. Nothing was less attractive to me than a high-handed male.

Right?

"You're not attracted to me," I said bluntly, reminding my brain and the stupidly damp flesh between my thighs to pull it together.

"That's bullshit—"

"No, it's not. It's your scent, Austin. The *desire* of Hunters has a particular smell—"

"Right, the fabled mating scent."

"—and you have never emitted that smell until now."

Austin sniffed himself. "I'm pretty sure I don't smell like anything, but even if I did, doesn't that prove that I *am* attracted to you? You're the only one here, Selene. I'm only looking at you."

I hesitated, briefly seduced by the logic in his words.

"No." I shook my head. "No. If you desired me, you would have given some indication before now."

"Maybe... Okay, fine." Austin ran his hands through his hair. "Maybe I was being blind to what was right in front of me. I didn't *see* you, Selene, but I'm seeing you now. I see how smart and accomplished you are, how hard you work. How *caring* you are—I see it with how you act with your sister and Oriana. And how you act with me."

I don't care about you.

That's what I should have said.

And I didn't. Not really. Or I shouldn't. There was no benefit to it—I couldn't keep him. Austin would move on with one of the higher-born females at court, and I'd have to witness their happiness every day. I would be a professional about it, of course, but a very bitter, unhappy professional.

"Are you going to lie to me, Selene?" Austin asked casually. "Act like there's nothing going on here?"

"There wasn't until a few seconds ago."

"We both know that's not true. There was always *something*. It was just growing into what it is now."

Austin took a step toward me, his eyes bright with an intensity that I hadn't seen before. Usually, he was so relaxed that I'd struggled to imagine how he could hold the attention of thousands on stage. Not now. Now I understood Austin's charismatic draw entirely.

I'd already been attracted to him. It wasn't fair that he had this secret weapon at his disposal too.

Plus that *scent*.

It was more potent than the most delicious fear I'd ever smelled in the human realm. Austin took another step, and while that also violated my unwritten rule list, I didn't push him away.

But I could have.

Perhaps that was what made it so easy to stay in place, to let him come physically close to me in a way that I would find incredibly off-putting from anyone else.

With claws and teeth and brute strength, I could overpower him, and there was nothing he could do to stop me.

"I want to kiss you," Austin said with a knee-shaking level of certainty. "But you already know that."

"No, I don't."

"Don't you? Maybe I'm not explaining myself clearly enough."

I hesitated. "Soren and Astrid are mates. Bound to each other. For them to kiss... Well, perhaps you don't want what they—"

"I think I might want exactly what they have."

That was...

I wasn't even going to acknowledge that.

Austin took another step closer. "Will you let me kiss you, Selene? Will you do me the honor?"

"I doubt it will be an honor. I don't think I'll be any good at it—"

Before I could come up with another excuse, Austin pressed his palms to the wall either side of my head, so close our noses almost touched.

The scent of his desire went from a steady hum to a full-force storm, saturating the air around us, turning my insides liquid.

"It's unfair how good you smell," I whispered, trying not to inhale and yet greedily gulping it down all at once.

Austin grinned with such a savage intensity, anyone would think he was the one with fangs. "I'll take whatever advantage I can get. The way you look, smell, talk, act, *exist*—nothing about you is fair, Selene."

That wasn't true. This was part of the game, part of the act of seduction. Words meant to flatter, compliments to appeal to my ego. I knew that. I expected that.

His scent didn't lie, though.

And maybe it was the heavy layer of *truth* in the way he smelled combined with how very close he was to my face that gave me pause. Logically, I knew his teeth couldn't harm me, he had no horns that could maim me, and he appeared to be speaking honestly when he said he liked me...

I jolted, banging my head on the stone wall behind me and startling Austin back a step.

"Selene?"

"Sorry! I'm sorry." His scent had soured, and I felt awful that I had frightened him.

"Don't apologize, are you okay? You hit your head."

"I'm fine." My head throbbed a little, but it would heal up once I visited the energy stores. "I don't... I don't do this often. I don't like having anyone *close* to me. They might use it against me. Or mock me. It makes me vulnerable." The words felt like knives in my throat, but I pushed on, needing Austin to understand that my reticence wasn't because of him.

He gave me a long, considering look, and I couldn't decide if I was embarrassed or grateful that he seemed to be taking my concern seriously.

"I'd never mock you. This is far too precious for that. And you're a lot stronger than me, Selene," he said slowly. "You could rip my throat out with your claws or your teeth before I could so much as blink. But if it'd make you feel better, you can tie me up, I don't mind."

"You don't?"

Austin shrugged. "For your pleasure, I'd prefer to have use of my hands, but I can get creative. If you want to keep going, that is."

I didn't actually want the responsibility of having Austin tied up at my mercy, but the fact that he'd offered soothed some of my worry.

"Never mind. No tying up necessary. I do want to keep going." I blew out a long breath, unsure of how to proceed. I'd never brought anyone back to my apartment before—for intimacy or otherwise. And while I *enjoyed* sex, if the strict set of conditions I had in order to engage in it weren't satisfied, I went without.

My conditions definitely weren't satisfied now.

The most important one—that I had a fast and easy escape readily available—had never been *less* satisfied. Though I supposed, if it came down to it, I could always restrain Austin and physically remove him from my apartment.

"Tell me what you need," Austin said solemnly, careful to maintain a small amount of space between us. "Not to make you feel *good*, not just yet, though I am dying to know. To make you feel *safe*."

"I'm being ridiculous. The only way you could physically hurt me would be if you were carrying a silver blade."

"You're not being ridiculous. And obviously, I'm not carrying a knife, but I'd be more than happy to take my clothes off so you could see that for yourself."

That gave me pause. "Alright. But in my bedroom. Away from the windows."

SELENE

CHAPTER 13

I led Austin up the stairs, to the bedroom on the mezzanine above the kitchen and bathroom, walled off from the wider room but without a door.

The moment we were inside the space, he was moving. Austin didn't hesitate, nor did he brag—something most Shade males had done if I expressed even the slightest amount of interest in them dropping their shadows. The ones from the valley where I'd grown up acted like I was debasing myself for sleeping with someone with less power, as though it was some kind of statement on my self-esteem and place in the world. The ones I'd encountered since I left Mistwood had more power and egos to match it, and acted as though any interest I showed in them was akin to begging for scraps from my betters.

It was almost enough to put me off the whole concept of sex in general.

But Austin simply undressed, shedding the cumbersome-looking layers of dark human clothes to reveal pinkish skin and faint brown body hair, as well as an array of inked drawings that I was eager to explore.

With every inch of skin he unveiled, a sense of duty grew within me, as well as something else. Something akin to gratitude.

He might not want me to point it out, but in comparison to me, Austin *was* fragile. And he was entrusting me with him. With his body and his safety. With his *pleasure*.

It was a responsibility and a gift.

"No knives, as you can see." Austin spread his arms wide, letting me look my fill, but it wasn't weapons I was interested in examining.

Austin's cock was nothing like a Shade male's cock. There was no bulbous knot at the base, threatening to tear me in two.

No, it wasn't like a Shade's cock at all.

But it was *very* similar in shape to the toy I favored for pleasuring myself. Long. Curved. Elegant. The perfect width for me to clamp around, for my cunt to clasp and stimulate until I was drowsy with satisfaction.

Would Austin enjoy that as much as I would? It didn't seem possible, and yet the shape of him...

Austin cleared his throat. "I'm not going to last long if you keep looking at it like that."

"You'll last just fine." It was a statement and a challenge. My pussy fluttered, anticipating the perfect stretch of him.

Except we couldn't.

He was too virile for that. I could tell as much just by looking at him.

"I would like to see you touch yourself," I said hoarsely. It wasn't quite a command, which was unusual for me when it came to intimacy, but I didn't feel the need for it.

Because Austin wasn't fighting for the upper hand, I wasn't fighting to hold on to it.

He wrapped his hand around his cock, a blunt fingernail touching the tip of his thumb without piercing the skin, and began moving his fist up and down in a mesmerizing rhythm. Could I ever touch him like that? It was probably too risky.

"Slower," I ordered as he picked up his pace. "I want to see what you're doing."

Austin groaned. "I know for a fact that you have better eyesight than me. This is just about torturing me."

I shrugged—an annoying gesture I'd picked up from him. "Perhaps."

He did as I asked though, and I watched entranced as he slid his fist up and down his length, occasionally circling the fat head of his cock with his thumb. Shiny liquid beaded at the tip, and I salivated as though his seed was a particularly rare and expensive delicacy on offer.

Could he touch *me*? My flesh was too delicate even for my own claws, but his dull fingers...

"What are you thinking about?" Austin rasped.

"I'm wondering what your fingers would feel like on me. *In* me. I'm wondering if I would like it."

Austin hunched forward as though my words had pained him. "Please let me try. I'll never ask for anything else."

I considered him. "I like it when you beg. It seems like the least you can do after scheming your way into being my charge."

"Maybe my subconscious already knew then that I was obsessed with you." A pretty lie, but a lie nonetheless. We both knew that Austin wasn't obsessed with me then or now, and he'd never looked at me with any kind of interest before today.

"Want me to get on my knees?" Austin asked casually.

"Not this time." I wasn't opposed to the idea, but I felt a sudden surge of self-consciousness. My body was not human. I would look different to what he was used to.

I was vain enough to care about it. Before my nerves could get the best of me, I let my shadows fall away, quickly removing the holsters around my thighs where I kept my blades.

Austin sucked in a breath, eyes greedily tracing my form. For a brief moment, I worried that he'd find me displeasing—too different from his usual lovers, too hard where human females were soft—but the scent of desire he was emitting only grew thicker and sweeter.

"You're incredible, Selene." Austin reached out as though to touch me in the way that he explored everything with his fingers, before seemingly remembering that he was giving me physical space to lead this interaction.

"You can touch," I told him, stepping forward. Strange, to realize that I trusted *him* to touch me more than I trusted *myself* to touch him. Those thin red lines that my claws had raked over the back of his hand were imprinted in my memory.

Austin's fingertips brushed against my skin, starting at my wrists before moving up my arms, his movements growing firmer and more confident as he went. His lips tilted up as he rubbed surprisingly soothing circles into my shoulders, before letting his hands drift down, pausing above my breasts with an enquiring look. I nodded, encouraging him to keep going, my pussy convulsing in time with his explorations.

"Your skin is so..."

"Thick?" I suggested.

"*Smooth*." He looked so awed that I couldn't help but reach out and rub my palm over his bicep and down his forearm, finding the texture of the light dusting of hair that covered him surprisingly coarse, though not in an unpleasant way.

"Are you sensitive here?" he asked, brushing the pads of his thumbs over my nipples.

I shook my head, surprised at the question. Shade young were born with tiny sharp teeth and drank milk from their mother's breast for several months. I would not wish to be sensitive there.

Austin continued his explorations, his thumbs reverently caressing the ridged muscles of my abdomen before sliding lower. He glanced up at me through thick, pretty eyelashes, seeking reassurance as his touch settled on my mons.

My hold on the tight leash of control I always kept loosened a little further. "Go ahead."

A ripple of desire traveled down my spine at the first brush of his fingers over my labia. He sucked in a surprised breath, examining the tips of his fingers, already shining with arousal.

"You're so wet." He rubbed his thumb against his fingers, looking somewhat in awe as he examined the proof of my desire. I couldn't decide whether I was embarrassed or not. The attention was very flattering.

"It's my slick," I pointed out, just in case he wasn't aware.

"Slick," he repeated in a low murmur, sliding his damp fingers between my thighs again, pressing forward to part my flesh. I nearly jumped out of my skin at the first firm touch of his fingers. They were smaller than my toy or a partner, but far more dexterous. I was trembling almost instantly.

What would his tongue feel like?

Don't think about his tongue.

Austin's fingers circled and toyed, and while there did some to be some kind of pattern at play, I couldn't discern what it was. He was watching my reactions so intently that I had to look away, unnerved by the intensity of his gaze. Besides, I was struggling to focus on anything beyond the overwhelming pleasure.

"Bed!" I gasped, my pussy clenching around nothing. If my orgasm hit me now, I'd crumple to the floor where I stood.

Austin immediately took charge and I surprised myself by letting him. His clever fingers never stopped their teasing exploration as he maneuvered me backward to the bed. Each step sent a jolt of satisfaction throughout my body, and I collapsed onto the mattress without a single worry about how Austin was looming above me in the clearly dominant position.

"Tell me if it's too much," he murmured, kneeling on the bed by my hip. With excruciating patience, he slid one finger inside me, letting out a grunt of surprise as my walls contracted around him.

"Fuck," Austin groaned, squeezing the base of his shaft as he pumped one finger slowly inside me before adding a second. "You feel... holy shit."

I didn't ask him to elaborate. I didn't need to. Not when the girth and length of his cock was so un-Shade-like and yet so identical to the toys I used. I could tell just by *looking* at him that he would feel incredible, and it looked as though he was having a similar realization.

Don't lose your head, Selene. It would be a very bad idea to get pregnant right now.

My back arched as his two fingers stretched me in the most delicious way, his thumb stroking my over-sensitized flesh. He squeezed his cock again with his other hand, the head of it looking a slightly painful shade of purple, and it was that which sent me over the edge into oblivion.

He looked *agonized* with desire. Hungry and desperate and greedy.

It was beautiful.

"You're still going?" Austin asked in amazement, stroking and twisting his fingers relentlessly. I doubted he could escape my grip if he wanted to.

Did human orgasms not last as long? It usually took at least fifteen minutes to subside.

We may not have been having penetrative sex, but I was definitely feeding from Austin at least a little. The well of power in my chest that had been consistently low since the portal closed was filling. It wasn't a flood of energy, but a small and steady trickle, yet it was more potent than any fear I'd ever fed on in the human realm.

Eventually, the waves of bliss ebbed away to a gentle contentment, every part of my body feeling gloriously relaxed.

Slick pooled on the sheet beneath me, long shiny strands clinging to Austin's fingers as he eventually withdrew them, all but panting in need.

"I want to fuck you." He wrapped the slick soaked fingers around his cock, marking himself with my arousal. Possessive instincts I didn't know I had roared to the surface, wanting to see his cock covered in slick straight from the source. Wanting his scent mingled so thoroughly with mine that there was no telling where his ended and mine began.

The sudden ache in my teeth brought me sharply back to reality.

"We *can't*," I breathed, my legs still shaking. "You're extremely breedable."

"Fuck, Selene," Austin groaned, massaging his cock with an almost brutal intensity. "How is it so hot when you talk about breeding?"

By the night, I was aching for him in a way I'd never ached for anyone, but it didn't matter. We couldn't. We *couldn't*. The whole reason Shades used to capture and mate the Hunt*ed* was to feed from them and breed from them. I wanted a child desperately, but it seemed like something we should discuss first.

"Austin..."

"Okay, okay. You're right. You're totally right." Austin blew out a long breath. "Let me give you another orgasm."

"What? No, I need to return the—"

"Don't even finish that sentence. Lie back and let me worship you."

I had never thought of myself as a particularly selfish lover before and yet...

"Okay."

I wasn't strong enough to resist this.

AUSTIN

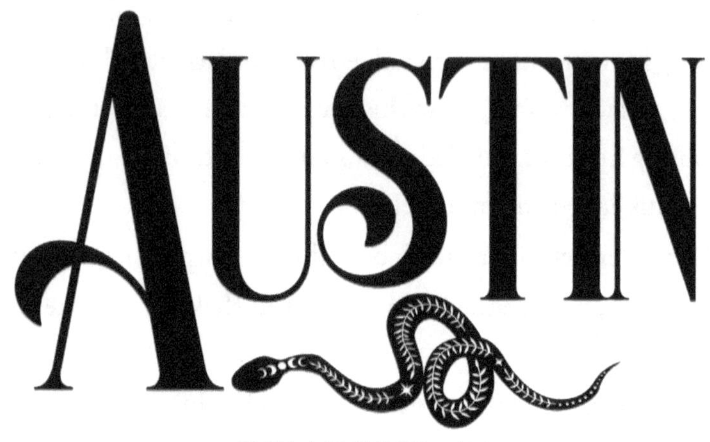

CHAPTER 14

Selene woke up before me. I slowly came to right as she was slipping out of the bed and heading downstairs, but I kept my eyes mostly closed in the interest of giving us both a minute to get our thoughts together. I doubted she let people stay in her bed very often, so I guessed she was feeling at least a little odd about waking up next to me.

And I couldn't even begin to unpick how *I* was feeling.

We hadn't had sex. She'd panicked when we tried to kiss. I'd snuck off to the bathroom before we fell asleep to take care of myself because my dick was so sore I was pretty sure it was going to fall off. I'd been very dedicated to Selene's pleasure, but objectively, I should have considered it kind of a failure of seduction for my part.

But I didn't. At all.

In fact, it may have been the best night of my life.

I was the only one who'd touched my dick, and yet it had been the most *intimate* experience I'd ever shared with anyone, and I knew in my bones that it wasn't a Shade-versus-Hunter thing. It was a *Selene* thing. I knew her, at least a little. I knew what it meant for her to let me get physically close to her. For her to let go and relax and enjoy herself.

Everything meant more because it was her.

It was kind of terrifying. I'd never really been at risk of developing real feelings for someone before, and I wasn't sure how I felt about it now.

What if I asked her for more and she rejected me? Just the thought had me breaking out in a cold sweat. I'd poured my heart and soul into my music a million times, I thought I knew what it was to open up and be vulnerable, but apparently I was completely wrong.

Being vulnerable with just one person whose opinion actually mattered to you was a hundred times more terrifying than laying my bleeding heart out for consumption by an audience. There was no stage separating us, no emotional distance, no excuses.

Fuck.

I dozed while Selene bathed, eventually rousing myself to head downstairs once I heard her pulling things out in the kitchen. *Just be normal, Austin. Don't make it weird.*

We're just a couple of buddies who shared an amazing night of no sex together. There's nothing to be awkward about.

"Good morning." *Nailed it. Chill as fuck.*

Selene set down the mystery black ceramic jar she was holding on the counter and turned to face me, pinning me with the full force of her emerald gaze.

Oh man, I was so scared and turned on, I didn't know what to think.

"I don't understand how this works in your world. Is your intention to never speak of last night again? If so, tell me now so I can comply."

I should have known Selene wouldn't let me *not* talk about it. She was blunt, and she liked clarity.

And I liked that about her.

"That's not my intention." It had been a little bit my intention, but when actually confronted with the idea, I found it abhorrent. I *was* afraid, but nothing worth fighting for came easy.

"Alright," she agreed easily. "I would prefer we not tell anyone else, though. They will have... opinions."

I didn't really care about any of those opinions, but if Selene wanted to keep me as her dirty little secret, I could roll with that. For now, at least.

"I want to do it again," I told her honestly. And again. And again. For however long she'd have me.

Selene continued to stare at me for an unnervingly long moment. "Okay then. Let me feed you first."

Oh. Oh, we were going to do it like *now*?

Okay. I could roll with that.

"There is a preserve my sister makes from fruit," Selene said, pulling a jar of mystery gray goop off a shelf. "It has no meat in it, of course. It may provide you with some nutritional value. I should have asked her for more yesterday for the other ex-Hunters to try."

She set out some bread she must have baked at some point, and a knife to spread the preserve, gesturing for me to go ahead and eat while she pulled bacon out of the larder for herself. My girl loved her some gray-con.

I unscrewed the jar on the preserve with a small amount of struggle that I think I managed to hide pretty successfully, sniffing it with low expectations because gray goop looked like the least appetizing thing ever. But it actually smelled kind of great? That did seem to be a shadow realm pattern. Even if it looked like sludge scraped out of the inside of a drainpipe, it'd probably taste surprisingly good.

"Callista made this?" I asked, using the knife to scoop out some and dabbing my fingertip on the blade so I could try a little. Selene watched me the whole time with her exasperated must-you-touch-everything face.

"It's how Callista makes a living. Our mother did the same before her. The family home is a small cottage surrounded by fruit trees. It will go to Oriana someday."

"How do you feel about that?" I licked the sweet, sour, slightly fizzy preserve off my finger, and immediately scooped a thick layer onto the bread. It was delicious.

"What do you mean?"

"Well, it was your family home too, right? It sounds like you've kind of removed yourself from the equation."

Selene was quiet for a long moment, stoking the fire in the cast-iron stove and setting a heavy skillet on the top to heat. "Callista sacrificed many years of her life to raise me. I like to think, regardless, that I would have always left the cottage to her and her offspring without a fight. As it stands, I have significantly more power than the Shades in Mistwood, and I never intended to stay there. When I reached my age of majority, I left right away."

"And went straight to the palace?"

"I started out as a guard at the Pit." She glanced at me, catching my blank look. "It's a prison."

"Got it. That must have been an intense environment."

She hummed thoughtfully, going quiet for a moment as the sound of sizzling bacon filled the room. "In some ways. Captain Soren noticed my potential and encouraged me to join the Guard proper at the palace. At the Pit, no one had particularly cared that I was from Mistwood other than some vague curiosity about how I was as powerful as I was. Once I came to the palace, the issue of my birthplace was much more pronounced."

"But you pushed through. Rose up the ranks. That's super impressive, Selene."

She shrugged—when had she started doing that?—carefully plucking the bacon off the skillet and constructing some kind of elaborate bacon-bread concoction with a bunch of other mystery ingredients.

"Captain Soren believed in my potential."

"He's a smart guy."

Selene snorted, always eager to deflect from any kind of praise. "Eat your breakfast. I'm concerned that you don't eat enough."

I let her change the subject for now, but I had no intention to stop giving Selene compliments.

"You really don't need to worry so much about me, you know. I'm more durable than I look."

Selene shot me a disbelieving look before taking a bite of her breakfast.

I finished eating before her, cleaning up my plate and taking some time to bathe since apparently we weren't in a rush this morning. I wasn't quite sure how Selene's shifts worked, but it seemed she had a later start today.

The water was as hot as I could stand it, and I sunk down until my chin touched the surface, closing my eyes and replaying the last twenty-four hours over in my mind.

"You're not attracted to me."

For all the very, *very* good memories yesterday held, those words were a low point. They weren't true—I was attracted to Selene—but the romantic feelings had come on suddenly, spurred on by actually *knowing* her, and I needed to reassure her that they were genuine. There was a depth to my attraction to Selene that I'd never experienced with anyone else in my life.

Fuck, I really wanted to make her feel good again. Good, and desired and beautiful. She got uncomfortable with intimate conversations, but *action*—well, action I could do. She couldn't argue with that. Selene had said as much herself when she pointed out the way my scent broadcast my feelings.

I got out of the bath and dried off, wrapping the towel around my hips. Before I left the bathroom, I paused to push the fabric a little lower, trying to showcase the maximum amount of abs possible. I had some seducing to do.

Shit, how *did* one go about seducing a Shade? Yesterday, we'd been all high on sexual tension and it had all happened naturally. Did I even *have* moves? I'd been sort of coasting by all my life on a combination of looks, talent, and moderate fame.

My dick was already hard at the thought of touching Selene again, so it was really inconvenient that my brain was picking now to have an existential crisis.

"Bed," Selene ordered the moment I stepped into the room.

"What?"

"You smell needy."

My historical trend of failing upward appeared to be continuing. "I am. Super needy. Let's go."

Selene led me up the stairs, her shadows vanishing into nothing as we reached the top. So convenient.

"How shall I tend to you, hm?" she mused, looking me over.

To be totally honest, she couldn't. Not really. Neither the claws nor the teeth were going anywhere near my dick and I would die on that hill. However, I also felt entirely fine with it? If I just got to make *her* feel good, I was completely sure I'd be satisfied. Her pleasure was my pleasure.

Was that a kink? It seemed like a kink.

"I want to tend to you. Will you lie on the bed for me?" Selene clearly liked to retain some measure of control, and I didn't want to push her.

She watched me carefully as she moved to the bed, lying on her back and propping herself up on her elbows. "What are you going to do?"

"Make you come with my tongue, if you're okay with that."

I was acting super cool about it, but I was quietly freaking out on the inside.

The thing was, I was really bad at eating pussy. I hadn't even tried since college after the repeated lackluster and/or outright super disappointed reactions.

Why was the clitoris so hard to find? Why did the most sensitive, powerful source of female pleasure play hard to get?

I hadn't gotten a good *look* between Selene's thighs, but I'd felt around when I was making her come on my fingers, and hadn't had an *a-ha! There it is!* moment. But she'd also orgasmed for, like, twenty minutes straight. So... maybe this wouldn't be a total disaster?

"I'm okay with that."

She was confident as fuck, spreading her legs for me the moment I kneeled on the end of the bed. I ran my palms up her thighs just because I could, just for the joy of touching her. Her skin was much smoother and thicker than mine, slightly leathery in texture, but fucking warm and super erotic.

I parted her with my thumbs, admiring the way her midnight black flesh shone with arousal, and as I tentatively ran a finger over her smooth, silky folds, she let out a full-body shudder.

That was promising.

Still no sign of the fabled clit, though.

Fuck, fuck, fuck.

"Do you have an area that's more sensitive?" I asked, sucking up my pride and communicating like a grown-ass man. *Look at me, trying new things.*

"You're touching it," Selene gasped, bucking her hips as my thumb shifted. Oh. *Oh.* I experimented again, stroking her silky flesh, noting the way that *every* movement had her twitching and writhing beneath me, slick pooling and dripping onto the bed.

Oh my god, it was just... all clit. All killer, no filler. Hypersensitive *everywhere.* There was no way I could fuck this up. This would be like eating pussy with a cheat code. Thank you, Shade gods.

All my hesitation vanished. I dived in all pudding cup and no spoon, ready to give Selene as many hours of orgasms as she could stand.

Or until she had to leave for work. Whichever came first.

But the second my tongue made contact with her pussy, I froze like I'd just licked an icy telephone pole. Not because I was stuck.

Because I was in heaven and I never wanted to leave.

"Your taste," I groaned, voice muffled by her flesh before I dived back in.

Selene's personality was a little prickly, but her slick tasted like strawberries that had been soaking for hours in champagne. Sweet and fruity and light on the tongue. Delicious. Perfection.

"Move," Selene demanded, writhing against my mouth. "Your tongue…"

I braced myself for a brutal hit to the ego, since I'd *seen* Shade tongues and felt a smidge insecure about my own.

"It's so silky," Selene groaned, entirely fucking herself against my face at this point. "So perfect. Just the right amount of stimulation."

Okay, there was definitely something to be said for this whole Shade-Hunter symbiosis, and it was all working out great in my favor.

Without any pressure hinging on finding one small, magical spot, I went to town, licking every inch of her for both her pleasure and mine. It wasn't as though it was a hardship when she tasted like my favorite flavor in the world. Eventually, her thighs began to tremble, and I slid one finger into her channel, letting her body get accustomed to the intrusion before adding a second, purely to enjoy the sensation of her pussy gripping my digits like it was trying to break them.

The part of me that liked my dick being attached to my body wondered if penetrative sex was even feasible. But there was a not-insignificant part of me that got off on the thrill of it. I mean, Selene could reach down right now and just Wolverine me directly in the eyeballs with her claws if she so desired.

I humped the mattress a little at the thought.

"I need more," Selene gasped, bucking against my fingers, reaching clumsily for something next to the bed, eventually grasping a small wooden chest and shoving it toward me.

I was pretty loathe to remove my fingers from her pussy, but curiosity had me moving. With a small click of the latch, the lid popped open, revealing a silvery-gray dildo that looked eerily similar in shape to my cock, with the exception of the flared, plug-like base.

What the...

That was a *human dick* dildo. Were our dicks the dragon dildos of the shadow realm?

"That kind of looks like my dick."

"You sound far too smug about that."

"I'm just saying. That's a pretty Austin-looking dick."

"Our kinds used to procreate and we're obviously very physically compatible," she pointed out primly, or at least going for prim while she was still writhing beneath me, desperate to come. That somewhat lessened my panic about penetrative sex between us being feasible. "Fuck me with it," Selene demanded, nudging me with her knee as her patience thinned.

"Since you asked so nicely..."

She was so slick that the dildo entered with relative ease, though the relentless clenching meant that it still took some effort. I watched, entranced, as I thrust the toy in gently, slowly picking up my pace as I learned what Selene liked. My dick ached, but I was too enraptured by Selene's pleasure—especially as she peaked and clenched so tightly that the dildo was locked into place— that I couldn't even comprehend touching myself.

But even as I experienced the best non sex of my life for the second day in a row, I couldn't turn off the quiet buzz of panic in the back of brain. This was so good, so right, so perfect. These feelings were not short-term fling feelings. These were *big* feelings.

And I couldn't think of a single reason outside of the sexual chemistry we shared why she'd want to keep me.

SELENE

CHAPTER 15

Usually, nothing put me in a good mood for the day better than an orgasm or several—I made myself come each morning as a matter of course, because it was good for my stress levels. Combined with the partial feeding I was doing from Austin, I *should* have felt excellent today, but I didn't.

I felt uneasy, and annoyingly unsatisfied considering how thoroughly Austin had pleasured me both last night and this morning.

It just didn't feel like *enough*. I was greedy for him in a way that I wasn't usually greedy for anyone. Was it just because of *what* he was?

Or *who*?

The latter was more dangerous.

As always, I made my way to the training grounds after my rotation and before dinner duty. Even that felt unsatisfying, I thought grimly. This was where I kept my skills sharp, demonstrated my commitment to my position for the members of the Guard who were forever watching and waiting for me to slip up. Usually, I relished the irritation my excessive training caused them, but not today.

What was Austin doing right now?

He'd taken his guitar to Elverston House and talked about working on a song. And he was safe there—logically I knew that. Still, the distance between us bothered me.

I threw myself into my workout, my muscles burning with exertion by the time I noticed Astrid entering the training ground alone. Perfect. She was by far the least unpleasant member of the Guard to spar with and was always up for a challenge.

"Why so stompy?" Astrid asked, snatching the baton I threw her out of midair with her good hand. "I've never seen you so... *heated*. You're usually much more aloof than this."

"I am just as aloof as always," I replied, far more defensively than I'd intended.

"No, you're not." Astrid went through the series of stretches and warmups that her fragile human body required. Had she ever tried yoga? "Works for me. Maybe you'll be distracted enough that I can actually beat you today."

"We both know that's not going to happen."

"Uh huh." She bounced on the balls of her feet for a few moments before dropping into a fighting stance. "I didn't even come here to spar, you know. I came here to check on you."

"If you're trying to distract me, it won't work." While I was fonder of Astrid than any ex-Hunter—except Austin—and more than most of the Guard, I wouldn't have called us friends.

Neither of us had friends. Except the males we were involved with, I supposed. Then again, it seemed disingenuous to compare our situations. Soren and Astrid were mated, in love, and bound for life.

Austin and I were friends who'd stumbled into bed together.

Astrid and I danced around each other, darting forward to attack, batons clashing before putting space between us again. While I was at no real risk of being defeated by Astrid—she was far slower and weaker than I was, even if her technique was admirable—today was the closest she'd ever come to besting me.

"You're so off your game," Astrid panted, holding up a hand to request a minute to catch her breath. "If I had a little more upper body strength, you'd be on your ass right now."

While I'd always taken care with her, knowing she wasn't as sturdy as a Shade, it was only after spending so much time with Austin and being responsible for his safety did I appreciate just how *fragile* she was.

"How is the captain comfortable with you being part of the Guard?" I asked sharply. What if I'd knocked her over? Human bones were like delicate little sticks.

"What?" Astrid straightened, frowning at me. "What the fuck is that supposed to mean? I think I've proven myself more than loyal to the shadow realm—"

"No, no, it's not that. Of course, you've proven your loyalty. But your body is extremely breakable. I don't think it's wise for you to be in the Guard. The captain should be taking better care of you."

Astrid spluttered indignantly. "*Breakable*?"

"If, by some miracle, you managed to knock me to the ground, I would be fine. Any minor injuries I sustained would be healed by feeding—it would be an inconvenience at best. Look at your hand," I pointed out, gesturing at the scar on her palm. Astrid had never recovered full use of it after her injury, and she believed she never would. "You were maimed and will forever stay that way."

What was Soren *thinking,* encouraging this madness?

"Sure. And yet, here I am. Sparring with you. Compensating for the lack of use in one hand by practicing with the other," Astrid replied slowly, giving me a strange look, chest still heaving as her breath returned to normal. "I'm not built like you, but I'm not made of glass either. And Soren trusts me to be able to handle myself. Where is all this coming from, Selene? Are you uncomfortable sparring with me?"

I made a frustrated sound of denial because *no*, that wasn't quite my problem. Besides, if Astrid was going to insist on this unwise course of action, it seemed better that she partner with me than any of the other members of the Guard who may not take adequate care with her safety.

"Or perhaps this isn't really about me," Astrid suggested, eyes narrowing shrewdly. "Maybe it's a different ex-Hunter's safety who you're actually worrying about."

The words I'd been holding in since the moment Austin had regained consciousness in this realm all came tumbling out at once. "He is an impossible charge to be responsible for keeping alive. He could die at any given moment. He could drink water incorrectly and *choke*."

"I mean, yeah, I guess. It's pretty unlikely, though. He could inhale an insect and choke. He could choke every time he puts food in his mouth. You will work yourself into a terror if you think of all the possible ways he could hurt himself."

"I've already worked myself into a terror," I shot back, throwing my hands up in exasperation, adding flying insects to my list of things to worry about. The shadow batons disappeared in a puff of smoke, my concentration too fractured to hold them in place. "Austin is as delicate as a newborn animal, and he doesn't seem to realize it at all. He's always *touching* everything—even things he has no knowledge of—practically inviting an injury!"

Astrid was almost smiling, which was a rather unsettling look on her since she was so rarely happy about anything. "What else?"

"He has no regard for his personal safety in general," I continued, the words flowing out of me before I could hold them back. "He wishes to accompany me wherever I go with seemingly no consideration for the risk factors. He claims he feels *safe* with me, which is unwise because I am only one Shade and there is only so much I can do. He says he..."

I hesitated, haunted slightly by the words he'd delivered with so much ease. Astrid waited patiently, not pushing me to confess. Perhaps that was why I found myself sharing more.

"I don't know. He says he *sees* me, whatever that means." I swallowed thickly, looking away. "That he sees my work ethic and other traits he deemed to be positive, I suppose."

It had sounded much better when he'd said it.

"Good," Astrid said simply.

"Good?"

"Of course. We all deserve to be seen." She shrugged as though it was nothing, but the words made something twist strangely in my chest. "How do you feel about it?"

"It's obviously ludicrous," I pointed out, my shadows rippling discontentedly. "He just hasn't met enough female Shades yet, and he's latched onto me as the closest available one. Perhaps what he *sees* is just what he wants to see. That's all it is."

After all, no one else had ever complimented the traits in me that he'd complimented. Perhaps I'd read too much sincerity into it.

"Selene," Astrid chided, tutting impatiently. "He's met plenty. He had a whole party to meet them."

"Well, he clearly needs another one," I insisted. "And he's been avoiding the dining hall where he would have an opportunity to get to know others. There are many eligible females at court who would give Austin a very comfortable life. They have apartments here at the palace, grand family estates around the realm, substantial incomes, and good breeding. And any one of them would snap him up as a mate. Austin has an abundance of exceptional options."

"Is it really so hard to believe that of all those exceptional options, he'd choose you?" Astrid asked softly.

"It's impossible to believe that. Ask *your* mate if you don't believe me. By every metric that matters, I have nothing to offer. This is how the shadow realm *works.*"

Astrid simply hadn't been here long enough to understand the nuances of Shade society. Besides, her mate was the Captain of the Guard and one of the most powerful Shades in the realm. Soren's family—though marred by the traitorous blight of his sister—was ancient and prestigious, and he'd been raised as a playmate to the royal children.

Realistically, how could Astrid know anything about what life was like for Shades outside of that small, elite circle? The entire time she'd been in this realm, she'd lived at court.

"I mean, you know how these things work better than I do," she conceded, mirroring my thoughts. "But I've encountered plenty of the snobby assholes at court who you claim to be so much better than you, and not only do I strongly disagree, I also really can't see Austin getting along with any of them. Verity, Tallulah, and Meera are surrounded by fancy court Shades and haven't committed to anyone either, and I'm pretty sure their difficulty relating to them is a big part of that. Some of us are from wealthier backgrounds than others, sure, but none of us grew up in palaces with servants and daily banquets. We all had, like, jobs and stuff."

Astrid wasn't one to say so much unless she felt the words were important, so I did give them some consideration. There *was* something to be said for Austin's background separating him from the Shades at court rather than uniting them, but would that matter in the long run?

The more time he spent in this realm, the more he would grow accustomed to the norms here. If Austin settled for me while he was hampered by his inexperience in this realm and influenced by my constant proximity to him, he would only grow to resent it later.

"Keep an open mind, Selene." Astrid flexed her injured hand gently. "Get to know him without any expectations and see where it goes. What's the worst that can happen?"

That I fall in love with him, and then he realizes what a poor option I really am.

Astrid sighed, staring into the distance, toward the direction of the palace. "Also, for what it's worth, the whole hierarchy thing is garbage, and Allerick can expect a lecture from me the next time we sit down together for family brunch. Actually, I'll lecture Ophelia, she's way more likely to get results with him than I am. But even if Allerick makes changes, you've got to back yourself, Selene. You're a fucking badass. You're probably the scariest being—Shade or human—I've ever met, and you know I fully intend that to be a compliment. If you got here, this high up in the Guard, this strong, this talented with *less* advantages than the others, that's a credit to your abilities, not a strike against them."

I swallowed thickly, the words bolstering me in a way I didn't know I needed. It wasn't quite enough to silence the doubts in my head telling me that I wasn't worthy of any of this, but it certainly helped.

"Come on," Astrid said, dropping back into position and holding out her good hand, waiting for a baton. "Let's get you out of your head."

CHAPTER 16

Elverston House was cold and uninspiring.

I understood that Selene had to go do her real job and that babysitting me all day wasn't totally feasible, but I'd been sulking about it for hours anyway. My vague plans to use this time wisely and write some new music had failed spectacularly.

How was anyone supposed to be creative in such a soulless building? Maybe I was being a little high maintenance, but I needed *something* to feed the muse, and the drab stone walls and frayed, moldering furniture weren't doing it for me.

I sighed dramatically, leaning my guitar against the ugly couch and flopping back on it, nearly impaling myself on a spring.

Why'd the others live here? Not that Tallulah or Verity were here now, they were out socializing or some shit, but there was no fucking way I was moving out of Selene's place to live here. *Either* of Selene's places. I'd offer to be her errand boy if she'd let me stay there. I'd be her on-call pussy licker if she'd let me. I had a healthy respect for sex workers, and my only marketable skills in this realm all appeared to be linked to my dick.

"Oh!" said a startled voice from the hallway. *Meera.* Even when startled, she had a distinct voice that I didn't need to turn around to recognize. Mostly because she was the only one in this house who was soft-spoken. Tallulah was pretty self-assured, and Verity was a whole force of nature. "I'm so sorry. I was out in the garden for so long, I didn't even realize we had company."

"Do I count as company?" I mused, staring up at the water-damaged ceiling. "Or am I just a fellow attendee of the Elverston Ex-Hunter Daycare, here for the day?"

Meera came to stand behind the couch, peering down at me. "Daycare?"

"Perhaps *prison* would be a better term," I agreed.

"You certainly have a flair for the... theatric." Meera raised an eyebrow at me. "I always wondered how anyone could possibly be comfortable performing on stage, but you seem like you'd be right at home with so many eyes on you."

"I would. I am." I let out another heavy sigh, my soul weighed down by boredom and the heavy responsibility of being a stifled creative genius.

"We can leave, you know," Meera continued, wholly unconcerned about my suffering. "Elverston House is a safe haven, a Shade-free sanctuary for us to get our bearings, but we're encouraged to explore. To find our own place here."

I jackknifed upright, knocking my guitar in the process, only just managing to grab the neck before it clattered to the ground. "I can leave? I don't have to stay here until Selene finishes work?"

Meera frowned. "Did Selene *tell* you that you had to stay here? I suppose that would change things a bit—"

I was already jumping to my feet, lovingly tucking my guitar back into its case. "Can I leave this here for a bit? It's kind of bulky to go wandering around with."

"I suppose." Meera was massaging her temples, which was a reaction I was used to invoking in women so I didn't pay it too much heed. "Maybe you should stay here. What exactly did Selene say?"

"She didn't make me *promise* to stay here or anything," I assured her, putting on my most responsible-looking expression. "I'm just going to go for a walk. Get some fresh air. Contemplate my future and what I'm going to do with my life now. That kind of thing."

I headed out of the dank sitting room, whistling some of the melody I'd been working on as I went because my muse had instantly perked up at the idea of getting out of here.

No one stopped me as I let myself out of the house and out through the garden of dead plants and sadness, turning at the gate in the direction of the palace, intending to swing right and head down to the training grounds. Selene had said she'd come and get me before dinner, so maybe I'd bump into her, even though I had no idea what time it was. Whatever. I'd just hang around the training grounds until Selene was done.

Huh. Maybe I could get a job there. After all, Astrid was an ex-Hunter and a gainfully employed member of the Guard. Granted, Astrid had been a Hunter protégé, and I'd done the bare minimum of basic training, but they must have junior positions or something, right?

"Austin!" Cosima waved at me from across the palace garden, accompanied by another female Shade that I didn't recognize. "Wait for us!"

Damn it. I should have stayed in the House of Sadness.

"Vita, this is *Austin*," Cosima said, sidling up next to me and pressing the whole side of her body against mine, reminding me of all the times I'd agreed to take a picture with a fan and they'd laughingly groped my ass while posing. Cosima wasn't groping me, but she wasn't exactly respecting my personal space either. "Where are you going? Is that guard not watching you anymore? We can accompany you."

"That's really okay—"

"Or you could come with us! Arius, the greatest explorer living today, is giving a speech at the palace about his most recent travels. He's from a grand estate called Sanlow, but his passion lies in exploring. It's been *years* since we've had such culture at court. The artists and great minds are all starting to come back now, hoping Queen Ophelia will... take more of an *interest* in the arts than her husband."

"Aren't you an artist?" Vita asked enthusiastically. "Cosima says you're an artist. Come on, Arius will be starting soon."

Sandwiched between the two of them, I was sort of swept up in the tide, finding my feet taking me toward the palace, already making plans to ditch them at the front steps. I was getting my bearings, but I definitely knew the path to the training grounds better from the palace anyway.

"Where's your warden?" Cosima asked. "Selah, isn't it?"

"Selene," I corrected, frowning. "She's not my *warden.*"

Okay, she was a little my warden, but they made it sound like an insult when it was literally Selene's job, and she was fucking excellent at it.

"Not that you *need* a warden," Cosima continued. "As we discussed at your welcome gathering. Vespera has been attempting to petition the king on your behalf, but I suppose he's too busy to talk to her..."

She trailed off, sounding vaguely uncomfortable, and I wondered if King Allerick was less busy and more actively avoiding her. That was a cheering thought.

"That's all totally unnecessary. I'm very happy where I am. If I was given the choice to stay anywhere, I'd stay with Selene." That wasn't saying too much, was it? She wanted to keep our whatever-it-was under wraps, which I totally respected, but I wasn't going to pretend that Selene wasn't my favorite Shade in the realm. I wasn't a good enough liar to pull that off.

"But she's... she's..." Cosima trailed off, looking to her friend in frustration.

"She's a *peasant,*" Vita whispered, glancing around. "No one knows how she has so much power. No one else from her part of the realm does."

"It's not natural," Cosima agreed sadly, shaking her head. "And everyone said as much when Captain Soren appointed her to the Guard. We couldn't believe it when she kept moving up through the ranks."

I considered myself a pretty affable guy for the most part. I didn't *like* negative emotions, so I channeled them elsewhere—usually into my music—so I didn't have to confront them in everyday life.

But now I was feeling *pissed*.

"Okay, well thanks for the lesson in classism. See you around."

"Wait!"

I was already walking away, breathing heavily with each step to get my emotions under control. Fuck, it was frustrating. There was so much more I wanted to say, but my hindbrain kept helpfully reminding me that if those two Shades turned on me, I'd be in ribbons before I could even defend myself. There was a weird twinging feeling in my chest at the realization of how *vulnerable* I was—a sensation I'd never particularly experienced in the human realm. It wasn't as though I was prone to getting into fights, but the knowledge that I'd be totally screwed if I did was very fucking humbling.

A reminder that I had *nothing* to offer Selene.

My mood was foul by the time I got to the training grounds, catching the tail end of Selene and Astrid sparring. Fortunately, Selene was busy enough to only shoot me a slightly impatient glance, though I was sure she'd tell me off later for wandering around on my own.

"Austin," Captain Soren said, scaring the bejeesus out of me as he came to stand beside me. Where had he even come from? How come he could move so quietly when he was so huge?

"Captain," I replied, acting like he hadn't just taken ten years off my life with his surprise entrance. Except he was discreetly leaning away and wrinkling his nose, so I guessed I wasn't really hiding anything since my sweat glands functioned like loudspeakers in this realm. "I'm glad I ran into you. I've been thinking about it, and I want to join the Guard."

Captain Soren turned, staring at me in silence for an unsettlingly long time. Whole civilizations rose and fell while he stood there, judging me.

"No."

No explanation, no justification, just a no. Cool, cool.

"How come? Astrid was allowed to join."

He scoffed. "Astrid is a lethal weapon, an asset we are beyond fortunate to have. Besides, I didn't want her to join either. It was good fortune that the king saw the potential that I was too blinded by my own hatred to recognize."

And they said romance was dead.

"How do you know I'm not a lethal weapon?"

"Are you?"

To lie or not to lie, that is the question.

"For sure," I told him with more confidence than I felt. "I'm an extremely badass ex-Hunter. Lots of training."

It wasn't a total lie. I did have quite a lot of training, even if most of it was from a decade ago and I hadn't really bothered to keep my skills sharp.

The badass part was one-hundred-percent false, but surely I could get by on charisma and rusty technique until I got up to speed?

"You can try out here tomorrow," Soren said eventually. "I'll send for you."

"Really? Thank you! I mean, thank you, Captain." I cleared my throat, trying to rein in my excitement. There was no guarantee that I was actually going to get in, but a trial was something. Shit, if nothing else, it was something to look forward to. Some kind of *purpose.*

I was very much looking forward to getting out of here and making Selene feel good—it was absolutely going to be the highlight of my day—but I probably needed to have a little more going in life than that to feel content.

Maybe.

Probably.

And I definitely needed some kind of career. Something to show Selene that I was marriage material. Mating material. All of the above.

"What are you doing here?" Selene snapped, making her shadow baton go *poof!* into nothing, and marching over to me. She was so fucking hot when she was fired up. Unlike with Cosima and Vita, there was no part of me that worried she was going to turn her rage on me, at least not in a physical way. No matter how much I annoyed Selene, I was always safe with her. "I said I'd come and collect you before dinner."

Astrid made her way to the edge of the training grounds, her face as red as a tomato, sweat cascading off her in waves. Maybe I should go for a run or something before this whole Guard tryout thing.

"I believe your charge is finding his days rather dull," Captain Soren said wryly. What? I'd never said that.

"I'm not surprised," Astrid replied. "Elverston House is pretty empty during the day now from what I hear, except for Meera."

"Meera spends most of her time in the garden," I volunteered, then paused to think about it. "She also likes me the least."

I was pretty confident she was actively avoiding me, and I wasn't offended about it at all. I wasn't everyone's cup of tea, and Meera seemed to prioritize peace and quiet.

Selene looked to Soren. "Perhaps a new plan for Austin's protection would be... sensible. Something that allows him more freedom."

She was clearly waiting for him to suggest something, but Soren was more interested in ushering Astrid away from the training grounds. "I'll defer to your judgment on this, Selene. You have handled his protection just fine so far."

"Thank you, Captain," Selene murmured, not sounding entirely grateful. The moment he and Astrid were out of earshot, she gave me her most unimpressed expression. "Why didn't you wait at Elverston House?"

I threw my hands up in exasperation. "It *is* boring there. And my muse doesn't like it."

"Your... muse?"

"Exactly. My muse. The thing that allows me to *create*. When my muse is unhappy, my creativity is stifled. It's very sad, you know."

"… is it?"

"*Yes*. Maybe if I could just hang out in Cartava all day—"

"Absolutely not." Selene shook her head. "I couldn't have you so far away from me."

"Because you'd miss me?" I asked hopefully.

Selene twisted to look at me for a long moment before turning back toward the barracks, not waiting for me before she took off at a brisk stride. Well, that wasn't a *no*. Or a yes, but still.

Not a no.

"I thought we were going to dinner?" I asked, jogging to keep up.

"I need to bathe. I intended to do so before collecting you from Elverston House, but since you decided to appear here of your own volition, you will just have to wait for me."

"I could wait. Or I could help?"

Selene paused, looking at me over her shoulder. "I suppose we'll get to dinner faster if you wash my back."

Oh, *fuck* yes. She might not be willing to admit it, and she may not be good at showing it, but Selene was totally into me.

SELENE

CHAPTER 17

I was already awake when the knock on my door came before first light. Austin was still sound asleep next to me, and absolutely not meant to be here. Quietly, I climbed out of bed and shoved open a window, hoping the scent of what we'd been doing last night would magically disappear.

"Selene," Carys said, dipping her head respectfully as I cracked the door open as little as possible. "The captain has requested that you bring Austin with you to the training grounds today."

My insides ran as cold as ice. "Did he say why?"

Carys took a step back as my shadows swirled around me, and I hurriedly pulled them back in, embarrassed by the loss of control. "He didn't. I believe they had some conversation yesterday?"

That was true enough. Austin and the captain had spoken while Astrid and I finished up at the training grounds, but as Austin was the one doing all the talking—complete with exaggerated hand movements—I hadn't given it much thought. After all, he was very fond of talking.

"Thank you, Carys," I said, dismissing her as quickly as possible. *Austin would be fine*, I reminded myself. Captain Soren had the utmost respect for the ex-Hunters. The only one he'd ever treated poorly was the one he was now mated to. I doubted there was anything to be worried about where Austin was concerned.

It was myself I should probably be worried for. Had someone noticed that Austin's room was empty last night? No one had noticed the two nights he'd stayed in Cartava. Or perhaps they had, and were keeping a record to present to the captain?

My stomach churned uneasily as I washed in silence and snuck out of the room to prepare a tray of food for us in the kitchens.

By the time I returned, Austin was awake, shooting me a beaming smile from the absurd-looking position he'd contorted himself into. For all I thought of him as fragile, Austin's limbs did things that frankly defied all laws of movement as I understood them.

"Good morning, darling. Did you sleep well?"

My mouth went dry at the casually delivered term of endearment. We couldn't go on like this. Someone was going to get hurt.

"I slept fine. You should have really slept in your room."

He hummed. "I promise I didn't ignore your instructions on purpose. I think we both just immediately fell asleep."

My skin felt hot and tight all over at the reminder of what we'd been doing *before* we fell asleep. It was frankly a wonder that he wasn't experiencing pain in his tongue and fingers after spending so long pleasuring me.

"I'm just finishing up my stretches. Go ahead and start breakfast without me."

"Why has Captain Soren asked for you to accompany me to the training grounds this morning?"

"That was quick." Austin took a few deep breaths, closing his eyes to focus, and I helped myself to a pile of charred meat in the meantime. Who knew how long his strange exercises would take.

Eventually, he unfolded himself, standing and stretching out his arms and legs before joining me at the table, still smiling as though he didn't have a care in the world.

He smiled more now, I realized. More than when he arrived here. Or at least more genuinely.

"You need more human food," I said, watching him rip apart the stack of flatbread I'd purchased for him before unscrewing one of the jars of preserves I'd brought back here for him to use as dip. "Vegetables and such."

"Probably," Austin agreed. "This is fine for now, though. Meera is hard at work on that garden."

"You never answered my question about why the captain wants to see you."

"Didn't I?"

"You know you didn't."

"Weird." Austin shoved a piece of bread in his mouth, preventing him from saying any more. He really was a trying creature when he wanted to be.

"Fine, keep your secrets. I'll find out soon enough," I muttered, shoving some cold, burned food in my mouth. Hopefully it wouldn't mean the end of my career.

"This is ludicrous," I snapped, watching Austin stumble back a step to avoid the brunt of Andrus' swing. "Why is Soren insisting on this?"

"He's not," Astrid replied, sounding more amused than distressed as she should be. "This is all Austin. Soren thinks he's bored. I think he's probably trying to impress you."

"Well, I am *not* impressed." That wasn't entirely true. Austin's *bravery* impressed me. The way he'd thrown himself wholeheartedly into this foolish endeavor was endearing in its own stupid way. "I'm extremely concerned for his safety."

"Probably wise," Astrid agreed. "Andrus won't do him any real damage on purpose, but Austin's technique is so sloppy, he may very well knock himself out at this rate."

"Is that meant to make me feel better?"

Astrid hesitated. "No? I could try that, though. Um. Don't worry about it? He'll probably be fine?"

"You're awful at this," I muttered. Though I wasn't confident I'd be able to do a better job if the situations were reversed.

"You could intervene," Astrid pointed out. "You're the second-in-command and in charge of Austin's safety. Soren would defer to your judgment in this."

Andrus blocked Austin's clumsy strike with ease, and while the impact of the colliding batons had Austin's arms shaking, he fell back into a slightly off-balance fighting stance, fully prepared to try again.

Tenacious. I hadn't realized just *how* tenacious he was before. "Austin doesn't like it when I point out how fragile he is."

"I can't imagine why." Astrid snorted.

My need to keep Austin safe was warring with the knowledge that he'd hate my interference. I could hardly judge him for his pride, I had plenty of my own.

I let out a heavy sigh, hoping Andrus had better control over his strength than I was giving him credit for. "No, I won't intervene."

"I think that's the right call." Astrid nodded curtly, crossing her arms. "Austin is finding his feet here in the shadow realm. We all are, but he seems more lost than the rest of us. I get that it's hard to watch him flounder, but he might *need* this."

As much as I wanted to tell Andrus to fuck off and tuck Austin safely away into his room at the barracks—better yet, *my* room—I knew Astrid had a point. Austin was *looking* for something. I was already taking more of his time and attention than was appropriate. The last thing I wanted to do was stand in his way.

"You're tense," Soren observed, looking at me as he came to stand next to Astrid, pressing his arm against hers.

An immense understatement.

"I'm responsible for Austin's safety in this realm. This is an unsafe activity."

"Well, he assured me that he was a badass Hunter," Soren said dryly. "So I'm sure he'll be fine."

Astrid made a strangled sound, uncharacteristically expressive. "That is a bald-faced lie."

"I'm aware of that," Soren assured her. "However, he clearly wanted an opportunity to prove himself, and doing so in this environment poses less risks than doing so anywhere else."

Soren was quiet for a long moment, watching as Andrus toyed with Austin, letting him dance closer before easily dodging obvious hits. Astrid's assessment of his technique as "sloppy" was partially true—he clearly had been trained at some point—but his movements were slow and unpracticed, even if I compared him to Astrid rather than the strength and speed of a Shade.

Without expending any effort, Andrus side-swiped Austin's ankles with his baton, knocking him to the ground. I took a step forward before I'd consciously decided to move, but Astrid's hand on my arm stopped me. "Let him get up on his own."

After an agonizingly long second lying on the ground, Austin rolled onto his side, pushing up to his feet with the same graceful fluidity he always used after his yoga routines, so I supposed he couldn't be *too* badly injured.

Austin shot Andrus a sheepish grin. "Maybe I'm slightly less badass than I remember."

"Maybe," Andrus agreed flatly, his baton disappearing into nothing. "If you're seeking some purpose here in the shadow realm, then perhaps you should ask the king and queen for another party."

Austin's face fell, and I shook off Astrid's grip to close the gap between us. "If Austin wants your unhelpful advice, he knows where to find you. Come, Austin. I want to check your injuries."

I could feel them all staring as I led him away, but I was too tightly wound with tension to even give them a back-off look over my shoulder. Was it not clear to everyone who'd attended the last party that Austin had been immensely uncomfortable? While I was still certain that he would find his mate among the court, it was cruel to put him into situations where he was so clearly unhappy.

Surely, they could see that. Even Andrus, with his limited emotional intelligence should be able to see that.

Actually, maybe not Andrus. That may have been asking too much of him.

"What were you thinking?" I hissed the moment we were out of earshot. "Andrus could have *killed* you."

"Everything here can kill me. I just wanted to see if I had a shot with the Guard. Like, maybe I'm a secret Astrid underneath all the tattoos and vegan leather."

"You are not an Astrid, you are an *Austin*. You are not meant to be part of the Guard."

Maybe Austin had been born into a warrior community, but that wasn't him. And I'd spent enough of my formative years struggling to fit into Mistwood to know that he should embrace who he was. That fighting against his nature would only hurt him in the end.

Austin sighed. "I'm seeing that now, though it's kind of a bummer. I guess I'm back at phase one again. Only good for breeding."

I stumbled to a stop, whirling around to face him. "You are good for *far* more than that. Who said that? Was it Andrus? I'll rip his tongue out myself."

Austin's scent sweetened so thickly I was almost choking on it, my body reacting viscerally to the intoxicating smell of his lust.

Don't react, I told myself firmly, my pussy already clenching around nothing, producing slick as though his scent had commanded me to.

"Everyone and no one," Austin replied gently. "Usually not in so many words."

Unsatisfied in more ways than one, I spun on my heel and marched back toward the barracks with Austin rushing to keep up. His scent was so enticing now that I wanted to get him back to the privacy of my room for multiple reasons, though he wasn't mine to want.

Fortunately, the corridor that led to the rooms was empty with everyone busy either at training or on duty. I didn't know how I'd react if someone else noticed Austin's scent.

The moment we were in my room, Austin breezed past me and threw himself down on my bed with a groan, as though he belonged there, lying on his back, spread out and deliciously vulnerable.

His head was tipped back, all but taunting me with his unmarked throat. Was he doing it on purpose?

"I should have stretched more. I swear I never had to deal with sore muscles as a teenager after training."

"Which muscles are sore?" I asked a little sharply, panic spiking at the idea of him being hurt. Should I get a healer? Could a Shade healer even help him?

One of the ex-Hunters had some kind of medical experience from memory. Meera, wasn't it? Perhaps I should have taken him to Elverston House instead of back to the barracks? Of course, I should have. It was idiotic to bring him here.

"All of them," Austin replied absently, stretching his limbs. I nearly swallowed my tongue as he arched his back, the thin white fabric of his shirt riding up to expose his stomach.

He had a very nice stomach. I wanted to run my claws over the thin line of hair that disappeared into his trousers.

"What will cure you? Do you need medicine? Shall I send for the ex-Hunter with the medical knowledge?"

Austin propped himself up on his elbows, smiling indulgently. "I'm fine, I promise. I just need a hot bath or something."

"Why didn't you say earlier?" I crossed to the bathroom, immediately turning on the flowing hot water. How was I meant to care for him if he didn't tell me what he needed?

"You worry too much." Austin was doing that strange, soft voice again. I never quite knew how to feel about it. It was so... affectionate.

"You don't worry enough. Get in the bath. I need to return to my rotation. Where would you like to spend your day?" I called over my shoulder.

There was a rustling sound, then Austin appeared, leaning against the bathroom door, mostly undressed. "You're giving me the choice?"

I swallowed, distracted by his bare skin.

"If you're going to volunteer yourself to join the Guard, then I'm sure you can keep yourself alive for a day without me tucking you away somewhere for safekeeping," I replied waspishly, reminding myself that I was annoyed.

"I'm touched by the faith you have in me. Truly."

I huffed. "You should be, I don't put my faith in anyone else. Don't make me regret it."

Austin smiled softly. "I won't, I value it too much. I'd like to stay here in the barracks. Though I left my guitar in Elverston House yesterday." He hesitated for a moment. "Maybe I could wander over and grab it?"

"That sounds very logical," I agreed, swallowing down my panic at the thought. He'd be fine. He'd be *fine*.

"Hey, Selene."

"What is it?"

"I'll be fine."

"I know that," I said curtly. "Get in the bath."

Eventually, I managed to drag myself away from the barracks, making for the palace to check all the guards were where they were meant to be. They had a habit of drifting apart like small children when there wasn't an active threat to look out for. I blamed their lack of discipline on their overly privileged upbringings.

"Selene," Carys said, jogging over to me, her face filled with concern. "Evrin isn't here."

"Again?" I sighed. Evrin usually monitored the in-between. Of all the Shades in the kingdom, he was the least inclined for company and enjoyed the solitude of walking through the oppressive, silent darkness alone for hours on end.

Carys hesitated, and I was reminded why I thought she'd do well in the Guard. She seemed to genuinely care about how others were perceived. "He seemed in very low spirits. I volunteered to cover his rounds."

He'd been in low spirits since the night of the ball. I hadn't yet raised it with Soren, but perhaps it was time. The in-between was suffocatingly isolated, and I'd always wondered how it was that Evrin had maintained his sanity up to this point. Perhaps he needed a change of scenery.

"I'll do his route," I said decisively, assessing Carys' experience in my head. She was strong and fast on her feet, but the in-between required a different kind of awareness. "Find Captain Soren and let him know I'm going in there. Then pair up with Galen, shadow his route."

After checking in with everyone else as the rotation started and making sure there were no other issues, I headed for the portal in front of the palace. It was still strange not seeing Soren around as much as usual, though I was happy for him that he had some kind of life outside of duty now.

I followed protocol by entering the in-between through the portal outside the palace so my energy signature was recorded, and as always, approached the human-side portals with extreme caution, although they continued to lie dormant. Before, they emitted a faint glow, a pull toward them that guided the Hunters who couldn't travel via shadows to where they needed to go. Now, they were extinguished, and almost grave-like in their dark stillness.

A slip of white caught my attention, and I inched my way closer, blade in hand and senses at full alert. I didn't expect to see any Hunters—they were incredibly vulnerable here even with the portals functioning—but I hadn't risen so far up the ranks by being inattentive in my duties.

There was no threat. Just a sheet of paper weighted down by a rock to stop it blowing away in the cross breezes that swept through the in-between.

We will give you five willing Hunter women in exchange for Austin Thibaut.

I almost laughed, carefully folding up the note so I could take it to the king. The Hunters had proved themselves liars when it came to making deals already. Neither the king nor the Council would make that mistake again. The fact that they were liars also threw some doubt on their claim that the women were "willing." King Allerick would rather have none than take any against their will.

The thought of what they would *do* with Austin if they got their hands on him sobered me. Did they want to kill him? Or were they just eager to get him back?

I hoped we never had to find out.

I exited the portal quickly, tracking down Soren at the energy stores. He scanned the note but didn't say anything with so many others around, just gestured for me to follow him through the palace and quietly instructing another guard to get Austin from Elverston House.

That made me even more tense. I didn't want to see Austin's safety in the hands of another Shade. They wouldn't protect him the way I did. They weren't his friend. They didn't care about his wellbeing the way they should.

What if they let Austin touch things? The man needed to be protected from himself.

The captain led me to a small sitting room where the king and queen were having their midday meal with Astrid and Prince Damen, with Levana standing watch. They all looked up in surprise as we entered, except for Astrid, who probably sensed us approaching through the mysterious mate bond.

"I'm guessing you're not bringing good news," King Allerick sighed, tugging the queen's seat closer to him as though to shield her from our words.

"The Hunters left a message in the in-between," Captain Soren said, passing it to the king to read without any preamble. I knew, in an abstract sort of way, that the king, the prince, and the captain were all close friends who'd grown up together at court, but being in their inner sanctum showcased the relationships more explicitly than I'd ever seen them.

Without the formality of the court around, Prince Damen leaned over sideways to read the note, dodging irritated flicks of King Allerick's shadows, encouraging him backward. With a frustrated huff, Captain Soren seized the back of Prince Damen's chair, dragging him out of reach while the prince laughed in delight, brightening the countenances of everyone else at the table.

The king passed the paper to Queen Ophelia, who made a noise of disgust, sliding it along to Astrid. "Typical. Obviously, there's no question of us taking them up on that offer. Aside from the fact that their word is meaningless, we don't trade in *people*. If Austin wants to stay, he's welcome to stay. If more want to come, then we'll find a way to get them here."

"Austin figured out how to get here, and it's not like he's some master strategist," Astrid pointed out, shooting me an apologetic glance.

"He was so drunk he immediately passed out when he arrived," I replied wryly. There was no need for Astrid to be apologetic—while he was often underestimated, Austin's journey here had been the furthest possible thing from strategic.

Strangely, it wasn't a strike against him in my mind, despite my own tendency to assess a situation from every angle before acting. I *liked* Austin's impulsiveness.

So long as I was nearby to make sure he was safe from harm.

"Exactly." Astrid grinned, though it had a slightly feral edge. "Don't underestimate the power of a motivated and disillusioned Hunter."

There was a knock on the door before Verner, one of the senior guards who I often put on rotation with Andrus to balance his temperament, pushed it open, gesturing for Austin to enter.

"Ooh, a party," Austin said cheerfully, swaggering into the room with a truly baffling amount of cheer and coming to stand next to me. "What are we celebrating?"

"We aren't," I told him shortly. "The Hunters have offered an exchange for you."

"Oh." He turned to face the king and queen. "Are you going to take them up on it?"

"Absolutely not," the queen said decisively.

"Cool, sounds good to me. Hey, are you still working?" Austin asked, turning to face me. "I'm really fearful for my safety now, and I feel like I need you to personally watch over me."

He made no attempt to sound sincere, and I found myself wanting to *smile* rather than feeling annoyed as I should.

"Yes, you sound terrified," Astrid observed. "Don't you even want to know the details?"

"I'm not a smart man, but I'm sure I can work out the gist of it. You guys need Hunter lust energy, so they've offered a bunch *more* Hunters in exchange for sending one itty, bitty Hunter back. Am I close?"

Austin smiled breezily, delivering the words with quiet confidence.

"Dead accurate," Astrid replied, eyebrows raised, apparently not realizing before now that Austin was far more astute than he presented himself as.

Austin shrugged. "Though, some of the sacrificial offerings might be Hunters who actually want to be here. It'd be cool if we could have some kind of communication system. A secret one, though. For the rebel Hunters who want to get out. Obviously, stealing a portal key isn't an option for most of them, which limits the possibilities for getting here."

Now everyone was looking shocked.

"You should offer your opinions more often," I said, giving Austin a pointed look. "You have much value to add."

"Let's not get carried away," he laughed. "I'm just a pretty face. A content-creating singer."

"You're massively selling yourself short," Queen Ophelia said, shaking her head. "Some kind of communication network is a great idea."

"Maybe we could have collection points in the human realm that Soren and I could check at random," Astrid mused. "Anything with a schedule would open us up to vulnerability if we were betrayed."

Soren made a sound of discontent, and I was guessing that even that idea was too much of a risk to Astrid's safety for him to go along with.

She shot him a cocky half smile. "Relax, Cap. We're just throwing around ideas."

"Throw around ideas later. We need to update the Guard, just in case the Hunters do decide to reopen the portal and try to follow through with an exchange," Soren clipped.

"Elders first," King Allerick interjected, kissing his wife's temple in a surprising show of intimacy before standing. I supposed I'd always known they were attracted to one another—her scent announced that to the entire realm—but the tenderness, especially in front of spectators, had taken me slightly by surprise. "Soren, probably best you come with me, the Elders will want to discuss it with you."

"I'll talk to the Guard," I assured Soren. Astrid was already standing, moving to my side.

"Alright, let's do this." While Astrid had a specific role within the Guard as part of the Queen's security, she was now highly respected by almost everyone. I imagined many members of the Guard would rather take orders from her than me. Astrid rolled her shoulders, raising an eyebrow at Austin. "You know, no one cared at all when the rest of us made the move to the shadow realm. You've got some heavy hitters in your corner, Austin Thibaut."

"Lucky me." He laughed it off but wasn't quite fast enough to hide the hint of frustration in his eyes.

Another frustration added to the sense of purpose and belonging he was clearly already struggling with.

I was a problem solver, it was something I prided myself on. But I didn't know how to solve this.

CHAPTER 18

Astrid accompanied Selene and me out of the sitting room and through the confusing circular corridors of the palace. Astrid and Selene were making plans of some kind, figuring out who needed to know what information and when, but I wasn't going to pretend like I had anything of value to add to that conversation.

I was more focused on the absolute and easy acceptance from King Allerick and Queen Ophelia of my staying here. They'd always *said* I was welcome to stay, but maybe I hadn't believed them? I'd always been more of a *concept* than a *person* where other people were concerned. My talent was what everyone saw first, and I really hadn't had a chance to showcase that here.

While there was a chance they just wanted me here for *breeding* purposes—thanks, Rainy—they would be better off with five new ex-Hunters than one me in that case.

Maybe, just maybe, in this realm... Being Austin was enough?

I sure as shit wasn't getting into the Guard anytime soon. The one thing I'd really attempted since I'd gotten here and I'd failed miserably, yet they were still willing to keep me.

"Are you distressed?" Selene asked, leaning in close to sniff me. "You don't smell distressed."

"I'm not distressed. I wonder if I'll ever get used to the smelling thing," I mused. "Are you used to it, Astrid?"

She shrugged. "I am notably less *scented* than other ex-Hunters. Apparently, I don't emote very much."

Well, that was easy to believe.

"The Hunters are really willing to ruffle some feathers to get you back," Astrid added, giving me an assessing look. She could have been impressed, indifferent, or carving me up to feed to dancing dogs in her head, it was honestly impossible to tell.

"Maybe my public statement did more harm than good," I sighed, conceding that I may not have thought through the consequences of my actions fully. The whiskey probably hadn't helped.

"Or maybe they just really like you," Astrid countered, raising an eyebrow.

"Of course, they really like him." Selene sounded so offended on my behalf that even Astrid couldn't maintain her mask of total indifference.

"The Hunters don't really like me," I clarified, reaching out to briefly stroke Selene's arm while Astrid wasn't looking. "I mean, some of them liked my music, but I never really pulled my weight in the group. Either it's human fans of my music making things difficult for them, or my grandfather pulling strings. The Thibaut family bankrolls the Council—they need to keep Grandfather on their good side."

"It's a big source of funding for them. There's no other Hunter family with those kinds of resources to step in and fill the gap if your grandfather pulls the money out," Astrid conceded.

"You're from a wealthy, powerful family?" Selene asked quietly. I doubted Astrid picked up the thread of vulnerability in her voice, but I heard it.

"Yes." There was no use denying it, and explanations about how I'd been cut off and living in a rat-infested shrine to black mold before I came here would only sound like excuses. "The Thibauts were one of the first Hunter families to make the journey to the new world, and they built a name and fortune for themselves there."

Astrid nodded along in agreement. "Councilors will come and go, but Austin's rich grandaddy will always be there, haunting them with his threats of withdrawing funds."

I shot Selene a wry smile. "He's not a nice man, even by regular Hunter standards. He had eight children, and between them, I have twenty-something cousins. I lose count."

"Tallulah being one of them, though she has a different last name," Astrid added, tilting her head to the side thoughtfully. "Weird that I've never thought of her as a privileged, Hunter, trust-fund baby when I've definitely thought of you that way. Maybe the surname had a bigger impact than I realized."

Astrid really didn't pull her punches.

"Or maybe it's just that I was treated like a privileged, Hunter, trust-fund baby, and she wasn't. When I wanted to do something outside of approved Hunter activities, my creativity was indulged. For *years*, even when my success was... *moderate*, as Tallulah says. When she didn't meet their exacting criteria, she was exiled for it, same as your sister." I paused for a moment, mulling it over. "It's probably garden-variety sexism, though I never thought of it that way before. I definitely feel like a dick for not noticing it earlier."

"Better late than never," Astrid replied, patting me on the arm in a way that was definitely meant to be affectionately condescending, but had Selene tensing as though she was about to claw Astrid's face off. "Huh, I just thought of something."

We all came to a stop in front of some bushes, and maybe I was just imagining things but I was *sure* the leaves looked kind of green.

"Originally, many more Hunters came through the portal with me after making a stand against the Hunters Council, but a lot of them had to return to tie up loose ends before committing to a move here."

What a novel, organized concept. I'd definitely bear that in mind for future inter realm migrations.

"Does this relate to Austin's suggestion of having a safe method of communicating with disillusioned Hunters?" Selene asked, picking up the point of the conversation way faster than I did.

"It does. One of them was the woman who developed the app that Hunters use to communicate with," Astrid said, borderline triumphant though it was hard to tell with her flat affect.

Unfortunately, since Selene didn't know what an app was, that pronouncement probably didn't have the impact Astrid hoped for.

"So, she's like a tech geek or something?" I asked. "You want to create some kind of digital messaging system? That's a little risky, no? And doesn't the tech geek want to move here? In which case, it has to be something that maintains itself."

Astrid exhaled, looking relieved that at least someone knew what she was talking about.

"Harlow doesn't actually want to move here. Well, she did, but then she came here and realized that she'd never have the internet again and changed her mind."

"Fair enough." I didn't really miss the internet specifically, but there were things about the human realm that I missed. Food, mostly. A digital music library. Headphones. Electricity. Gollum the rat.

Well, I didn't *miss* him, per se. I just wanted to know how he was doing.

"But she's also like, I don't know, an anarchist or something," Astrid continued. "I'm confident she'd be willing to help set up some kind of system. It would need to be private, even from her. Or maybe it can be some kind of combination of physical and digital. Like a virtual bat signal that can be tracked to a physical location…" she trailed off, undoubtedly considering the multitude of privacy issues that would need to be taken into account.

"It's a solid idea," I said, not wanting her to get disheartened. "But it's a *big* one. It's not the kind of project that's going to happen overnight."

Astrid pursed her lips. "Yes, I suppose so. I'll visit her regardless. Harlow may have heard something about you or the Council's plans."

"Is that safe? I don't want you to put yourself at risk for information about me." Nothing was worth putting Astrid or any of the others in danger.

"I'll be fine," Astrid assured me, looking vaguely unsettled at the idea of someone worrying about her safety. "Soren is mostly a liability in the human realm, but he'd never let me go alone. He can whisk me away if it all goes to shit."

She nodded once to herself, seemingly satisfied with this course of action. "Okay, I'm going to head to Elverston House and fill the others in on this new and ridiculous development. See you guys later."

Without Astrid there as a buffer, it was clear that Selene was still tense, and I had the distinct impression that if I made a misstep I might lose her forever. She may not want to admit it to anyone, not even herself, but Selene's tough exterior hid a delicate interior where more insecurities than I knew about warred for dominance in her head.

I hadn't necessarily intended to hide the fact that I was from a wealthy family—I had so little to do with them that it barely felt like I was related to them at all. But I had grown up with a lot of privilege like the assholes here at court who treated her as less than. The idea that she'd consign me to the same category as them in her head was terrifying.

"Where are we going?" I asked, keeping my tone light and breezy. *No pressure, darling. It's just me. The same Austin that I was this morning.*

"I shouldn't leave the grounds."

"Barracks, then?" I suggested.

Selene looked at me for a long moment before turning back to face the looming palace behind her. Her face gave nothing away, but I could of sworn I *felt* her internal battle.

"You don't want to join in the feast?"

I laughed quietly. "No, Selene, I don't. I want to go curl up on your horribly uncomfortable bed with you and stay there for as long as possible. Can we do that?"

"We can go back to the barracks," she replied cautiously.

But that wasn't what I'd asked her. I blew out a breath, speed-walking to keep up as she set off through the gardens.

This was an obstacle, but I was going into it determined not to let it defeat me, because Selene was everything and that was worth fighting for.

SELENE

CHAPTER 19

It was unusual for there to be silence between Austin and me.

Not on my end, of course, but he *always* chattered. Constantly made observations about trivial things, asked baffling questions, and touched everything within reach.

Not today, though. We made our way back to the barracks in a silence that didn't feel entirely comfortable, and I wished that I had tonight off so we could at least be uncomfortable together in Cartava, surrounded by distractions.

Instead, I'd have to sit in my plain, impersonal room at the barracks, and wonder the entire time what Austin thought of my very working-class existence and if he was missing the wealth and comfort he'd been born into.

Almost certainly, I imagined.

There were families here at court who weren't *in* positions of power but were strong enough and wealthy enough to be adjacent to it. To influence outcomes to their own benefit, and whose children and grandchildren would go on to do the same. I knew those Shades, I guarded them here at court. I let the insults they hurled at me bounce off without acknowledging them.

None of them would be happy to give up the lives they currently enjoyed to slum it in the barracks, that was for certain.

"I'm coming to your room," Austin announced. "Or you're coming to mine. One way or the other, we're talking this out."

"Is that so?" I murmured, waiting for his pushy confidence to chafe, though it never did.

"That is so."

"Fine. Come to my room then." If he were anyone else, I'd have insisted on going into their space so I could remove myself when I was ready, but with Austin...

My room was more comfortable, and I wanted him to be comfortable.

I was soft where he was concerned.

"Talk to me, darling," Austin demanded gently, closing the door to my room behind him and taking a seat at the small table, patiently waiting for me to do the same.

I paced for a few moments before going to sit down, almost immediately standing up again to resume walking. The movement helped me focus.

"We should ask Vespera to organize another event for you."

Austin snorted, lounging back in the chair and drumming his fingertips lightly on the table, looking entirely at ease. "Absolutely not."

"Austin—"

"Selene," he interjected in a singsong voice. "You're panicking, and I get that. But you know I'm nothing like those snobby idiots. You know how I feel about you."

I opened my mouth to point out that no, I didn't, not really, but changed my mind. The point wasn't to talk about whatever misguided emotions he was experiencing. The point was to quickly and neatly end this messy arrangement before it grew any more complicated. He wasn't meant for me. I'd already known that, and this new revelation only solidified my thoughts.

"Selene," Austin said softly, coming to a stop in front of me, gently grabbing my arms and sliding his hands down to grip mine. I watched the gesture avidly, fascinated by it. No one was ever gentle with me. No one ever thought they needed to be. "You know me. Do you really think I'm like them? Do you really think I have the same superficial, shitty priorities they do?"

I'd seen Austin in Mistwood. Seen the way he'd interacted with Oriana. And how he'd never complained about the barracks, or even my apartment which certainly wasn't some grand estate.

"No, I don't think that. But you should get to know the others. There's a good chance you'd have more in common with them—"

"I'm not interested."

"But you *might* be—"

"Can I kiss you?"

That silenced my arguing. "If you want to try again."

I hadn't exactly done well the first time. Austin didn't hesitate, pulling me toward him with a firmness that would have perhaps felt alarming a few days ago but felt entirely natural now.

"I'll always try again. I'm not giving up on you." And then his lips were brushing against mine, and my head was spinning from both his words and the sensation. It was gentle at first, and while I couldn't decide if I *liked* the physical feeling, the closeness and intimacy of it were incredibly potent. I'd never had anyone so close to my *face* before, to my throat, to the erogenous zone at the base of my horns.

But his movements didn't *stay* gentle.

His tongue swiped my lower lip, and mine all but shot out in a panic, protecting him from my teeth.

Austin smiled against my mouth, chest pressing against mine, pushing me back against the wall. I hadn't even realized we'd been moving.

"That's it. Give me more."

His tongue flicked the end of mine, and it was so silky smooth that all my hesitation melted.

I was still careful, worried that my teeth would hurt him, but that just meant everything about it was gentle and tender in a way that intimacy generally wasn't for me. This was... romantic.

As if he knew I was going to start panicking again, he pulled back, dropping the lightest of kisses on my lips in the process. His eyes were heavy-lidded as he shot me a lazy smile, the rich scent of his desire filling the small space.

Austin's hands came up to cup my jaw, his thumbs stroking over my cheekbones. The eagerness in his eyes to touch my horns was obvious, but he never pushed his luck.

Whatever it was that he *wanted*, Austin either waited for me to offer it or helped me when I found the words too difficult to speak out loud.

I trusted Austin.

I could trust *myself* with him. He was my friend. Maybe the first I'd ever had.

Hadn't I been trying to end things? I'd gotten sidetracked.

Carefully, I gripped his wrists, guiding his hands up to the base of my horns. They were uncomfortable when scratched, and not an area that Shades tended to devote much attention to on each other, but Austin's soft, clawless fingertips...

I groaned loudly, half melting into the wall behind me, my hips coming to press flush against his.

"Oh, I think you like that," Austin breathed, experimentally giving the base of each horn a gentle squeeze. "Can I kiss your throat?"

I'd never let anyone near my throat in my life. I should tell him no. I should tell him I hate the idea. I *should* hate the idea.

"Okay."

His hands stayed on my horns as he leaned forward, and I tipped my head back to give him better access, feeling his hot breath on my skin a moment before the silky press of his lips.

"This is a very bad idea," I murmured, remembering where we were. "You smell so…"

"So what?" he asked, mouth moving against the column of my neck in a way I found surprisingly erotic.

"So… *fuckable.*"

Austin groaned, pressing his face into my throat, his hips rocking against me as his cock strained in his pants. My shadows did nothing to hold slick, and the front of his trousers was damp with my arousal almost instantly.

"I love it when you curse. You're usually so *proper.*"

"There's no other word for it. You smell *fuckable,*" I repeated. "And everyone in the barracks will scent it."

Guilt crept up my spine at how okay I was with that idea. *More* than okay. I wanted them to smell Austin's desire and know that it was for me and me alone. It wasn't an impulse I was proud of. I'd been the one to request we keep this between us.

Austin released my horns and undid his trousers, his cock weeping through the thin fabric of his underwear. My legs parted of their own accord as he gripped the base of his shaft, guiding it forward and rubbing the fat head in teasing circles over my sensitive flesh through the slightly abrasive fabric. I gasped at the intensity of it, my thighs shaking almost instantly at the sensation.

"I think you like it," he whispered, eyes filled with mischief. "I think you like the idea of those pretentious assholes slavering at your door, lusting after my scent. Do you want to share me?"

"Never," I hissed, pushing him a few steps back to the bed, only just managing to temper my strength as I nudged him down onto the mattress. "I will *never* share you."

"Good," he choked out, sucking in a surprised breath as I shredded the sides of his boxers with my claws, the tips leaving the faintest red lines on his thighs as I yanked the fabric away. "Holy shit, that was sexy."

My chest was heaving as I tried to catch my breath, tried to get myself back under control. I wanted his cock inside me more than *anything*, but we couldn't. We *couldn't*. It was a terrible idea. We'd both regret it.

"I want the taste of your slick on my tongue."

I exhaled slightly. Good. Yes. That was a practical alternative. I tilted my head to the side, watching him impatiently.

"Well?" I prompted. "Aren't you going to move?"

"Why? I'm in a good spot right here. You can put that sweet cunt right on my mouth."

He couldn't mean... "You want me to *kneel* over you?"

"Kneel, sit, smother me. I'm pretty open to all options."

I tentatively kneeled on the edge of the mattress, shuffling forward on my knees before straddling his stomach. "You're certain? I've never done that before."

It was a very vulnerable position for Austin, and no one else had ever let themselves be that exposed with me.

"I'm very certain, and I'm even more certain you'll like it, but if you don't, just tell me and we'll stop."

I nodded, his words giving me the reassurance I needed to make the journey up the rest of his body, settling my thighs either side of his head.

Austin did his best to wrap his arms around my thick thighs, parting my labia with his thumbs and leaning up to lick every inch of me that he could reach. The first touch of him had me jumping, slamming my hands against the wall behind the bed to steady myself, my claws screeching against the stone.

There was nothing sophisticated about his technique. It was messy and sloppy and *loud*, and it only heightened the experience. It was all pleasure, completely devoid of vanity.

"Austin," I rasped, jolting as he flattened his tongue and licked my cunt like it was his favorite ice cream. "That feels... indescribable."

He seemed to take my words as a challenge, picking up his pace and tugging my body more firmly down on his face, increasing the pressure.

Was he okay? Was this hurting him? My orgasm loomed, making it hard to focus. I had to trust him, though. I had to trust that he knew his own limits.

"I don't want to come yet," I breathed, struggling not to as his nose bumped my sensitive flesh and he gulped down my slick as though it was life-giving nectar. "I want your cock."

That made him pause.

"Not fully. We can't. Just... a little. I want to feel it."

Austin groaned, the mattress shifting slightly in response to his writhing movements.

"Is that a yes?"

"Do you want your toy?" His voice was muffled, mouth still pressed against my pussy.

"No. I want you. Just a little." There was one thing I *particularly* wanted to try. Something I'd dreamed about, that I'd never be willing to try with anyone else...

I climbed off him, flattered at Austin's disgruntled sound as though I was depriving him of a great treat.

"I trust you," I told him solemnly, meaning every word.

Austin sat up, wiping his shining mouth with the back of his hand. "And I'm very fucking grateful for it. Tell me what you want me to do."

"I had a dream last night..." Trembling slightly with nerves, I laid down on my stomach, giving Austin my back. Immediately, he moved in closer, running his hands over my body, kneading my muscles, gently squeezing my ass, helping me to relax.

"You're so sexy," he murmured, running his thumb over the back of my thighs, tracing the defined muscle there. "Where do you want me?"

I swallowed thickly. "Over me. With your cock between my thighs."

He made a slightly strangled sound, climbing over my body, his cock nestling between my legs. "This is playing with fire, darling."

"I know. But you'll be good."

He made a muffled sound of pain, pressing his mouth to my shoulder. With some careful maneuvering, he pressed his cock at my entrance, not pushing in. I tightened my thighs, encouraging him to thrust through my folds, stimulating nerves I didn't know existed.

"Fuuuuuck," Austin rasped. "Your slick is… holy shit."

His voice was a rasp in my ear, making me shudder. This was a kind of intimacy I'd never experienced before. His entire body was covering mine, leaving me vulnerable in a way I usually never allowed.

Austin rearranged us slightly, sliding his arm that had been next to my head beneath my torso and pushing his wrist into my palm.

"This wasn't dangerous enough?" I gasped, my thumb claw brushing over his vein.

"This is your insurance policy. You're giving me a lot of trust right now, and I'm giving you mine. If you slice me here with your claws, I'll bleed out and die," he murmured, his voice a seductive croon. I immediately tried to release him, but Austin pressed his hand in tighter. "I trust you too."

I still shifted a little so that my claws were pressing into the top of his hand—the place where I'd first accidentally scratched him—rather than his veins, but I didn't let go. I doubted I'd have been able to even if I wanted to.

Austin braced his weight on his forearms, the coarse hair on his chest rubbing against my back as he rolled his hips, his breathing labored.

I couldn't speak after that, I didn't think he could either. The slick made it easy for him to move, and I kept my thighs tensed as much as possible, squeezing the base of his cock, but this *was* a dangerous game.

More than anything we'd done so far, this was filling my energy reserve. Austin was an odd mixture of heady and light, and that was exactly what it felt like to feed from him. Rich and decadent, yet bright and airy. He was the perfect mixture of contradictions.

My cunt clenched around nothing, *aching* to be filled. I'd never wanted to *fuck* more in my life, but I couldn't bring myself to stop even for a moment to get my toy. Austin shifted his hand to cup my breast, and it was the possessiveness of it rather than the sensation that inched me over the edge. My teeth sunk through the pillow as I tried to muffle the sound from the rest of the barracks, ripping through the fabric instantly.

"Fuck!" Austin rasped, pulling back clumsily, the hot splash of his cum hitting the back of my thigh. He immediately moved, lying on his side and pulling me into him, molding himself to the curves of my body and holding me through the waves of pleasure that seemed to drag on forever.

Slick had pooled on the bed beneath us, and the entire room reeked of arousal. I needed to open a window. Strip the bed. Try minimize the evidence of what we'd been doing in here.

But my legs felt too weak to carry me, and I was far too content in Austin's embrace.

"What are you doing to me?" I asked, my voice unrecognizable.

"I could ask you the same question," he murmured sleepily. "You're addictive. I hope I'm addictive for you, too."

I hummed, rubbing the soft pad of my thumb over the veins in his wrist, the tip of my claw occasionally scratching his skin. "You say that now."

"And I'll keep saying it until you believe me," he assured me, kissing my shoulder once, and then a few more times for good measure. "However long it takes."

"We'll see."

"Yes, we will."

AUSTIN

CHAPTER 20

For the first time in months, maybe even years, I was itching to sit down with a pen and paper and *write*. Even the cold, damp aura of sadness that hung over Elverston House couldn't stop me. I was so filled with feeling that writing felt like the only answer, the only outlet for the emotion bubbling up inside me—both positive and negative.

The beautiful mysterious Shade who was cold as ice on the outside and burned as hot as the sun on the inside.

My lover who gave me every part of herself, and my love—my *love*—who kept her heart safely hidden away.

My pride that wanted the whole world—this realm and every other—to know she was mine, and that same pride that balked at not having anything to offer her.

We were a mess of beautiful contradictions, Selene and I. Two different kinds of beings from totally different backgrounds, muddling our way toward each other because that's where we *belonged*, even if we didn't quite understand how.

The more time I spent with her, the more fixated on the idea of a *life* with her I became. I'd seen snippets of Selene's life—more, I was pretty sure, than most people saw—and I wanted to be a part of it more than I'd ever wanted anything.

I just needed to find a reason for her to keep me. It wasn't self-pity, not entirely. I had nothing going for me in this world. No moderate levels of fame. No worthwhile talent since the kind of music I made wasn't a *thing* here. No income. I'd failed epically at joining the Guard. I couldn't protect, provide, or materially add any net positives to Selene's life.

Aside from the fact that she seemed fond of all the ways I could make her come, I couldn't think of any other reason why she'd entertain any sort of future with me. And while I wasn't above using my dick to get in the door as it were, I really hoped to have something more to offer.

I would. I'd find something. This wasn't a problem I was about to leave unsolved.

The words poured out, about inevitability and struggle. About wanting and holding back. It wasn't a smooth, linear love story.

It was better. The ideas were flowing. The words were kind of there. The riff sounded fucking awesome. I was *creating*, after months of not being able to create, and it kind of felt like I'd gotten my superpowers back.

I hummed a few lines of the chorus, experimenting with the melody, wanting something different. Something that fit this realm better—not the stuffy formal choir music favored at court, but the lilting, poetic style of the folk music at the fair. Something that felt like a *story*.

"That's pretty." I looked up, finding Ophelia leaning in the doorway, startling me out of the zone. "You write your own songs?"

"I used to. I've been so uninspired for the past few months that I feel like a fraud calling myself a songwriter."

"That didn't sound uninspired." She stepped into the room, taking a seat on the armchair opposite me.

"I guess being here has been inspiring." I smiled to myself like a dope. My muse was awake and kicking, filled with ideas that all revolved around a certain Shade with eyes like glowing laser emeralds.

Maybe Selene was my muse now?

"Good! I actually came here to speak to you about your music."

"Oh?"

"Well, no. I came here because all of us ex-Hunters are meeting for wine and cheese in the drawing room soon—I hope you'll join us, it's a semi regular thing we do. But I did want to ask about your music." Ophelia fidgeted with her skirt, looking sheepish. "I love the shadow realm. I do. But the music scene here is a little lacking. I mean, it's mostly choirs."

"It's mostly choirs *here*. At court," I clarified. "There's a little more variety in the rest of the realm."

She blinked. "There is?"

"Don't do a lot of traveling around your realm, Your Majesty?" I teased, though I was kind of serious. I wasn't sure the Shades in Mistwood actually wanted royal attention, but it wasn't sitting right with me that whole segments of the population were just wholesale ignored.

"Probably not as much as I should have done." Ophelia's face flamed red, and I felt a bit bad for embarrassing her. "We've traveled a little, and I'd like to do more, but sometimes I feel like it's not my place to push, you know? I didn't grow up in this realm. I definitely wasn't a princess, I have the most basic understanding of politics in the human realm, and I just don't know how this all works. But there's an advantage to seeing things with fresh eyes as well, and I need to get better at making the most of it."

I nodded, figuring I'd already said more than I was qualified to say. I didn't know this realm very well, and I didn't know Ophelia at all. I was just a dude who made up songs.

"I didn't realize you'd ever left the palace grounds," Ophelia added, raising an eyebrow at me.

"It would hardly be fair on Selene to be stuck here all the time just to keep an eye on me."

"I guess I thought she *wanted* to be here, though that was a total assumption and I should have asked. I haven't had much of a chance to speak to her."

I had plenty of thoughts about that too, but I didn't want to get in trouble with Selene by voicing them.

"What kind of music is there in other parts of the realm?" Ophelia asked, relaxing into the armchair.

"Folk music would be the closest description, I guess. It's a very distinct sound—lots of woodwinds and percussion instruments, no strings. The songs are stories though, handed down among generations, and each song has its own dance that goes with it. I guess this place can feel kind of serious if you spend all your time at court, but there's a lot of laughter and... I don't know, community, I guess? In other parts of the realm."

I glanced down at the paper in front of me, realizing that I'd been more inspired by that than I thought. Where in the human realm, my lyrics had always been kind of abstract, this song definitely had a narrative.

"Would you sing it in front of the court?" Ophelia asked, following my gaze.

"I don't know. It's not finished yet." I hesitated, wanting to say more but unsure if I should. We'd originally agreed—at Selene's behest—to keep whatever was happening between us quiet. But aside from the fact that she was certain everyone in the barracks knew because of our scent, I also kind of hated hiding it. It felt like she'd suggested it for my benefit, like she thought of herself as a dirty little secret when she was anything but. "It's about Selene."

Ophelia laughed. "I gathered that from the moon goddess references. You don't want her to hear it?"

"I want her to hear it, but I don't know if she wants to hear it. Does that make sense?"

Ophelia smiled gently. "There's been a lot of gossip about the two of you. I guess the courtiers had their own ideas about who you would be interested in, and for some reason, Selene wasn't on that list."

"Classism," I replied bluntly. "I'm not going into detail because it's not my story to tell, but that's the answer."

"I really need to book that trip," Ophelia said faintly.

"Probably," I sighed, setting my guitar aside and standing up to pace in front of the couch. "I guess this is just a sentient-being problem. Human, Hunter, Shade, it doesn't matter. We create hierarchies to make sense of the world and our place in it, but they're inherently oppressive. If you're at the bottom, you're clawing your way up for whatever scraps are left. Am I a revolutionary now? This feels like my big Les Mis moment."

I grabbed my sweater and held it to the sky, waving it around like a flag and propping one foot up on the couch. *Vive la révolution*, and all that jazz.

"Please don't cut off my head," Ophelia laughed while I tossed the sweater aside and flopped back onto the couch. "Even if I could be doing more. I *will* do more."

"I believe you. You have a real aura of optimism around you."

"I suppose I guessed there was some snobbery involved in the gossip, but I assumed it was because Selene actually has a job while they all sit around all day."

"It's a little deeper than that. God, it's honestly baffling. Selene's background is a feature, not a bug. She's *interesting*. And so fucking dedicated. She puts in the work, she cares about her job, she never let her background— which could have easily been an obstacle—stop her from rising up in the ranks. That didn't happen by chance, it happened because she wanted it. I really admire that, you know?"

"Yes, I can definitely tell," Ophelia said with a soft smile.

"I just want the forever with her. The Shade version of a white picket fence and a minibus full of convertible car seats."

"She... doesn't feel the same way?"

I rested my hands on my stomach, staring up at the ceiling and fully committing myself to this impromptu therapy session with the Queen of the Shades.

"It's not that. She does *like* me. The pressure on her here at court is more than she lets on," I said carefully, not wanting to divulge Selene's innermost insecurities behind her back.

I didn't care what the court thought about Selene. It'd be nice if they could see her through my eyes, but ultimately I wanted *Selene* to see herself through my eyes. To see all the incredible things about her that she dismissed as nothing. To maybe make all the idiots who hadn't *seen* her before really see her now.

My moon goddess. My Selene.

I jackknifed upright, locking eyes with a startled Ophelia. "You want me to perform in front of the court?"

"Well, only if you want to—"

"In front of *everyone*?"

"If that's okay—"

I jumped up, pacing again. "Oh, it's more than okay. A captive audience of non believers and the love of my life all in one place?"

If only I'd had this kind of motivation at the *The Headliner* finale. Those dogs could have danced the fucking *Nutcracker* and still wouldn't have beat me.

"This is perfect. I'll finish the song and woo her with a grand gesture."

Ophelia hummed. "Grand gestures are a tricky business, are you sure you've thought this through?"

"Absolutely. It'll be romantic. Very eighties teen romance movie. I just need to finish the song—"

"Nuh uh, you're coming to a gray wine-and-cheese session first. You absolutely have *not* thought this through, and we're going to have a brainstorming session with the others before you scare Selene off forever."

Okay. Okay, I could work with that. *Girl's night, here I come.*

This whole thing felt super taboo. Like I'd climbed through a girl's window in high school to crash their slumber party or something. I'd nabbed the seat closest to the door in what I guessed had once been a glamorous formal sitting room, ready to make my escape as soon as it was socially acceptable. The stiff tufted armchair hard as rocks beneath me. Why was fancy furniture so uncomfortable? What was even the point in owning uncomfortable furniture?

Nothing in Selene's apartment was uncomfortable. I wished I was there instead.

Meera, Verity, and Tallulah were sitting together on an equally uncomfortable-looking couch, a large blanket draped across all three of them, while Ophelia and Astrid were sitting on the other side of the coffee table on large armchairs, kitty-corner to one another.

"Wine?" Ophelia asked, glancing up at me as she poured a silvery-looking wine into goblets.

I grimaced. "I'm good, thanks. I'll stick to water."

Astrid gave me a knowing smirk, having seen the state I'd shown up here in. On the one hand, coming here had been the best decision I'd ever made—drunk or otherwise. But it could have also gone spectacularly wrong. The alcohol hadn't been giving me the answers I'd needed for what was going wrong in my life, it had just made the questions feel less urgent.

Ophelia slid a glass of water over to me and encouraged me to help myself to the array of grayscale snacks in the center of the table.

"So, er, welcome, Austin." She shifted slightly in her chair, looking momentarily flustered.

"It's weird having you and your Y chromosome here," Tallulah supplied helpfully, shooting me a bright smile. "But we're very happy to have you here."

"Are you going to censor yourselves on his account?" Astrid asked, looking very specifically at Verity.

Verity shrugged, unapologetic. "I'm an untamable beast, but I'll do my best."

"No need to censor yourselves on my account. What do you usually do at these hangouts?" I asked, watching what selection of gray items Meera picked out since she didn't eat meat either.

"We gossip, mostly," Ophelia replied with a shrug. "Talk about what we've got going on. Courtships, friendships, questions, and concerns. It's all on the table."

"As you know, Ophelia and Astrid have Shade mates," Tallulah added, bringing me up to speed. "Meera is courting. I... well, I thought I was going to be courting, but I guess not. Verity doesn't know what she's doing."

"Excuse you," Verity gasped, pressing a hand to her chest in mock outrage. "I know exactly what I'm doing. I didn't before, granted, but *now* I have a goal, and I'm working toward it."

"What's your goal?" Ophelia asked curiously. Astrid was sitting next to her sister, acting disinterested, but I got the distinct impression that Astrid was actually a lot more into this whole conversation than she let on.

"To find a Shade who matches my weird. I'm not hiding it anymore. I'm letting the weird *out*. As someone who has very much *settled* in the past, I'm not settling this time. If he isn't perfect for me, I don't want him." Verity nodded firmly to herself as though that settled it.

"It's good to have standards?" Ophelia agreed tentatively. Maybe she was worried there wasn't anyone weird enough for Verity here.

"I'm not courting anyone," Meera said, shooting Tallulah a reproachful look. "We're just friends."

"Mm, does he know that?" Tallulah teased. "Because he looks at you like he's imagining what your future babies will look like." Meera blushed furiously, staring down at her hands, and my cousin took pity on her and turned her attention to me instead. "What about you, Austin?"

I only *just* managed to suppress a laugh at the expectant way they were all looking at me, all while attempting to act totally natural. Almost as though there was a particular theory that they wanted confirmed. A certain Shade who may have already caught my eye.

I could have just thrown them the catch they were so clearly fishing for, but I wanted to make them work for it a little.

"What about me?"

"Oh, you know. How are you settling in? What have you been up to?" Tallulah asked casually over the rim of her goblet before taking a sip of wine.

"What's up with you and Selene?" Astrid added bluntly. Tallulah choked on her mouthful, and Ophelia shot her sister a slightly exasperated look.

"Well, that's an easy question. Selene is a perfect goddess, and I want to worship at her altar."

I had a sneaking suspicion Astrid already knew that, though. Her and Selene both had that fierce I-don't-need-friends energy, but I suspected they may have inadvertently found friendship in each other.

"Oh boy," Tallulah muttered, downing another swig of wine. I got the distinct impression my arrival in this realm hadn't been good for my cousin's stress levels.

"How's that going for you?" Meera asked politely.

"Did you have some ground to make up after the first impression you made?" Verity added, smirking.

"I definitely did," I sighed, flopping back into my chair and regretting it instantly when the hard back jarred my shoulders. "I think I've mostly redeemed myself? She's hard to read. Sometimes I think she really likes me, other times I'm pretty sure she's really annoyed with me."

"Aw, Austin!" Tallulah squealed. "Did you get body snatched when you came through the portal? I've never known you to get tied up over, well, anyone. Any*thing*, other than your music."

"Trust me, I'm as surprised as you are," I replied. *There was really something to be said for this whole girl chat thing,* I decided. I felt better already just talking about this stuff. "It snuck up on me. Once I got to know Selene, I got a little obsessed with her."

"That's so romantic," Verity sighed. "That's what I want. But not a *little* obsessed, I want a lot obsessed. I want him to be unhinged with love for me. I want him to tie me to his bed and ravish me. Is that so much to ask?"

"This is the censored version of Verity," Tallulah told me with a laugh.

"You're welcome," Verity replied. "Anyway, are you next to be mated off, Austin? Maybe you should just stick your neck out—literally—and see what happens? If she bites you, you're claimed, no take backs."

"Yeah, I'd prefer something with a little more... talking and agreement and stuff first." Ophelia exhaled slightly at my words. "I don't want Selene to resent me, and honestly, I've foisted my company on her enough as it is. But I was thinking of a grand gesture, what do you all think of this..."

SELENE

CHAPTER 21

I'm going to suggest to the captain that I take over guard duty for the Hunter man," Andrus said casually, rapidly forming and unforming a shadow baton. He was clearly trying to get a reaction out of me, and I gave him absolutely nothing.

Andrus was a pest. He wasn't worth an iota of my attention.

"Don't you want to know why?" he pressed.

"No." I did, but that was beside the point.

Andrus was silent for a few moments, his batons growing more messily formed with each passing second. This was why I'd been promoted over him, though he was incapable of seeing that. Andrus was terrible at keeping his emotions in check, though stars forbid I point that out since he liked to act as though he had none. Anger didn't count, apparently.

"You're keeping him away from court," Andrus said, running out of patience as I knew he would. "No one else has had a chance to get to know him. They've been complaining, you know."

I didn't bother responding. That conversation was for Austin. Perhaps the captain. No one else.

"The barracks reek of your coupling. You're clearly trying to keep him for yourself," Andrus accused. "You are using your proximity to him to your advantage."

"Am I?" I murmured, keeping my gaze trained on the newest recruits who were sparring closest to me, ensuring they didn't actually do too much damage to one another in their attempts to impress us.

"Don't bother denying it. The entire Guard knows."

"I don't bother with anything where you're concerned, Andrus," I replied flatly, though his words hit harder than I let on.

I *was* trying to keep Austin for myself. Whether it was intentional or not ultimately didn't matter because the result was the same—he wasn't getting opportunities to meet anyone else. How could he know if he actually even liked me if he didn't get a chance to spend time with others?

I was demanding far more of Austin than I was entitled to.

Andrus didn't need to know that though.

"You're not denying it because you can't."

"Austin is more than capable of vocalizing his wants, and he is averse to the ostentatious displays of attention he's received so far. However, if he must show his face at dinner to prove I am not holding him hostage, I'm sure he will cooperate."

"If you want to prove you're not holding him hostage, assign his care to me," Andrus challenged.

"Austin is a sentient adult being, not a child to be passed between minders. He requested me specifically to the king. Take your concerns up with them."

"You don't deserve this position," Andrus hissed, turning fully to face me, his shadows writhing at his feet like snakes. I had hoped to avoid drawing attention, but it appeared Andrus was going to be uncooperative on that front.

"I'm the only member of the Guard who earned my place here on merit rather than family name. You have never once demonstrated your suitability for leadership, Andrus. You have plenty of raw power and potential, it's a real shame that you're hindered by your own ego. Spar with Verner, I'd like to see you both working on improving your control."

His hands flexed at his side for a moment, and I prepared myself for a fight if it came down to it, but eventually, he slunk across the pitch to where Verner was practicing, ignoring the quiet taunts of the rest of the Guard.

"Back to it!" I ordered, surveying the gossips with disdain. "Save your petty words for the feast hall, they have no place in my domain."

"Well handled," Soren said, startling me with his presence. "Though you could have been harsher with Andrus. I wouldn't have objected if you'd sent him to do guard duty at the Pit until he'd learned some humility."

"It wouldn't have worked. Andrus is always looking for reasons to blame me. Sending him to the Pit would have further fueled his resentment."

"A very logical call. I'm not sure I possess the restraint to have made it myself."

I was honored that he thought as much. Captain Soren had taken a chance on me when the rest of the Guard would have seen me turned away at the palace doors. I owed him everything.

"Did you happen to hear—"

"I did."

"... You don't have any concerns?" I asked eventually.

"I don't."

You should. I am too possessive over him.

"All the ex-Hunters met today in Elverston House. They drink wine, socialize, that sort of thing. Austin joined them. While Astrid won't tell me exactly what goes on at these things, she's comfortable that Austin is happy where he is, and I trust my mate's judgment. I'll take over here—Astrid is due to join me shortly, and you should probably ensure that Austin doesn't go wandering and try to join another organization he's not suitable for."

I snorted before I could stop myself, mortified at showing such casual amusement in front of the captain. He didn't seem disapproving of it, at least.

"Thank you, Soren," I said quietly, excusing myself from the training grounds. I wasn't good at expressing myself, but my gratitude was for more than just him supervising the rest of the training session. He'd had confidence in my abilities before I'd had confidence in them myself.

Austin was already outside Elverston House when I arrived at the border that Shades weren't allowed to cross. I watched him for a moment as Meera pointed out things in the soil—presumably the plants she was attempting to grow—and the way his entire face lit up when he spotted me made most of the entire aggravation of the Andrus encounter vanish.

Most of it.

No one in my entire life had ever looked so happy to see me.

"There you are! Are you done for the day? Where are we going?"

"It would probably be good for you to attend the feast in the dining hall."

Austin's face fell, and there was an immediate twist in my gut that I'd been responsible for it.

"I know I probably should. I've been great at avoiding the dining hall so far, but I was really hoping to spend the night with just you. Ideally, in Cartava."

Why was I finding it so difficult to stick to my original course of action? As a general rule, I found it very easy to hold to my decisions once I'd made them. There was no room for second-guessing myself when I was leading the Guard into a fight. Being *certain* was one of my greatest strengths.

And it was failing me completely.

"It would be best for you to attend the feast," I reiterated, lacking any real conviction.

"Best for who?" Austin asked, drawing himself up straighter and crossing his arms over his chest. His expression was as arrogant as ever, but there was a hint of what I thought may have been a challenge in his eyes.

I wished there wasn't. He was unfairly attractive enough as it was.

"There are many Shades here at court who wish to get to know you. They have pointed out—rightly—that I am taking up an inordinate amount of your time—"

Austin snorted. "*I'm* taking up *your* time, Selene. I'm the one that's always following you around, begging you to take me places rather than ditching me with another suitable guard and giving you a break. I like your company. I only want to spend time with you."

"You shouldn't say things like that," I replied quietly.

"Even if it's the truth?"

Even then.

I couldn't find the words I needed. There was an excuse somewhere that would have worked—a justification that sounded entirely plausible and motivated only by logic—but my mind refused to conjure it. Everything I came up with sounded too...

Emotionally invested.

Too jealous, too eager, too *wanting.*

Too inappropriate-in-every-way for a sexual relationship that had started out—at best—on the basis of curiosity and convenience on his part.

"I won't force the issue," I said with a resigned sigh. "We can go to Cartava to eat before returning to the barracks."

I emphasized the last few words heavily. We couldn't continue on the way we'd been going. It was drawing too much attention, and I was forming attachments that I couldn't afford to form.

Austin hummed the entire journey from the outskirts of Elverston House to my apartment, occasionally singing a few disjointed lines of a song while we traversed the in-between, his wrist warm and solid beneath my palm. It was different from the usual humming that he'd done ever since he'd arrived in the shadow realm. He repeated small sections over and over again with slight changes, as though he was playing with them, trying to find the exact right combination.

I wanted to ask, but I also didn't want him to stop. Austin's brain was a fascinating thing, and he very rarely gave anyone any kind of insight into it, content to let everyone think he was disinterested and lazy.

The heat of Cartava was heady and welcoming, the sounds of the patrons drinking and dining on the laneways providing a comforting sense of home. *This* was where I felt like myself. In this damp, sweaty city on the sea, filled with misfits and loners, Shades of business and bored socialites. Cartava was for everyone.

After covering Austin in shadows, I maintained my firm grip on him as we climbed the winding tower staircase to my apartment, wondering how much he could see in the dim orb light with his inferior vision.

"I love cities," Austin sighed, abruptly ceasing his humming.

"Do you?" Although he'd seemed fond of Cartava, I'd assumed that was just because it *wasn't* court.

"For sure. I've always lived in cities." Austin kept talking as I loosed my shadows to unlock the door. "There's something very freeing about getting lost in the current of people just going about their day, everyone minding their business and not giving a shit what you're doing."

"That is one of the things I like most about Cartava," I agreed quietly, closing the door and locking it behind him. Though it was a little disconcerting hearing the words from him.

It would be easier not to get attached if we didn't have so much in common.

"I'm guessing there's a seedy underbelly somewhere, but I hadn't seen it yet," Austin continued with a lazy grin as the shadows fell away. "So far, it was all just glossy and shiny and good vibes, and I never wanted to leave."

"From my experience, that is more of a human realm issue. Cartava is the only city in the shadow realm. Keeping it as a reputable center of culture and community is important to those of us who live here because the very idea of it is abhorrent to some Shades." I hesitated for a moment. "My residence here isn't something I would speak openly about at court."

Austin snorted. "As if they're the arbiters on taste."

I smiled at that, heading for the kitchen. I wasn't really in the mood to cook tonight. Usually, I didn't cook nearly as much as I had been—the restaurants were my favorite part of Cartava—but I couldn't take Austin out there with just me to protect him. Briefly, I contemplated leaving him here for a moment and going out to get something before dismissing that idea too.

Then again, he'd been okay in Mistwood. No one *wanted* to hurt the ex-Hunters who'd come here—not now that we were forbidden from traveling to the human realm to feed. It was only the ex-Hunters who lived here keeping us alive.

Austin would be revered, if anything.

"Everything okay?" Austin asked, careful to step into my line of sight before resting a hand on my forearm.

"We could... go out."

"Out?"

"For dinner."

His eyes lit up instantly, and I was filled with guilt at how much I'd been keeping him hidden away from the world. Of course, there had been plenty of times where he'd asked for that, but there was a difference between wanting space from the tiny bubble that was life at court and not wanting to go out at all.

"Do I get to wear a shadow costume?"

I nearly dismissed the idea out of hand—obviously there was no point trying to disguise him as a Shade, up close it was very clear that he wasn't.

But I didn't have to *disguise* him. He could just *wear* my shadows.

I draped them over his existing clothes, crossing them above his hips and letting them trail a little behind him like a long jacket. Sweeping and majestic, and just a little flamboyant. It suited Austin perfectly.

Austin looked down, his arms spread, turning one way then the other and looking over his back as he examined them.

"This is the coolest thing I've ever worn," Austin said in awe, raising his head to meet my gaze. "Thank you."

"It's nothing," I mumbled, embarrassed by the gratitude in his expression.

"No, it's not, or you wouldn't have told me not to read into it the first time." Austin winked, fiddling with something behind his neck. He pulled one of his thin gold chains free, latching the miniscule clasp my claws would have never managed so it made a loop once more.

"For you," he said simply.

"Oh no, I couldn't—"

"Please?"

"Stop that. Stop doing that thing with your eyes." Somehow, he'd made them look rounder and more pitiful, and it was making my chest twist in a funny way.

"Can I put it on you? I've seen Shades at court wear chains over their horns."

"Silver chains," I pointed out. "These are far more valuable."

"Good." He held up the chain, waiting for me to lower my head so he could drape them over my horns. My throat felt tight as I bowed my head. It was a gesture of submission, but it didn't feel like I was conceding any of myself to Austin. If anything, it felt like he was conceding some of himself to me.

"Pretty," he murmured, the metal clinking against my horns as he arranged it. I straightened as he lowered his hands, refusing to go and look in the mirror just in case I liked what I saw too much.

"Come on. There's a place nearby that serves sweet food. It has no meat in it."

"Dessert for dinner, I'm all about it."

I wasn't the only one trying to keep my emotions in check.

We made our way downstairs, and Austin asked questions about everything from the stones under our feet to how the orbs above us maintained their glow. Apparently, the shadows I'd used to cover his face impacted his vision more than I realized.

There was no one on my street, but when we turned onto the crowded laneway lined by restaurants, the buzz of conversation immediately died at the sight of Austin.

His hand slipped easily into mine as if it belonged there, tangling our fingers together. Nothing about his scent indicated he was afraid—of course not, he was never afraid of anything—and he sent beaming smiles at everyone as we slowly made our way up the silent street. Even the vendors poked their heads out of the narrow doorways that led to their kitchens, gawking at us.

"We can leave if you're uncomfortable," I whispered.

Austin turned his grin on me, and it was one of his genuine ones. One that made his eyes wrinkle at the sides. "Are you kidding? This is great. It may not seem like it because I've been hiding away at court, but I really do love attention. It just has to be the right kind of attention. I'm very particular, you see."

"Is that so," I murmured, indulging his ridiculousness on this occasion since he seemed to be enjoying himself so much.

The dessert vendor was already standing in the doorway, watching us with interest. She seemed as ancient as Cartava itself, and no one in the realm made more delicious sweets.

"Who is this?" she asked in the old language of Cartava, having no interest in learning any others.

"Austin," I replied, speaking up a little louder for the benefit of the other Shades listening in. "He's a former Hunter from the human realm."

My speech was clunky—I hadn't learned this language growing up. Mistwood had its own dialect.

"He's *your* former Hunter," she cackled. "Are you doing your part to contribute to the stores? They're looking a little low, last I checked."

There was some booming laughter from nearby, and Austin trained his trusting gaze on me.

"They're asking if I've been adding to the stores," I mumbled.

"Oh. Have you?" He frowned as though the idea hadn't occurred to him.

"I haven't been *taking* from the stores." Our intimacy had meant I fed a little from him, but I suspected we would need to lock together fully for me to get the full impact of it. The trickle of energy had been enough for me to subsist off though.

Austin hummed thoughtfully while I ordered a selection of desserts so he had plenty to try.

"Come!" one of the Shades nearby announced in English. "Sit with us—we have plenty of room here for both of you."

The interaction reminded me so much of that first feast night when Vespera had insisted Austin sit next to her, except it was entirely different. I was included this time.

"My name is Mursat," he announced as Austin took the seat between him and I, more than happy to make conversation with this group of new Shades. He really was far more sociable by nature than I was.

"I'm Austin, nice to meet you. Are you from Cartava?"

And that was all it took. One question and they were entirely engrossed in conversation, occasionally speaking with some of the Shades at the surrounding tables who were crowding in close to hear Austin speak.

While I was silent, more than happy to listen and then to distribute the dishes between our plates once it arrived, I didn't feel excluded. It was a good reminder of why I'd moved here.

"This is so good," Austin said, turning to face me with wide eyes, holding the crumbly tart in his fingers. "Can we come here again?"

There was that clawing sensation in my throat again. That desire to promise Austin the world, knowing I couldn't give it to him. Knowing there were others who could.

"Sure."

"You said you were some kind of musician?" Mursat asked. "Will you sing for us?"

The crowd cheered in support for this idea, stamping loudly on the cobblestones.

Austin looked at me. "What do you think?"

I couldn't help but smile at the infectious enthusiasm of the crowd. "If you'd like to, then of course, go ahead."

"On the table!" Mursat insisted, gesturing for everyone to clear away their plates and goblets. "Come, come! Everyone else, shut it!"

Austin climbed on the stool, and I watched with some wariness as he jumped onto the table, hoping he wasn't about to injure himself somehow. "I really wish I had my guitar, but it's cool. We'll just do it a cappella. Years ago, I came second in a talent competition with this song. I *did* lose to dancing animals—" Everyone laughed at this, and Austin almost glowed, his smile was so bright. "—but I'm hoping it's still a pretty good tune, even if the Hopping Hounds won the trophy. Okay, here we go."

Austin closed his eyes, taking a deep breath before opening them, fingers tapping against his thigh in a silent beat.

He was always so cheerful that the rough, soulful timbre of his voice took me by surprise. I'd always known that there was more to Austin than appeared on the surface, but he sung like someone who was intimately acquainted with pain, and I doubted any of the Shades present had expected that.

Austin sung about struggling to find a sense of belonging, of feeling like everyone else had already had it all figured out and wondering why you weren't there yet. It was beautiful and poignant and universal, and I was more curious than ever about the dancing dogs. Were they really more talented than this?

I could see those around me listening contemplatively, being drawn in slowly by the unique sound. It wasn't like any other music I'd heard in the Shade realm, and it took me a moment to get accustomed to it, but I definitely *liked* the sound. And this was a good audience for it—Cartava was unpretentious and open to try new things in a way the rest of the realm often wasn't.

The melody grew more upbeat as the song progressed, the words more optimistic in tone, more open to the idea that we were all struggling in our own way and that was something that united us rather than divided us. The Shades around us stamped their feet in time to the beat as the song picked up tempo, and I joined in, feeling myself smiling like an idiot as I watched Austin moving up and down the table as he sung.

It was impossible not to feel joy watching him, not when he was so clearly enjoying himself. Austin was a born entertainer.

AUSTIN

CHAPTER 22

I was so high off the buzz of performing for an engaged and excited audience that I all but dragged Selene back to the apartment, needing to get her alone. The adrenaline was coursing through my veins, looking for an outlet, and I wanted that outlet to come in the form of many, many orgasms. For Selene.

I could wait.

"Are you going to get on the bed and let me eat your pussy?" I demanded the moment we were in the apartment, letting myself be just a little authoritative.

"I don't think we're going to make it to the bed," Selene replied, crossing the room and dropping to the floor instead, the mass of oversized cushions supporting her back. She dropped her thighs open, shadows disappearing as she waited for my brain to come back online.

It was so unexpectedly bold and sexy that it took me a moment to catch up. I dropped to my knees with a thud, lying on the ground between her spread legs, my mouth already watering for another taste of her champagne-cum.

"You really want to do this again?" she asked doubtfully, staring down the line of her body at me.

"I assure you, I'm going to want to do this all the time."

I used my thumbs to spread her then flattened my tongue and licked a long stripe up her sensitive flesh, groaning at the sugary-sweet taste that instantly coated my tastebuds. Vaguely, I was reminded of the way that most things in nature, at least in the human realm, that were sweet were safe to eat. Both in the fact that Selene's cunt was safe to eat—huge bonus for me—but that she herself was safe for me.

That even when I'd been antagonizing her, I'd always recognized her as my safety.

"How are you so good at this?" Selene gasped, jolting up off the cushions. I lightly pressed a forearm over her hips, not quite pinning her to the ground, but giving her the illusion of being held down.

One day. One day she'd trust me enough to let me properly hold her down, and I'd reward her by eating her pussy until I got lockjaw.

"Don't answer that," she said after a beat. "I don't want to know about all your experience."

I looked up at her with a savage grin, my lips sticky with her arousal. "I'm a greedy man, Selene. This is not a habit of mine with anyone but you."

She looked pleased by that, and I silently patted myself on the back for my history of being a lazy, selfish lover.

I resumed my clumsy yet somehow excellent ministrations, gently teasing Selene's opening with my thumb, my cock aching to be inside her.

Was she feeding from me right now? I was definitely too busy to ask, but I hoped so. There was something very heady about the idea that I was *nourishing* her through intimacy. Each day with Selene unlocked a kink I didn't know I had.

Her pussy fluttered and clenched, and I knew she wanted something to clamp down on. Giving her my fingers didn't feel like enough, but there was no way we were pausing now to go grab the dildo, so fingers would have to do.

Selene arched her back as I filled her, her cunt clamping down *hard* as she came almost instantly. Just as I knew she would. It was never a mystery with her, I *knew* her body, I was more attuned to *her* needs than my own.

What a fucking privilege.

I murmured words of comfort to Selene as she came down from her high, gently stroking circles on her hip with my free hand, the contact non sexual and entirely meant to comfort. Eventually, she blinked at me blearily, pussy still occasionally contracting around me.

"That was amazing," she mumbled, body limp. I pressed a kiss to her stomach before disentangling myself.

"Wait here, I'll get a damp cloth."

I cleaned up in the bathroom before getting Selene a cloth, marveling at how *good* I felt without coming. I wasn't opposed to the idea, but I also kind of loved the thought of just snuggling with Selene now until it was time to go back to the barracks.

She was sitting up when I came back in the room, cleaning up herself before grimacing at the puddle on the floor and disappearing for more supplies. I personally was a big fan of the slick, but it definitely presented some logistical issues.

Once she was satisfied with the state of the floor, Selene headed into the kitchen to make us tea before we headed back.

"I'm pushing it," Selene sighed. "But it's been such a perfect night, I don't want it to end."

Hope inflated in my chest like a balloon as I took my usual seat at the table, knowing she preferred me out of her way in the kitchen.

"I didn't even ask if you liked the song," I laughed, realizing I'd basically tackled her the moment I'd gotten off the table and dragged her back here.

Selene smiled, pumping water from the manual faucet into the kettle. "I did. It was wonderful."

"Oh, good. Ophelia asked me to perform some of my music for the court in a few days. Introduce some less staid music to the shadow realm. I pointed out that there was actually more variety than just choir jams, but you had to leave the sanctity of the palace to experience it."

She paused, midway through filling the kettle. "Please tell me you didn't speak to the queen like that."

"I wasn't really thinking of her as *the queen* at the time. Just some regular lady from Denver, you know? I guess I should watch my words more," I replied absently.

"You are a filthy liar, Austin," Selene murmured, giving me her most unimpressed look. "I know you are very astute and aware of your words when you're not up to your strange, overly mobile eyeballs in liquor."

"Leave my eyeballs out of this," I laughed. "Okay, I was maybe trying to guilt Queen Ophelia a little. Shouldn't the king and queen be doing like... royal tours or something? In the human realm, I was always of the Algernon Sidney school of thought that monarchy was 'founded upon human depravity,' but that is me taking a very anthropocentric view of things. Obviously, I'm aware that things work differently here. I just can't help but think that the royal couple could be *doing* a little more, you know? Why is Mistwood *so* abandoned by the rest of the realm?"

"I can't believe you pretend to a vapid idiot," she sighed, lighting the stove. "Worse, that others *believe* you are."

"Maybe I'm a good actor."

"I don't think so. I think their minds are already made up about you because of how you present yourself and your chosen career, and they don't bother to look any further. And you don't bother to correct them."

There was probably something to that. People didn't want those kinds of thoughts from me. They wanted easily digestible musical *content*, and a pretty, brooding, sad-boy face.

I shrugged, eager to change the subject. I liked that Selene *didn't* see me as a superficial idiot, and I didn't want to remind her that everyone else did. But that was a little bit my fault too. I needed to push back harder. Be my authentic self a little more openly.

"How do you feel about me performing in front of the court?"

"How do I *feel* about it?" Selene repeated, confused. "It hardly matters."

"Your feelings are the only ones that matter to me."

She straightened, giving me a long look. "You shouldn't say things like that to me."

Danger, my brain supplied helpfully.

"Because you're not ready to hear them?" I didn't want to push Selene beyond her comfort zone. But I *did* want to give her a little nudge. It was too easy for her to pretend like I wasn't serious about her otherwise.

"You should save them for someone else."

I snorted. "No. You don't deserve happiness any less than the wealthy Shades at court, Selene. If that's why you're holding out on me, why you want *me* to hold back, then I am respectfully declining, and I will continue to woo you until you believe that you're it for me."

Selene looked ready to run, and that nice balloon of hope I'd been carrying around in my chest deflated rapidly, but not all the way. I wasn't going to give up, and she needed time to see that.

As Astrid had pointed out, we *didn't* know how the shadow realm would react to Selene and me. Maybe her fear was entirely warranted, and I was being too glib about it. Maybe we'd never be an accepted couple at the palace, even though no one here in Cartava had blinked an eye, and they hadn't really in Mistwood either.

But Selene had worked hard for her career at court. I couldn't realistically ask her to give that up just to be with me.

"It can't happen, Austin." She was trying to sound cool and calm, but the tremble in her voice gave her away. "I can't give you what you deserve. Perhaps... perhaps we shouldn't, you know, anymore. It's confusing things. Tonight was perfect. Maybe this is the right place to... leave it. On this final, wonderful memory."

Ah, I got it now. When Selene had called this night perfect the first time, it hadn't been in joyous acknowledgment. It was in resigned acceptance. Did Selene even realize she accepted bad things as though they were her due, but balked at the idea of anything good?

"If that's what you really want," I told her, each word felt like a stab in my heart, but if you love something, set it free.

Right?

Fuck, that sounded like the dumbest advice ever.

"I'll never pressure you for more than you're willing to give, Selene," I added. "If you want this to be done, we'll be done. But I'm not giving up hope."

It was cold comfort that Selene looked as agonized as I felt.

"Even if I asked you to?" she asked, almost desperately.

My smile felt as fragile as glass. "You can ask me to leave you alone, that's completely your right, but you can't ask me to give up hope, Selene. That's mine, and I'm not willing to part with it."

Selene's shadows rippled in agitation as she doused the small, flickering flame in the stove. "I should return you to court."

"If that will make you happy, dar— Selene."

She gave me a look as though it was entirely obvious that it wouldn't, but she returned me back to court in silence anyway, leaving me at the border of Elverston House and walking out of my life.

"What are you doing here?" Tallulah said, startling in surprise to find me in the kitchen a few hours later, a pile of half-burned sticks in the grate in front of me. How was it apparently *so* easy to accidentally start a house fire and yet incredibly difficult to on-purpose start a fire for warmth in a controlled environment? Someone was lying.

"I'll be staying here for the foreseeable future, riding out my emotional breakdown, but I didn't know which rooms were taken so I thought I'd hang out in the kitchen until you were all back from dinner."

Verity and Meera appeared in the doorway behind Tallulah, peering in and getting an up-close view of my misery.

"We'll give you some privacy," Meera murmured, backing away before returning a moment later to drag Verity with her.

"Here, let me do that," Tallulah offered. I moved out of the way, plonking myself down on a stool while she puttered around the fireplace, doing some kind of sorcery and having it burning in no time. Not to go *full* self-pity, but I couldn't do anything right.

"Do you want to talk about it?" she asked eventually, filling the kettle and bringing it over to hang above the fire.

"I gently broached the idea of being in love with Selene. She didn't take it well."

"You gently... what?"

"You all said that I might terrify her if I made a big announcement in front of *everyone*, so I took that on board, and was going with a softer approach, which I intended to follow up with the performance that was *for* her but not in an overt way." The words were all tumbling out of me now. The grand plan that I thought struck the balance of intimate and yet public enough to tell all the uptight pricks at court to go fuck themselves. Maybe I should have to stuck to my pretty-boy-shallow-thoughts-lane.

"The thing is, I kind of knew she wasn't going to take it well," I continued. "Because Selene has basically been told her entire life that she doesn't belong or that she's not good enough and you can only hear that shit so many times before you internalize it, but I'd hoped I could ease her into, you know, falling in love with me. Anyway, she broke up with me even though we weren't officially together and dropped me here."

I slumped forward, resting my elbow on my knee and propping my chin on my hand. On the plus side, at no point had Selene said she didn't care about me. This was about what *other* people thought. That wasn't an unsurmountable hurdle, was it? I still had the performance to do. A public platform to make a statement, though I'd have to be very careful not to make things worse.

"Right. Um, yeah. Are you okay?" Tallulah asked, floundering a bit for something to say.

I hummed, tapping my foot restlessly on the ground. "No. Selene is all alone right now, probably stressing out, and I'm not okay with that. But I have to tread carefully. This is a real pivotal moment, Tallulah. It could go either way."

"Could it?" Tallulah blinked at me. "It sort of sounds like it's already gone one way."

Not yet. I refused to believe that.

I stood up, my fingers itching for my guitar. "Where can I crash? I've got a song to finish and a soulmate to win over."

"I guess you could have Astrid's old room, she's moved out now—"

"Perfect."

I would now be entering my Sad Boy Era, but I was going to come out on the other side with some fucking *art* and my girl.

SELENE

CHAPTER 23

Nothing in this kitchen was worth eating. I stormed out of the barracks in a foul mood that was only partly attributable to hunger, not letting myself think of the reason I *was* upset. Thinking about it didn't help. It didn't change anything. Some hurts were better left unexamined.

"Ah, there you are."

I grimaced at Kael's sudden appearance. He wasn't a member of the Guard, didn't even have family members who were. There was no reason for him to be hanging around the training grounds.

"Kael," I clipped. "Are you lost?"

"What? No. I was looking for you."

"In my capacity as lieutenant?"

My voice was sharper than was appropriate, given his station at court versus mine. But I just couldn't find it in me to temper myself.

"No. Because I wished to spend time with you." He puffed his chest out self-importantly, and I wondered why I'd never noticed how obnoxious his mannerisms were before. "I have noted that other guards seem to be minding the Hunter male now. I am glad to see you are relieved of your duties where that is concerned. You presumably have more time available now."

"Not really."

Kael didn't take this as the disinterest I'd hoped for.

"Of course, Captain Soren was recently telling me that he's giving you more responsibility within the Guard—we're old friends, you know. Grew up together. I was very impressed to hear of your success within your position. It made me think of that conversation two years ago—"

"The one where you told me there was no female at court you would be less inclined to have a child with than me?" I clarified.

He had the grace to look at least a little sheepish at the reminder. "That was then. Things have changed."

"*I* haven't changed. You thought my lineage unworthy of your family. My lineage is the same as it always has been." I walked past him, heading toward the palace. Unfortunately, Kael followed.

"I was hasty in my words."

"You were honest." Privately, I suspected that my spending so much time with Austin had made Kael jealous in the way that children became jealous over toys they hadn't wanted to play with until someone else was. It seemed arrogant to voice such a thought, though. There was nothing about *me* that would inspire jealousy in a Shade like Kael.

Then again, he was far more pompous than I'd initially realized. Perhaps no one else had wanted him and he'd come back to ask me to bear his heir out of desperation.

"I would like to revisit the subject." Kael was all but jogging to keep up with me.

"I would not. If you'll excuse me, I have work to do."

Kael's interruption certainly didn't improve my mood. Several hours later, I was still fuming from the indignity of it all. Of him having the *nerve* to approach me as if his cruel rejection was something that could just be *revisited* at a time that was convenient to him.

No, I wasn't from some prestigious family, but that didn't mean I wasn't worthy of *respect*. My time still mattered. My feelings still mattered.

"Do you set the schedules for the guards on your own?" Carys asked, trying to make small talk as she trailed me through the grounds. I'd already come through once and set a few things amiss in the hopes she would point them out on this rotation. It would be a good indicator that she was ready for some solo duties.

"Yes." Being Soren's second-in-command mostly meant doing a lot of administrative work, and listening to Andrus and Galen complain about how they could do it better.

"Are you attending Austin's performance later?"

I swallowed around the painful lump in my throat at the casual mention of his name. At the mention of the performance I'd been trying desperately not to think about. "As it will draw a significant crowd, yes, I will be there to ensure it all goes smoothly."

And to prevent a stampede of court females, eager to be the first to place their mark on a male ex-Hunter and claim him for their own. His appeal wasn't going to *lessen* after he'd performed for them. Even if they didn't like his music, Austin was so handsome and charismatic that it probably wouldn't influence them either way.

I hated that for him.

Austin wanted to be *seen*. Not for his talent or for an abstract idea of him, but for *himself*.

"And as his, um, friend too, right? I think he really likes you," Carys said hesitantly, clearly unsure of breaching the formal gap of professionalism that had always existed between us. "Since the moment he arrived here, he's only had eyes for you."

"That was just an attempt to irritate me," I explained, though I had no idea why because I was not in the habit of explaining myself. "Austin basically tricked me into guarding him."

"But why would he do that if not to spend time with you?"

"I don't know. Because he's clever and likes getting his own way," I groused, though I actually admired that about him. I just didn't like *talking* about it or remembering in any way that he could never be mine. "You haven't noticed any of the out-of-place items I set out."

Carys stammered, and I felt a little bad for embarrassing her, but it was important that she take this dull part of the job seriously if she wanted to move on to greater responsibility.

"I'm sorry, Selene. You've been so patient with me, I didn't mean to let you down."

"You didn't," I replied automatically, surprised that she would think so. "You're just not ready to move on to solo duties yet. You'll get there. If you want to," I added, because I wasn't entirely sure. Carys, like many of the Guard, was a second-born who wasn't going to inherit the family estate. This was a very respectable career, but it wasn't the lifeline for them that it had once been for me.

"I *didn't* want to," Carys admitted. "Originally, this was just something my parents wanted for me, and I wasn't that interested. But you inspired me. You always treated the Guard like a serious career rather than just a backup option, and it started to make me think about how I could do the same."

"Oh. Well, I'm glad." I cleared my throat, my foul mood morphing into awkwardness.

"I think it's really great that you're not *from* here," Carys continued, oblivious to my discomfort. "You bring fresh ideas and a new respect for the work we're doing. Captain Soren knew what he was doing when he promoted you."

"Thank you." If she kept talking, I might quit out of sheer panic. "I'm going to return to the training grounds now. You should finish up. Go, er, get ready for the performance."

"Right! I'll see you there. I'm so excited!" She bounded away with an enthusiasm I'd never once in my life possessed, while I redid my route a final time to fix all the things I'd set awry for Carys' test.

I was procrastinating.

The training grounds had been something of a haven for me over the past few days, but I was spending so much time there that I was starting to attract comments. The barracks were stifling, though. Lonely and miserable, full of reminders of Austin. And my apartment...

I had always adored my apartment, but I was strongly considering selling it. Every time I went into the kitchen, I remembered that awful last conversation with him and lost my appetite.

No matter how many times I reminded myself that it had been the right decision, the only decision, I couldn't help but resent the situation I found myself in.

The situation I'd *put* myself in, even if it were the lesser of two evils. Austin would find someone better for him, and they would have a good life together. He shouldn't have to sacrifice his social standing for me.

It was my own stupid fault for getting entangled with him in the first place. Worse, for developing feelings for him.

As much as I hated my lonely room at the barracks, I couldn't face the whispers at the training ground. Instead, I filled up the bathtub and soaked in the hottest water I could stand until I couldn't put off going to the dining hall any longer.

How was Austin feeling? Was he nervous? He was probably wandering around, as cocky as could be, flashing everyone that carefree smile while his clever mind went over all the details, the inner workings hidden away from the world, exactly where he wanted them.

With a heavy sigh, I dried off and reattached my weapons, covering them with my shadows before leaving the barracks. Luck must have been on my side, because the only guards I saw were ones who were, at the very least, ambivalent about me, rather than of the Andrus-and-Galen persuasion.

I didn't have the patience for them today.

Wait, who was—

"Oriana?" I gasped, freezing mid step. Callista rounded the corner, looking harried as she rushed after her wayward offspring. "Callista? What are you doing here?"

Callista grabbed Oriana, giving her daughter a disapproving look before towing her behind a leafy bush, tipping her head at me to follow.

Baffled, I stumbled after her, half wondering if I was sleep-deprived and imagining things.

"What are you doing here?" I repeated, leaning in close to talk to my sister since she was glancing around nervously. "Are you okay? Do you need my help?"

"What? No, of course not." Callista snorted. "We're here for the show, of course."

"The show?" I blinked at her.

"*Austin's* show," Oriana said slowly, looking at me as though I was dense. "Did you forget? He'll be sad if you forgot."

"No, no, I remembered. Of course, I remembered. I just... I didn't know you were attending," I finished lamely.

"Austin sent a messenger from the palace to invite us." Callista straightened, looking very smug. "The messenger didn't know where we lived, so he had to visit a few houses in the valley to find us. Caused quite a stir, he did, asking after us like that."

Callista would be dining out on that for years.

"Why all the secrecy then?" I asked, gesturing vaguely at the bush. "You're an invited guest of the star performer."

"Well, yes, but we don't want anyone to see us with you. Austin can do as he pleases, invite all sorts of rabble, he's not from around here. It wouldn't look good for you to be seen talking to us."

Oriana didn't so much as blink at this bleak assessment, which made my chest hurt all the more.

Except no one had been firmer in that belief than me.

"No, that isn't right—"

"Don't you go feeling bad," Callista said sternly. "We couldn't be more proud of you, Selene, we just don't want to get you in any trouble. We'll be off to the hall now—Oriana, no more running off, I mean it. We're like little bugs here at court, I don't want you getting squished under one of these courtly types."

"I'll accompany you—"

"No, you won't, I won't hear of it," Callista said firmly, already towing Oriana away. She paused for a moment before disappearing around the bush, giving me a long look. "Don't you miss that man's concert, Selene. I don't know what's going on between you, but I saw the way he looked at you, and I heard the way you talked about him. If you don't show up, you'll break both of your hearts."

With that, she was off, and I was left wondering what had just happened and why I felt so awful.

It hadn't been *my* idea for everyone to treat me as less than because of where I was from. I hadn't *asked* to be looked down upon. And yet I couldn't help but feel like I was at fault, at least where Callista and Oriana were concerned.

I wasn't ashamed of them. I wasn't ashamed to be related to them.

I was a little ashamed that they thought I might be.

And maybe...

Maybe I was more than a little ashamed that I'd let those negative voices talk me out of the best thing that had ever happened to me. Maybe the reaction would have been overwhelmingly bad if Austin and I had pursued a relationship. Maybe I would have been fired. But at least he'd have been able to see that for himself and make an informed decision rather than me making it for him. I couldn't help but feel like I'd given up without really trying, especially when he'd been willing to fight for me.

It was probably too late now. I'd made my decision, and I had to own that. But I was going to hold my head high, and at the very least, stop letting so much of the poison that had been poured into my ears define the choices I made.

Feeling more calm and certain than I had in days, I straightened my shoulders and headed for the dining hall. For the first time in my life, I had no first plan, let alone a backup, but it was strangely okay.

I was going to back *myself*.

AUSTIN

CHAPTER 24

There was no spotlight, no MC, no backstage area.

No pressure? I couldn't quite decide on that. I wasn't really feeling a tremendous amount of pressure to *impress*—my music was very much not the norm here, and while it had gone down pretty well in Cartava, I was expecting polite bewilderment here at best.

Choir music, it was not.

The pressure was all coming from within. From the endless bubbling well of stress that had kept me up most nights this week, scribbling rhymes and strumming chords as quietly as I could so I didn't disturb the others. My room at Elverston House looked like a crime scene, if someone had gotten a little carried away with the hostage notes.

Taking a steadying breath, I stepped out of the side door into the dining hall, wandering up the stairs to the dais with my guitar as cool as could be. There was a stool set out at the front for me, but that was it as far as staging went. The Shades were still talking quietly among themselves, watching me— or rather my guitar—with interest, but there definitely wasn't any fanfare. No sea of phones looking back at me from the audience instead of faces. The entire room was illuminated, and I could see all the way to the back where Selene had just slipped through the doors, looking like a fucking warrior goddess staring up at me.

There was also no drink in my hand to get me through the show. I didn't need it.

A noise from the front distracted me as Oriana wriggled through the legs of the courtiers standing closest to the dais, waving excitedly at me while Callista attempted to elbow her way through to get to her daughter.

"You made it! It's so good to see you," I said, grinning at Oriana. I wasn't lying, but I also wanted to say a subtle fuck you to all the judgmental Shades standing around, looking at Oriana and Callista with abject disdain. "I don't know if you should be running away from your mom though—"

"Play the music!" Oriana encouraged as Callista caught up to her, dragging her daughter back against her and looking harried.

I laughed, strumming the opening chords. "I mean, I was going to do this huge speech, but maybe I should just give the audience what they want."

That got a few laughs—the loudest coming from Ophelia, who was hanging off her husband's arm with a smile that looked borderline painful. This had been her idea, I guessed she was worried it was going to go terribly.

Which it wasn't, because this was the best song I'd ever written, hands down.

"I'll keep my introduction short and sweet. My name is Austin. I was a musician in the human realm, but I live here now, and I love it—thank you for making me feel so welcome." There were a few murmurs of approval because ass-kissing was truly a universal language. "Anyway, I wrote this song. It's called *Luna*, and it's dedicated to the love of my life—you know who you are, darling."

Before they could really start whispering, I started playing the opening chords louder, finding my rhythm.

I'd told Tallulah that I wasn't going to put Selene on the spot, and I mostly meant that, but I couldn't avoid it entirely. Not when so much of her apprehension stemmed from what everyone else thought.

As much as I hated it, their opinions affected Selene. And I hoped I could show her that they didn't have to. That they didn't deserve space in her mind. That *I* sure as shit didn't care about what they thought.

So I sang my fucking heart out.

I sang about my lover and the changing phases of the moon and how I'd be there through every one of them. Through darkness and light and everything in between, my lover was mine and I was hers.

I knew the crowd didn't necessarily *get* it, but most of them were swaying along with me as I sang—except for Oriana, who was having a full-blown dance party of one at the front. Even the snobby Shades that had been watching her with distaste in the beginning were now happily enjoying the mini show she was staging.

But that wasn't who dominated my attention.

As always, when Selene was in the room, I found it impossible to focus on anyone else. She wasn't watching me as a performer like the rest of the room was. She watched me like she *knew* me, like she was *proud* of me.

It was fucking heady.

No one had ever looked at me like that.

Tell me what I have to do to keep you. Tell me what I have to do so you'll make me yours.

I finished the song on an upbeat note because I wanted life to imitate art, just barely managing to stay sitting on the stool when all the Shades started stamping their feet on the floor. It might take a few performances to get used to that.

Ophelia was already moving up the steps, and I leaned my guitar against the stool, quickly jogging down to the main floor in case she decided to ask me for an encore before dinner service began.

I had something much more important I needed to be doing.

I pushed through the crowd of Shades, smiling politely at their compliments but not pausing in my search for Selene. Where had she gone? I'd *just* seen here. Oriana found me first, slipping through a startled courtier's legs and grabbing my hand.

"Quick! There's a male trying to make a baby with Selene!"

I nearly choked on my own tongue. "What did you just say?"

"Come on, come on! You have to tell him to go away!"

We could definitely agree on that. I let Oriana lead the way, finding Selene at the back of the room with an irate-looking Callista by her side, glaring at a guy I recognized from around court. From his weird, failed attempt at flirting with Selene before.

Kael.

"Austin," Selene said on a relieved exhale. "I'm sorry, I should have been waiting by the stage for you—"

"He hardly needs a guard at this moment," Kael clipped, attempting to steal back Selene's attention.

Fuck that.

"I don't need Selene to *guard* me, I need her to be *obsessed* with me. Like I'm obsessed with her. I doubt she'll reach that level, but I'm forever hopeful. Did you like the song, darling?" I added casually, as if she hadn't broken up with me then avoided me all week.

"It was beautiful," Selene said quietly, staring at me with unabashed intensity. She looked *a little* obsessed with me, in all honesty. More than she ever had before.

"Oh, good," Callista sighed. "You're going to put an end to this nonsense and finally tell each other how you feel. Come on, Oriana. This isn't for us. We'll see you later, come visit, won't you?"

"What? But I want to stay!" Oriana whined.

"Are you sure?" Selene asked, looking torn between going after her sister, responding to what I'd said, and dealing with Kael. My girl was already drafting a plan of attack in her head, figuring out which fire to put out first.

"Oh, yes. I really don't like it here, you know," Callista laughed, taking Oriana's hand and heading for the doors.

"Probably for the best," Kael said approvingly, watching them leave.

"What's that supposed to mean?" Selene asked sharply, gesturing for me to move closer to her side, eyeing the room warily. The plan of attack appeared to be to keep me within arm's reach at all times and deal with Kael first.

I was fine with that. The sooner he was out of the way, the better.

"You know why," Kael replied impatiently, turning his glare on me. "Does he need to be here? It's clear he's developed an unhealthy attachment to you."

"That is clear," I agreed.

"You should leave, *man*. Selene and I are talking."

"Austin stays. You and I have nothing to discuss." Selene had briefly looked like she was floundering, probably because she was usually more behind-the-scenes and right now she was garnering a lot of attention, but she was back on form.

"*I'm* a little curious as to what you're discussing," I said mildly while *make a baby* floated around in my head on repeat. For sure that had been a misunderstanding. Oriana had just heard wrong.

Selene scoffed. "Kael has now decided that I am worthy of bearing his child."

Well, fuck.

"I have not *now decided*," Kael groused. "I have had sufficient time to observe you in your role and establish that your strength was commendable enough to endear you to me. I did not even change my mind having seen your family."

"Why would that make you change your mind?" I asked, shoving down my spike of rage and doing my most genuinely curious face. By the way Kael wrinkled his nose, I guessed I hadn't entirely succeeded in hiding my emotional response.

"Because I'm from a *weak* family that doesn't belong at court. Because I don't belong at court, or at least that's what he told me the last time we spoke." Selene's words were flat, and while she didn't appear to still be nursing a crush on this guy, jealousy coated my tongue in bitterness anyway. I'd never claimed to be rational where Selene was concerned.

"It's true that you are not from an established family line of powerful Shades," Kael agreed as though they were totally on the same page about this. "However, you have risen to become one of the most powerful females at court, and I would be foolish to overlook that—"

"Then you were foolish," I pointed out.

"—and I am ready for us to begin trying to conceive."

"No thank you," Selene replied evenly. Which wasn't quite the fuck-off-and-never-return speech I was hoping for, but that wasn't really her style. Selene was polite. She didn't make a scene. She also didn't indulge other people's stupidity.

"You can't possibly think…" Kael trailed off, openly staring at me for a moment before returning his attention to her. "*Him?* You can't possibly think they'll let you have him. He's the first male Hunter in this realm. He'll be marked by someone from a more prestigious line. You know this, Selene."

"First of all," I began. "The king and queen were all *we want you to be comfortable here* so no one is making me do anything." Where were they anyway? They'd only been a few feet away. "Second of all, I'm not a fucking chew toy to be argued over. Selene is my choice, if she'll have me."

Everyone in our general vicinity went silent, and the hush seemed to ripple over the entire room, the Shades at the back craning their necks to try to catch a glimpse of what was going on.

This wasn't exactly how I envisioned The Big Moment going. I'd planned on the song combined with the dedication being just obvious enough to get everyone talking while I squirreled her away for a private grand confession. But this was fine too. Selene was here—that was definitely the most important part—and I was great in front of a crowd.

"I told you I was going to hold out hope," I reminded her, not bothering with the charming Austin Smile, but giving her a real one instead. "And I am. As you probably picked up from the song. But if the metaphors were too subtle, I've got about fifteen more in my head all about you."

Selene glanced at the crowd pressing in on us, but her shadows were still and steady around her. She wasn't nervous, at least. And I definitely wasn't. This was *Selene*. She understood me like no one else did. She saw me more clearly than anyone else ever had.

"Be very sure, Austin," she murmured, surveying the crowd once more before her gaze settled on me. The message was clear. *They're listening. Don't say something you'll regret.*

"I am very sure that I'm in love with you, darling. If I were the one with the sharp teeth, I'd have already claimed you by now because I wouldn't be able to fucking stop myself."

Was that too much? Tallulah had edged around the crowd, and I could see her out of the corner of my eye looking impressed in a horrified sort of way. On reflection, I was much more charismatic in song form.

"You don't have to say it back," I assured her, knowing that she'd hate feeling that vulnerable in front of everyone. "Maybe you don't feel the same way at all. I think you feel *something* for me though—"

"I do," Selene interjected, taking a step closer to me. "Of course I do, you know I do."

There was clearly still a part of her that was waiting for the other shoe to drop, but she was also being really fucking brave. Selene was opening herself up to me in front of all these people who claimed she wasn't good enough for me, and that took more courage than I'd ever had in my life.

"Are you going to give me a chance, darling?" I asked, holding my hand out to her.

"I'm not sure I stood a chance *against* you," she said with a wry smile, carefully sliding her palm into mine, her claws pressing on the veins across the back of my hand. "You're very charming when you want to be."

"That's not why you like me, though."

"No," she agreed. "It's not."

Her hand trembled *ever so slightly* in mine as she straightened, surveying the room imperiously, daring anyone to challenge her.

Courageous as fuck. And as much as I'd love to think my songwriting was epic enough to inspire this, there was no way. My guess was Selene hadn't enjoyed our week apart either.

Obvious.

We were soulmates.

I squeezed her fingers gently, staring at her with all the adoration I felt—no cocky mask required. Anyone who saw me right now would know that Selene was it for me, and that was exactly what I wanted them to see.

"Hunter man," Kael said, stepping forward with an air of importance and a boatload of arrogance. "Before you commit to this course of action, I would advise you to think carefully about what your circumstances will be, and what you will be depriving Selene of. I have an apartment at the palace, I'm the heir to my family's estate—"

"And you turned her down," I pointed out, shaking my head in mock disappointment. "What an idiot."

"I was being *cautious*," he hissed, possibly aggravated by the tittering crowd. "As you should be if you don't want to spend the rest of your miserable days at her family *shack* in Mistwood."

"What a fucking asshole, you were seriously into this guy?" I asked Selene in disbelief. "I'm now incredibly grateful you said I wasn't your type if your type is *that*."

She nudged me affectionately with her elbow. "I was wrong about my type."

"I'm sorry, did you say Mistwood?" another voice piped up. "You're from Mistwood?"

Selene

CHAPTER 25

My relief, my *joy*, was tempered by the fact that there were so many Shades surrounding us, clearly eager to contribute their opinions—including whoever had just spoken—and I wanted nothing more than to whisk Austin away back to the sanctuary of our apartment to claim him as my own.

Because Austin was mine and I was never going to let him go.

I'd needed this, though Austin had realized that before I had. I needed the certainty of public words, witnessed by those who'd always looked down on me. I needed them to see that Austin was genuine in his feelings for me. Genuine and unashamed.

"Yes, I'm from Mistwood," I murmured, not turning to look at the male who'd spoken. In the past, I'd have struggled even admitting as much, but I didn't find it hard to say the words this time. The captain was the only one responsible for my job, and he knew where I'd come from and had promoted me anyway.

I didn't need to give the opinions of so many as much weight as I'd been giving them.

"How old are you?"

That question startled both Austin and me into turning around and facing the speaker. *Arius*. I knew *of* him because of the tales from his travels, but he didn't spend time at court.

He had... distinctly shaped horns. Ones that almost met in the middle before sharply curving outwards on either side. I'd only ever seen that particular shape before in the mirror.

Austin shifted closer to my side, still holding on tightly to my hand. Suddenly, the gossiping courtiers were silent, everyone watching avidly.

This I could have happily done without an audience.

"I'm twenty-nine," I replied, internally commending myself on the cool steadiness of my voice.

Arius had gone completely still, even the shadows he was wearing seemed to have frozen like a sheet of ice. I felt the kind of agitated, restless fear that I hadn't experienced since I'd first joined the Guard and realized I was able to defend myself.

For a horrible moment, I felt like the small child whose parentage had been whispered about behind my back whenever they thought I wasn't paying attention. In those days, I'd been filled with a mixture of resentment that I was an orphan and a futile hope that my parents would magically return for me some day. Childish dreams of a wealthy, adoring father who'd come and rescue me from a life where I didn't fit in. Or the more morbid ones of a mother who wasn't *actually* dead, but being kept away from me for some reason. That if I just got strong enough, or did my chores fast enough, or applied myself more in my lessons, that I'd prove myself worthy of her return.

I didn't miss those dreams.

Austin's blunt fingertips trailed over my arm, grounding me with his presence. My shadows had been stirring restlessly around me, and his gentle touch gave me the sense of calm I needed to pull them back.

"I'm right here," he reassured me, his voice low and soothing. I nodded once, struggling to find words.

"Arius," King Allerick said, the crowd easily parting to let him through. Of course, the royal couple were here too, witnessing that moment between Austin and me. Did that mean they had no objections? "Did you have something to say to our Lieutenant?"

The king asked the question as if he already knew the answer, and there were some pointed whispers being exchanged by the crowd along with some not-so-covert gestures at our horns.

"Alura. That's your mother's name. Isn't it?" Arius hunched forward slightly, trying to make himself smaller, his expression cautious.

"Yes." The old wound of grief in my chest flared at hearing it said aloud, and I was glad Callista had left already. She'd have either burst into tears or attacked him. I'm not sure I'd have had it in me to stop her if it was the latter.

"You're… It's… Well, you appear to be my child. I would hazard a guess that you are anyway, given your age and where you're from and your abilities. Alura and I… And, well, no Shades like me had passed through Mistwood in many generations. And then there's your horns…" he trailed off, perhaps realizing that everyone was hanging on to each word.

I had imagined many times over the years what it would be like to meet my father. It had never been this awkward in my imagination. He wasn't the swooping, gallant hero I'd pictured, that was for certain. Then again, I'm not sure I would have wanted that, not now. I didn't need a hero. I'd saved myself.

"Well, look at that," King Allerick drawled, saving me from having to formulate a response. "Kael, how fortunate that you no longer need to concern yourself with where these two will live. Unless more surprise offspring appear in the wake of Arius' travels, it would appear that Selene is the heir to the family seat at Sanlow."

I blinked, glad that Austin leaned in harder at that moment, his arm pressed tightly against mine, feeling warm and solid and dependable.

The hall filled with whispers, with analysis of the king's proclamation, and what it meant for their opinion of me. I could see the court weighing up their options right in front of me, deciding whether or not they would treat me with some modicum of respect now because of my lineage, and the very concept of it made me feel sick.

I twisted to face Austin, trying to ascertain if his opinion of me had changed. While his expressions were more nuanced than a Shade's and I couldn't always read the finer details, I didn't *think* he was looking at me any differently.

"Sanlow is a significant estate," I told him quietly. "It has large land holdings, and it's an ancient house. An ancient and well-respected family."

"Okay." He said the word as if it was light and easy. As though I was suggesting a restaurant for dinner, and he had no real preference either way.

I was panicking slightly, though I didn't think it showed on the outside. "I thought this was what I wanted, but I don't want it. I like my life as it is. I don't want to be a courtier."

Austin's lips twitched. "So long as you're happy, I'm happy."

"But it would mean arguments like Kael's that I'm not worthy of you wouldn't be an issue."

Austin's eyes flashed with irritation. "It's already a non issue. Kael's an idiot, Selene. Put that out of your mind and think about what it is that *you* want."

Were there times when I'd thought to myself that life would be easier if I was from one of the grand families at court? Most definitely.

But Callista and Oriana would never be welcome in this world. And I wouldn't be either, not really. Those who'd looked down on me before would look down on me still. They'd just be forced to do it from across the dining table instead.

The voices around us were getting louder, though I didn't care to listen to what they had to say.

"It would give you a better life," I whispered, hating the idea of taking that opportunity away from him.

Austin grinned at me, showcasing that smile I liked so much. "Selene, since the moment I arrived here, I've been trying to figure out how to wheedle my way into your existing life, just the way it is. I don't care if you have a castle and a fancy title or if we split our time between the barracks and Cartava. I love you. I just want you."

"I just want you too," I whispered, wanting to return his words properly but hating that there were so many others around who might hear them. I could be vulnerable for Austin, but no one else. Only he got that side of me.

Arius was inching closer, careful to keep himself squarely in my field of vision, so he at least had some good defensive instincts. From what I knew of him, Arius was a scholarly type who traveled the realm, recording his findings in letters published by another wealthy Shade for the masses.

He was in every way, my complete opposite.

Austin followed my line of sight, shooting me a comforting smile and lifting my hand to press a kiss to my knuckles. "I'm not going anywhere, Selene. No matter what you decide."

I nodded, my shadows shifting restlessly around me as Arius cautiously approached.

"Um, hello." Arius' shadows flitted around him as he approached, reflecting his nervous energy. I looked for similarities between us other than the horns, but the more I looked, the more differences I found. He was fidgety and hunched forward to make himself seem smaller and less powerful than he was—a posture I'd never assumed in my life. My eyes were green, like my mother's and Callista's and Oriana's. A Mistwood color, found far more often there than at court. Arius' were purple like Prince Damen's, likely from some shared ancestor because all of the court families were related.

I supposed that included me now.

"Hello."

Arius shifted his weight, claws clicking together as he twitched and squirmed. "You're very beautiful. Like your mother."

"Thanks. She died giving birth to me."

Arius made a strangled sound of surprise, rearing back. "I had no idea. I had no idea that she was even with child. The chances are always so slim… I have no other children. Or I don't think I do. I supposed I thought that someone would write if they were carrying my offspring. Not that I'm blaming her, of course…"

"She couldn't." I cleared my throat uncomfortably. "She could read a little, but she wouldn't have been able to write a letter."

From what Callista had said, our grandmother didn't have much regard for education—something my mother had sought to rectify with Callista, and Callista had encouraged with me.

In spite of myself, I felt my bitterness morphing into something less sharp, less acrid.

Perhaps, if my mother had lived, she would have told me about Arius, and I'd have tracked him down myself. Or maybe she wouldn't have told me, and then I'd at least have someone to direct my rage at, but I didn't. My mother was dead, and Arius was a stranger to me, but I felt more at peace with my parentage than I ever had.

Callista had cared for me like I was her own, at great personal sacrifice. She loved me like she loved her own daughter. I was *lucky* to be raised by someone who had given me such unconditional love and support throughout my entire life, parent or no.

"I don't want your title. I don't need anything from you." A tension in my chest eased at saying the words out loud.

"Yes, I can see that you're very accomplished in your own right. It's very impressive, of course. Lieutenant of the Guard. My child." Arius laughed nervously. "My father would have been very taken with you. I've never been much of a warrior myself, as you can probably tell."

I could tell.

"As the court—the king himself—recognized you as my heir, you may inherit Sanlow anyway," Arius said apologetically, returning to his hunching posture. "I have no intention of siring more children, I always assumed the estate would go to my cousin on my death. Do with Sanlow what you wish when it comes to be yours—I've never spent a great deal of time there. There's so much world to see, it seems a shame to stay in one place."

On that topic, we could probably find some common ground. I loved my apartment, but one of the things I *specifically* loved about it was that it was low maintenance and I could come and go as I pleased.

"Perhaps, if you were open to it, we might spend some time getting to know one another?" Arius asked. "Of course, I would like to meet your mate as well."

Austin's scent sweetened slightly, perhaps with pride, though the label wasn't entirely accurate. Not yet, at least.

Once we were alone, it would be.

"That sounds... agreeable," I replied tentatively. "I— w*e* live in Cartava when we're not at court. Maybe you could meet us there, away from all the spectators at court."

"Cartava? I adore Cartava." Arius sounded excited, and I was right in thinking we'd stumbled onto a mutual father-daughter interest. Cartava offered plenty of intrigues for a keen explorer to sink his fangs into. "It's one of my favorite places in the whole realm, I—"

But before he could finish speaking, Captain Soren's shout cut him off, silencing the hall with one sentence.

"Hunters have just come through the portal!"

AUSTIN

CHAPTER 26

On an objective level, I understood that the Hunters showing up here was a serious thing that I should take seriously, but I was too smug for serious things right now.

It was probably a good thing Selene was too uncomfortable with big displays of emotion to tell me she loved me in front of the whole court. I'd be insufferable.

I all but sauntered out of the hall, jostled by Shade guards on every side, as the entire court made their way on to the palace steps to gawk at the Hunters. I wasn't entirely sure this was what Captain Soren had been going for when he'd announced they were here, but apparently, everyone was feeling nosy and not at all threatened while they were on their own turf.

"Is it wise for you to be here?" Astrid asked, yanking me to a stop at the top of the stairs that led down to the garden and portal. "You know they're here for you, right?"

"He knows," Selene replied, staring straight ahead, not letting me play dumb.

"It only makes sense that if they're here for me, I should be the one to tell them to get fucked. I'm pretty sure that's in *The Art of War*."

"Can you please be serious for one whole second and consider your safety?" Astrid replied, exasperated.

I snorted. "My girlfriend is a badass, I'll be fine."

Astrid *almost* smiled. *Almost.* "Well, that's true enough. I don't envy her trying to keep you out of trouble though. You should be on a leash."

"Darling, would you be into that?"

Selene huffed impatiently, though I could tell she was a little bit amused beneath all the exasperation. "Just be good for the next five minutes, *please*. Be good, say nothing to antagonize them, and I'll reward you thoroughly for it later."

"How thoroughly?"

"*Thoroughly.*"

I could work with that. We could circle back to the leash idea.

Selene and I came to a stop at the front of the crowd while Astrid situated herself next to Captain Soren, closer to the portal and the three Hunters standing there.

It was hard to take it seriously since the vibe of the Shades piling out of the palace was borderline bacchanalian in nature. In this realm, the Shades had nothing to fear from Hunters, and it really showed. If these snobs knew any of the folksy rural songs, we'd be having ourselves a party right now.

It was a different vibe over on the Hunter side, though. I vaguely recognized Bradley from Grandfather's holiday parties and knew that he was on the Council, and I assumed the other two were councilors though I couldn't be sure. They were standing with their backs to the portal, looking *very* uncomfortable.

"Do they smell bad?" I asked Selene.

She snorted. "They're too far away to tell, but I presume so."

"What do you want?" King Allerick drawled, neatly sidestepping Soren who was doing his valiant best to stand between the Hunters and the king.

"We're not here to fight," Bradley announced hurriedly, holding his hands up. This was so dumb. The Hunters who'd shown up were one step away from a weird hand symbol and announcing they came in peace. It was embarrassing. I was embarrassed for them.

"You'd get your ass kicked if you were," Astrid replied, almost pleasantly.

"We're not here to fight," Bradley repeated doggedly, catching himself mid glare and looking away from Astrid. Soren bristled, his shadows shifting ominously. "We just want Austin."

"It's *so* hard being famous," I told Selene seriously, raising my voice to catch their attention. "Everyone wants a piece of me."

"Be good," Selene reminded me, her posture entirely relaxed.

"Right, right." I turned my attention to the Hunters. "Sorry to cause you an unnecessary trip, but I'm really happy here in the shadow realm. You can head on home now. Back to your evil lair to resume plotting our downfall, or whatever it is you do."

"What happened to not antagonizing them?" Selene asked, exasperated.

"I'm pretty confident I never agreed to that."

"We have a message from your grandfather, Austin."

"Well, that's definitely not going to convince me to come back."

Bradley ignored me. "He says that you were given everything you could have ever wanted. That your wishes were indulged in a way that no other Hunter's were. That returning and publicly putting to rest the rumors about your disappearance is the least you can do."

"Don't listen to them, Austin! If you go back they'll kill you!"

I recognized Tallulah's voice from the back of the crowd, but by the time I spotted her, she was being carried inside bridal-style by a Shade I didn't know. Though she didn't appear to be upset about it, so maybe it was the mystery Shade from the ball?

"I wasn't going to!" I called back before she vanished inside the palace.

"Are you sure?" Cosima asked, startling me. Apparently, she'd been standing behind me the whole time. "I don't want you to get killed or anything, but are you positive you want to stay here? You may be the only man who ever chooses to live in this realm. You're giving up everything."

"I'm gaining a lot more than I'm giving up," I replied easily, running my hand over Selene's palm. "Not just the kind of love that I wasn't sure existed, but a *life*. A community. A sense of fulfillment I never had in the human realm."

I didn't say it because it was distressing even in my own head, but if I'd kept going the way I'd been going, I'd have probably been on the fast track to liver failure in my forties. I hadn't just fallen in love with Selene when I came here. I'd fallen in love with *myself* again. I remembered what it felt like to have gratitude for my mind and for my body. To want to care for those things.

Selene exhaled slightly. Maybe she'd worry less once she bit me? Was the mating mark like an insurance policy?

"Tell them to go away," Selene commanded, her bossy voice sending all the blood in my body to my dick. "I have plans for you, and they all require the privacy of our apartment."

Only Bradley's sour expression stopped me from springing a full-blown boner right there in front of the crowd. It was more of a semi.

"I can take care of the rumors just fine," I told Bradley. "I don't need to return to the human realm with you. Grandfather is right that my wishes were indulged like no other Hunter's, but that's not a strike against me. It's a strike against all of *you* and this absurd system you've come up with. If you think this little group of us here will be the last defectors, you're fucking delusional. Anyway, I'll get off my soapbox, I frankly have way better things to be doing."

Bradley looked ready to argue, but Soren took a menacing step forward while Astrid flipped a dagger in her good hand like a psychopath. A lid for every pot, as they said. Those two were perfect for each other.

"You will never be able to return," Bradley warned, already stepping back toward the portal. "As far as the human realm is concerned, Austin Thibaut will be a tragic statistic. You set that narrative up yourself before you left."

He and his colleagues vanished into the portal before I could respond. Not that I could have refuted his point, not really. But I hadn't intended to either.

A mysterious death? After my cryptic message to fans? The Hunters didn't realize the gift they were giving us.

"Well, that was disappointing," Astrid sighed, somehow disappearing the knife she'd been twirling right before my eyes and striding over to us. "My one opportunity to stab a councilor without dealing with the American legal system and they decide to be peaceful. What are you thinking about? You look oddly gleeful."

"You do," Selene agreed, standing far closer than she usually let herself stand in public. I wanted to preen like a cat. "In your mischievous sort of way."

"You wound me. I'm very un-mischievous really. Other people keep putting me in mischievous situations."

"What are you plotting?" Selene pressed.

"Nothing *really*. I mean it could be something. It's an idea. I guess it depends on how devoted we are to keeping the secret."

"The secret? As in the secret of the Shades? And the shadow realm?" Astrid narrowed her eyes. "Are you planning on starting a podcast or something? The humans wouldn't believe us if we told them."

"Wouldn't believe *them*," I corrected. "The Hunters. The Council. Can you imagine if some dedicated internet sleuth follows some strategically placed breadcrumbs from a supposed-to-be-dead guy back to the Hunters Council? They'll think it's some kind of cult of conspiracy theorists, skulking around under the cover of darkness to hunt ghost monsters. The memes make themselves."

"What is a meme?" Selene asked.

"I don't think I can explain it without sounding like I made it up," I replied after a beat.

She nodded sagely. "Like the dancing dogs."

Astrid hummed thoughtfully. "There might be something to that idea, but we'd have to give it some proper consideration. If it forces the Council to disband, we might end up *worse* off. Better the devil you know, as they say."

"Yeah, we should definitely have a brainstorming session. Anyway, Selene and I have to go. We have plans."

Astrid's lips twitched. "I know. We all know. I'll pack up your guitar if you want to leave directly—"

"Thanks! I'll grab it off you later." I grabbed Selene's hand, grinning at her sound of surprise and tugging her toward the entry room. "Come on, I was promised thorough rewards."

"*If* you said nothing to antagonize them. Which you immediately did."

"It hardly seems my fault that they're so easily antagonized."

Selene shook her head, coming to a stop once we were away from the crowd, forcing me to halt or let her go. And I was never going to let her go.

"What is it?" I asked.

She hesitated, taking a deep, steadying breath.

"I want you to know that I love you," Selene said eventually, steeling herself to hold my gaze. "I don't know if I'll ever have the confidence to just announce it in front of a crowd the way you did, though I wish I could."

"I don't care about that," I told her, softening my smile and pulling her toward me to press a chaste kiss against her lips. "You don't ever have to tell me again if saying the words makes you uncomfortable. So long as you *feel* it. But I probably won't ever stop telling you how much I love you, so you'll have to get used to hearing it."

"I think I'll be just fine with that," Selene assured me, returning my brief kiss with one of her own, only hesitating for a moment with the foreign gesture. "Come on. I need you alone."

I felt nothing but relief as the oppressive humid heat of Cartava descended on us the moment we exited the entry room. I *welcomed* it. It reminded me of sweat-soaked orgasms and the taste of strawberry champagne on my tongue, and I sincerely looked forward to those being future memories as well.

"Shall we celebrate? Go out to eat?" I asked, letting Selene tow me back to the apartment.

She looked back at me over her shoulder, unimpressed. "Less of your human jokes, more walking."

"Yes ma'am."

There was no secret shadow cloak or anything covering me up this time. I was walking through the streets of Cartava as bold as brass, waving and smiling at the Shades who paused in the middle of what they were doing to stare at me. A few waved back with some level of familiarity, perhaps diners from that restaurant we'd visited a week ago.

"I think we're attracting some attention."

"Good. I want them all to know who you belong to."

I nearly tripped over my own feet. Probably from the sudden loss of blood in my top head. And then there were no words because we were both walking as fast as we could without breaking into a sprint to get to the privacy of the apartment.

It was going to hurt. I knew that. I'd seen the scars on Astrid and Ophelia. They were very teeth shaped, there was no getting around it. But I was mentally entirely okay with that because the pain would be worth it. The pain would result in something incredible.

Maybe this was how women felt about childbirth.

I caught my breath at the top of the stairs while Selene unlocked the door, ushering me inside. She didn't bother throwing open the shuttered windows this time.

"Bed," she demanded, pointing at the stairs.

"If you insist," I laughed, darting out of the way of the barest wisp of a shadow whip she sent my way. I loved it when Selene was playful. Over time, hopefully, she'd realize she didn't have to be quite so gentle with me.

But we had forever to get to that point.

I stripped as I walked, leaving a trail of clothes behind me as I ascended the stairs.

Selene was hot on my heels, pinning me against the wall the moment we reached the mezzanine floor, her shadows having vanished at some point, claws lightly indenting the skin at my wrists.

"Kiss me," she ordered, physically in charge but still ceding a little control to me, waiting for me to bridge the distance between us.

I didn't hesitate, our mouths colliding with a little less finesse than I'd intended but I was too desperate to taste her to care. The occasional scratch of teeth against my tongue always made Selene pull back a little, but I fucking loved it. It was thrilling but in a way that made me feel entirely secure because I knew she'd never deliberately hurt me.

"We should talk," I gasped, pulling back before I lost control entirely.

"*Now?*" she asked incredulously, fingers flexing around my wrists.

"Babies. We should talk about babies." Probably. Right? I was pretty ready to throw caution to the wind, but I wasn't the one who'd be pregnant for however long Shades were pregnant for. "Do you want them?"

Selene shifted back slightly, blinking at me in surprise. "Yes. I do."

"Same," I replied, cool and casual while my mind supplied images of me stuffing her full of as much cum as possible until she was carrying my child. "Are you ready for that now? It's okay if you're not—"

"I am." There was the faintest dripping sound of her slick hitting the wooden floor. Okay, it seemed like we were both on the same page.

"I'm going to get you very fucking pregnant," I told her solemnly. "Get on the bed."

She grinned, exposing the mouthful of sharp teeth that would soon be embedded in my skin. "I thought I gave the orders here."

"Not when I'm breeding you. I'm in charge of that."

Selene didn't release my wrists, but allowed me to maneuver her back to the bed, dragging me down on top of her as she laid on her back, my cock nestled perfectly between her damp thighs. I was thrusting before I even realized it, grinding against her folds, getting her slick flowing even faster.

"Tell me to slow down, darling. Tell me to eat your pussy and make you come on my fingers so I know you're ready for me," I demanded hoarsely, already urging her legs apart, stimulating her most sensitive areas with each shallow thrust.

I could feel myself slipping lower, one agonizing second away from *just the tip*.

"No. I'm ready. I want you *now*, Austin."

I groaned, pressing my mouth to her shoulder to muffle the sound. "I'm trying to be gentle."

She scoffed. "You don't need to be gentle with me."

"I know. I just want to be." No one else ever was. I was going to give Selene all the tenderness she'd been missing out on.

She hummed in agreement. "But not today."

Before I even registered what was happening, she'd hooked one leg over me, her heel digging into the back of my thigh. She leaned up, the side of her horns brushing against my head as she brought her mouth to my ear, fangs scraping teasingly against my skin.

"Fuck me," Selene whispered. "*Please.*"

Oh, that *please*. That please was just for me.

I had no hope of holding out after that. My cock pressed forward, no hands required since Selene's pussy all but pulled me in, clasping rhythmically around me. I swallowed a strangled gasp at the feel of her before I'd even pushed forward an inch. I knew from using my hands that her cunt pulsated and gripped to an insane degree, but my cock was a million times more sensitive than my fingers.

"Do that again," I all but begged, the sensation making my vision go white for a moment from pleasure.

"You like it?" Selene asked tentatively. "I don't have any control over it."

"I more than like it. *How* am I meant to last when you feel this good? I'm going to come in like three seconds. Oh, fuck. I'm going to humiliate myself," I muttered.

"You'll last for me." She used her leg to tug me toward her, and I let myself rock forward, pushing my cock into her hot, soaked channel thrust by thrust. The *grip* of her pussy blew my mind. For a moment, I couldn't decide if she was pulling me in or pushing me out, but once I got to about halfway, it felt more as though she'd never let me go.

"You good, darling?" I rasped, settling my hands either side of her head and massaging the base of her horns.

"I'm very, *very* good. Give me more, I want all of you."

"Patience," I teased, pressing in a little more. The pulsing squeezes, the blazing heat, the soft texture of her... It was all too much and exactly right at the same time.

With one last thrust that took all of the self-control I possessed, our bodies were flush, both of us panting like we'd run a marathon. The base of my spine was tingling like crazy, but I didn't want to come yet. I didn't want this to be over. Fuck, we'd barely even started.

I gave Selene's horns just enough of a squeeze to make her gasp before rallying myself and fucking her properly in long, hard strokes, gritting my teeth against my orgasm like I was scaling a mountain in a blizzard rather than having the best sex of my life. Her vagina was doing some kind of witchcraft on me and I never wanted to leave this bed.

Don't come, don't come, don't come.

Once Selene peaked, I knew with absolute certainty that I would follow. Her orgasms lasted, like, twenty minutes minimum.

Claws scraped over my scalp and down my back, not quite breaking the skin but leaving a faint sting as the scratches were exposed to the thick evening air. The sheets were soaked, the room saturated in the scent of strawberry-champagne arousal. It was *decadent.*

I changed my angle, grinding against her with each movement, and Selene came with a gasp, ripping her hands away from my body just in time to tear long shreds into the sheets. There was no holding back against that. Her pussy had me in a stranglehold, pulling an orgasm straight out of my fucking *soul.*

Time blurred, the long minutes of her pleasure drawing out my own, and to my surprise, I found that my dick was still very much at full mast. Was I just matching Selene's energy? Giving her what she needed by staying hard despite *just* coming?

I could get used to this.

"I need to bite you," Selene gasped, voice filled with desperate need that I'd never once heard from her before. "I'm sorry. I *need* it."

"Don't be sorry." I propped myself up, tilting my head back to give her access to my throat. "I need it too."

She whimpered, still very much in the throes of her orgasm. "On your back. I need to be in control, and I need you to stay very still."

There was no need for her to explain that she was loathe to hurt me, it was clear in every word, every movement. I took charge for a moment, rolling us so that I was on my back and tilting my head for her, doing my best to stay still while her pussy was still magically massaging my dick.

Selene braced her knees on either side of my hips, her warm, smooth body covering me. Yeah, the bite would hurt, but her presence, her skin against mine, was more comforting than anything in the world. It would hurt, but I'd be fine.

"It's going to be okay," I breathed, rocking my hips just a little bit.

"I don't want to hurt you. Austin, it will *hurt* you."

"Only for a little bit." I didn't know that for sure, but it'd heal. "And the small amount of pain will be worth it."

Selene's tongue swiped over a patch of throat and I groaned loudly at the rough texture on my oversensitive skin. "Don't tease. Give me your bite. Claim me."

Those were the two magic words. With a greedy growl that I felt all the way down to my toes, Selene's teeth breached my skin in one smooth movement.

Fucking finally. I was hers.

SELENE

CHAPTER 27

The most delicious meals, the best sex, and all my greatest professional accomplishments paled in comparison to the immense feeling of fulfillment I got as I marked Austin as mine. Claimed him. Branded him.

I grabbed his wrists, pinning him down as I extracted my teeth, swiping at the blood before focusing my full attention on wringing as many orgasms out of him as I could. The territorialism I'd felt where Austin was concerned hadn't lessened whatsoever. The feral edge of my greed for him had eased oh-so-slightly, but it had been replaced by something even more all-encompassing.

May the gods save anyone at court who thought to steal Austin from me. I would not be tempering my violence if that situation arose.

My pussy gripped him tightly, and his eyes rolled back, briefly showcasing an alarming amount of whiteness.

"Are you hurt?" I gritted out, hating that the trickle of blood running down his neck gave me a sense of possessive pride.

"I'm great," Austin slurred, giving me a dopey smile. "I also feel like I'm about to come again, which is kind of wild. This is a whole new level of stamina for me."

I hummed, dipping my head again to lick at the bitemark, an instinct I didn't know I had encouraging me to tend to it. My pussy was still fluttering and clenching with the after effects of pleasure, and while I was more than ready for another round, Austin looked as though he needed a moment to recover.

My sweet ex-Hunter with his soft human body. I would take care of him in all ways, keeping him safe from harm and only fucking him as much as he could handle.

And I was so *full.* Overfull, in fact. I would need to visit the energy stores to siphon at some point because I'd fed so thoroughly that I couldn't process all the power in my body.

Would it always be like this?

"Do you think you're pregnant?" Austin asked blearily, interrupting my thoughts as he grinned up at me. "I hope our babies look like you."

"Stop talking, I'm trying to give your delicate human body a break and that is not helping."

His grin widened, mischief brightening his drowsy features. "I'm going to breed you so fucking good, my mate. I won't stop until you're good and round with my baby—"

With a frustrated growl of affection, I sent out a whip of shadows to loop around his tongue, tugging at it a moment to get him to stop talking while I pinned his wrists to the bed with my hands and rolled my hips. If he wanted to fuck again, we'd fuck again.

"Holy shit," Austin whispered. "We are definitely experimenting more with that later."

"I think I might have lost some brain cells through my dick," Austin slurred, lying flat on his back on the bed, arms and legs thrown in every direction. His hair was sticking to his face, damp with sweat, and the bitemark at his neck was a satisfying dark pink in color.

He looked well used, and it gave me an inordinate sense of pride. I'd done that to him.

"Are you hungry?" I asked, silently hoping he'd say no because for once I was too exhausted to cook.

"No. Get in bed, I'm needy and I want a cuddle."

"I like that about you," I assured him, climbing onto the bed, fully prepared to give him space to spread out, but he immediately wrapped himself tightly around me.

"Mm, all mine," he mumbled into my shoulder, nuzzling my skin.

"All *mine*," I corrected, lightly running the tips of my claws over his forearm. "Bitten and claimed. You belong to me."

"Fuck yeah I do." He paused to press a few teasing kisses over my shoulder. "If you have any dark secrets to declare, you can let me know now. I'm entirely trapped and at your mercy."

I hummed in agreement. "I'm not interesting enough for dark secrets. Though there is something you should probably know…" I fidgeted with the silky gray sheet, careful not to let my claws snag on the fabric. I'd already ripped two sets today.

"What is it?" Austin asked, propping his head up on his hand so he could peer over my shoulder.

Should I say anything? It wasn't an activity I'd ever engaged in with someone else. I'd always managed just fine on my own, and it certainly wasn't *necessary* for me to be happy in our mating.

Then again, I wanted to be honest with Austin in every way. To share every part of myself with him.

"As you have probably realized, female Shades derive a great deal of pleasure from... clamping." I kept my gaze fixed determinedly on my claws, refusing to meet his eyes.

"You mean the, you know." He gestured vaguely at my lap. "Magical milking pussy thing."

"By the night," I muttered, torn between amused and exasperated. "Yes, *that*."

Austin nodded. "Alright..."

"For many females, it helps us sleep."

He nodded again, looking no less confused. With a steadying breath, I reached over to the small chest I kept next to the bed, pulling out my silvery-gray toy.

"Sleeping with this in helps me relax. I awake more refreshed."

Austin's cock stirred at my back, his scent growing thick and lush. Slick pooled almost instantly in response.

"Selene, my darling, are you telling me you'd like to fall asleep with my cock inside you? Please let those be the words you were about to say."

"Do you promise not to tease?"

He kissed my shoulder again. "I promise."

"Fine, yes, that's what I was going to say. Though I imagine you find it to be a very strange request."

"I mean, it's cockwarming, basically. I think. That's a thing that happens in my world."

"You've done this before?" I winced at the sharpness in my voice.

"Is my green-eyed monster jealous?" he murmured, one hand ghosting over my hip, toward the juncture of my thighs. "You don't need to be. I definitely haven't done this before. Have you? With someone else?"

"Of course not. I don't let others sleep in my bed."

And it would have been a logistical nightmare. Shade cocks with their bulbous, awful knots were entirely impractical for such a thing.

"Except me," he replied, his fingers parting me, sliding through slick instantly. "You're already so wet."

Austin knew the exact amount of pressure I needed, bringing me right to the edge before working his cock in slowly from behind while I clenched *hard* around him.

"Oh, fuck," Austin groaned, his cum filling me almost instantly. "I hadn't planned on doing that, you just feel so fucking good."

I was too lost in the throes of my own pleasure to answer with words. I reached back, gripping his ass, careful not to pierce his skin with my claws, and rocking my hips to take as much of him as I could.

How had I ever thought my cold impersonal toy was sufficient? Austin was warm and he smelled incredible, and his arms were wrapped around me like he'd never let me go.

"Austin," I whispered, pushing down to close that last tiny gap, the backs of my thighs pressing against the top of his. "This feels *perfect*. You are perfect."

"We're perfect for each other," he agreed, voice thick with emotion.

EPILOGUE

SIX MONTHS LATER

A tight, rhythmic pulse massaging my dick woke me up.

Ten out of ten, it was the best way to wake up in the morning, and absolutely one of the things I loved about Selene. One of the many. I'd loved her *before* the sex. This was just really the cherry on top of the strawberry champagne.

With a breathy, sleepy sigh, Selene arched her back, the tips of her thick hair brushing my chest while her pussy contracted around me. That small movement seemed to set off a chain reaction, her walls fluttering and clenching as she began to roll her hips.

I groaned before I could stop myself, fisting the sheet with one hand, the other resting on her growing belly. "Are you awake, darling?"

"I can't believe I got satisfaction from a toy. You feel so much better," Selene gasped.

Hell yeah, I did. My personal mission in life each day was to #ThibautHerBackOut.

"Are you going to get on your hands and knees for me?" I asked, pressing my hips tight against the smooth curve of her ass as her pussy wrung my cock a little tighter.

"We don't have time," Selene replied breathily, though she immediately shifted into position while I moved with her, all but dragged along by her clenching cunt. "You scheduled in a revolution for today. We have to get ready."

"Not until my wife is satisfied."

"I'm not your wife."

"Then hurry up and marry me," I groaned, bracing myself over her back and rolling my hips. Morning sex was always a languid affair. Selene's pussy seemed to form a vice around me in sleep, and it took a little bit to get her body to release me. It had gotten worse—which absolutely meant better—during pregnancy, which hadn't surprised me. In every way, Selene had wanted me closer when she'd realized she was expecting.

"Stop planning revolutions and we'll have a chance to arrange it," Selene groused, arching her back into a Bitilasana posture because she'd been enjoying working through the pregnancy yoga book Astrid had picked up for us as much as I had.

"Deal." I pressed a kiss to her shoulder, her skin hot from the thick early morning air of Cartava, and picked up the pace of my thrusts. For all that I wanted to lie here and enjoy the pulsing perfection that was Selene's pussy, I *had* made plans for us today and I didn't want to keep the royals waiting. "I'll play my part, but after that I'm done. Our little family is all that matters to me."

Once we were up and dressed, we headed out into the streets of Cartava to get breakfast on the way to the palace. While Selene still cooked, it was clear now that she'd mostly been doing it for my benefit—she *loved* restaurants, and we were slowly making our way through all of the ones we could find that offered at least one meat-free option on the menu.

She was going to cook tonight, though. Arius had stopped in from some far-flung corner of the realm with an enormous basket laden down with rare and unusual ingredients for Selene to experiment with. Emotionally, they may not have had the closest father-daughter relationship yet, but he was really making an effort to learn Selene's interests and connect with her.

"Austin!" Mursat called, lounging on a seat outside a small tea shop, cup in hand. "And Selene—you are glowing. When can we expect another show in Cartava? I want to bring my family in from the mountains to watch you perform."

"For you? Pick a date, my friend. I've got plenty of new material I'd love to share."

Mursat stamped the ground twice in approval, waving as we headed past him. "I will make it happen!"

"I'll perform less when the baby arrives," I promised Selene.

She gave me sideways look. "Why?"

"To... be at home more?"

"We will just both come to watch you." She shrugged. "I want the baby to love your music as I do."

"I might cry," I warned her. Selene showed her love through actions rather than words, which I was totally fine with, but it did make the words that much more sentimental. I was a puddle of goo on the floor whenever she told me she loved me.

Selene snorted. "You'll be doing most of the childcare during the day. If you'd like to sing in the evenings, then I want to be supportive of that."

"You're the best."

My troubadour career was getting off the ground, but Selene was the one with the more structured job, so it only made sense for me to be a stay-at-home dad. Besides, I really wanted to. I was under no illusion that it would be easy, and we were both unsure about what a Shade-Hunter baby would need, but there was nothing Selene and I couldn't figure out together. Plus, we had a great support network. Callista and Oriana were going to move in for the first couple of weeks to help out, Meera—who had doula experience—was going to be at the birth along with a Shade healer, and all of the other ex-Hunters were eager to meal prep and clean and do whatever else we needed to make life easier.

We were fucking blessed beyond measure.

After grabbing a bread-based breakfast—vegetarian for both of us this time—we headed through the portal to the palace where Astrid and Soren were already waiting.

Three enormous pots, almost as tall as me, had been placed at intervals along the palace steps, and they were overflowing with green leaves that stood in stark contrast to the black and gray building behind it. They'd been plants brought over from the human realm that Meera had grown, but either they'd set off a chain effect or we—the ex-Hunters—had. The gardens around the realm were sprouting more green leaves and red and gold flowers than ever.

Selene's shadows rippled uneasily, her grip tight on my hand. It wasn't safe for the baby if Selene went into her incorporeal form, which meant she'd be sitting this trip to the human realm out.

As much as Selene trusted Astrid and Soren to keep me safe, she was fretting.

"It'll be fine," I told her solemnly, squeezing her hand. "In and out, we'll be done in under an hour."

"And you'll be careful. And not antagonize anyone or take any foolish risks."

"I'll be on my best behavior," I promised.

"We'll make sure of it," Astrid added. "Harlow is good people. I've been working with her closely in getting the communication network set up. I don't say this lightly, but we can trust her."

Selene nodded, meeting the kiss I pressed to her lips with equal force, not caring that we had an audience. "I'll see you soon."

"I love you," I told her, following Astrid and Soren, not expecting her to say the words back.

"I love you too."

Harlow Miles had pixie cut hair dyed green at the ends, glasses so thick they looked like they might be bulletproof, and wore a black hoodie with a goth depiction of Cinderella on the front that I really wanted for myself.

"So, you moved to the shadow realm?" she asked conversationally, typing at a rate that seemed to defy human physics.

"I did. Astrid mentioned you visited."

Astrid and Soren were hovering at the back of the room, staying out of the small circle of light cast by Harlow's monitors.

"Mm. I really wanted to move there, you know? Like *so* bad. I read a lot of manga, and it really seemed like the universe was giving me an opportunity too good to pass up."

'*What is manga?*' Soren asked, his voice only audible to Astrid and me since we were mated into the Shade psychic network.

"But my entire *life* is online," Harlow continued. "I can't even imagine what it would be like to no longer have Friday night watch parties, you know? Don't you miss that?"

"The internet?" I thought about it for a moment. It had been an integral part of building my fan base, but it had also ravaged my self-esteem. "Not really."

I missed having an unlimited library of music at my fingertips, or any kind of device to play it on, but it had encouraged me to focus on my own craft I supposed. I'd played a few gigs in the shadow realm now, and the Shades seem to be growing accustomed to my humanesque style of music. The most successful shows were always in the bars around Cartava, because that's where all the coolest Shades lived.

"Jealous," Harlow sighed, slumping back in her hot-pink gamer chair. "Maybe I could just vacation in the shadow realm?"

"We can probably arrange something," Astrid replied dryly, saving me from answering.

"Perfect!" Harlow shot me a beaming smile, swinging around her chair and heading over to the far wall where she'd set up a filming area for me against a blank white wall.

It had a very hostage aesthetic, but that was kind of what we were going for.

'Are you sure about this?' Soren asked, not for the first time. And Selene trusted mine and Astrid's judgment when we'd gone through the finer details of this plan with Allerick, Ophelia and all the other bigwigs. They accepted that it was the right course of action, that it gave our side some power within the human realm and put the Hunters on the back foot, but they didn't like or understand the technology aspect of it. None of the Shades did. They were putting a lot of faith in us ex-Hunters to pull this off.

"I'm sure. It'll be fine," I assured Soren, making Harlow jump.

"We're leaving the second you're done speaking," Astrid grumbled. "It's one thing for me to visit this realm, you're a whole different security risk. I don't need some overenthusiastic Austinator tracking you down."

"The second I'm done speaking," I agreed. I wasn't super worried—Harlow had explained in a bunch of cyber tech terms all the ways that this was totally safe and secure—but I didn't want to hang around either. I wanted to get back to Selene.

"Alright," Harlow said, checking the settings on the camera. "We're good to go. You do your thing, we'll turn off the lights so you can *poof* back to the shadow realm, and I'll do *my* thing with the footage. Nothing gets posted until Astrid has reviewed it under... what was it, Astrid? Pain of death?"

"That sounds like her," I laughed, heading into the light. It wasn't until I was standing in front of the camera that I appreciated how much I *hadn't* missed this. Back in my new home, I did my gigs, chatted with the crowd, then went on my way, back to the apartment with my girl. There was none of this artifice, none of the primping and preening and mugging for the camera. It was just about the music and connecting with the audience, and it was fucking *authentic* and it *meant* something.

"I thought we were going for more of like a mysterious tone..." Harlow suggested, popping her head out from behind the viewfinder. "It's just that you look kind of pissed."

"Right, right. Sorry." I blew out a long breath, arranging my expression into something resembling somber. The artificial emotions were harder to pull off these days. "Ready."

"And three, two..." Harlow's voice trailed off as she silently held up one finger before gesturing at me to start.

"Hey guys. My name is Austin Thibaut, you may remember me from season eight of *The Headliner*. I posted on my social media a few months ago that I was going to live outside of the spotlight as a private citizen. I would have loved to leave it there, for me to live my life the way I'd chosen, but unfortunately I can't do that because there are people who want me dead. You may have even heard rumors that I'm *already* dead. I can assure you I'm not." I pulled a copy of today's newspaper out of my back pocket, holding it close to the lens to show the date printed. "I'm not dead. Not yet. And I'll never give up fighting them. But they're powerful. They have resources I can never match. To my Austinators, I love you. Take care of yourselves. I hope you all have wonderful lives, and I'll never forget your support—I'm so grateful for you."

It wasn't meant to be detailed. It wasn't meant to provide answers.

The opposite, in fact. It was meant to provoke questions and create trouble—two things I'd historically been pretty good at but never knew how to put to good use.

Harlow cut the recording, beaming at my heartfelt, emotional performance. "Just triple checking you know that this is going to kick the hornet's nest?"

I was already making my way toward Soren, who was hovering restlessly at the edge of the light circle. "That's the point. But I've done my part. But I've got to get home to my almost-wife now. We've got a happily ever after to live out."

THANK YOU

Thank you, reader! Without you, I wouldn't get to spend my days mulling over lady Shade anatomy and googling the abundance of weird facts that Austin had floating around in his head. I adore these characters, and I hope you did too. Let me know! I always love to hear from readers.

Steph at Rawls Reads Editing and Marcelle at Books Checked were the dream team on this project—thank you both so much for your amazing work and endless patience with me! I also have to thank my PA, Nikki, and all of my wonderful friends for putting up with me, especially during the editing phase when I am, frankly, unbearable. I love you all.

Originally, I was going to tell Meera's story next, but Verity is demanding attention, and I don't think I can say no to her. Until next time!

Colette R. xx

P.S. To keep up with the latest news and releases, join my Facebook Reader Group or subscribe to my newsletter.

ABOUTTHE AUTHOR

Colette Rhodes is a paranormal romance author from New Zealand. She loves to write about love in all its forms, and adores imperfect heroes and heroines who find perfection in each other. You'll often find her trying to justify her degree by including ancient history and mythological influences in her work.

If she's not writing, then you're almost certain to find her reading—ideally with a cup of tea in hand and a scented candle burning to match the mood.

Keep up with Colette here:
coletterhodes.com
@coletterhodes_author

ALSO BY COLETTE

SHADES OF SIN:

Luxuria

Superbia

Gula

Avaritia

Ira

Invidia

Acedia

STATE OF GRACE:

Run Riot

Silver Bullet

Wild Game

Dare Not

Saving Grace

ON THE SHELF:

Scheme

Excess

THREE BEARS DUET:

Gilded Mess

Golden Chaos

LITTLE RED DUET:

Scarlet Disaster

Seeing Red

KNOTTY BY NATURE:

(RH omegaverse with T.S. Snow)

Allure Part 1

Allure Part 2

EMPATH FOUND:

Empath Found: The Complete Trilogy

DEADLY DRAGONS:

The (Not) Cursed Dragon

The (Not) Satisfied Dragon

STANDALONE:

Dead of Spring (MF - Hades & Persephone retelling)

www.ingramcontent.com/pod-product-compliance
Lightning Source LLC
Chambersburg PA
CBHW021726190726
48289CB00008B/2709